# Belly Of The Beast

A NOVEL BY

**CALEB ALEXANDER**

This book is a work of fiction. Names, character, places and incident are the product of the author's imagination or are used fictitiously. Any resemblance to actual events, locals or persons, living or dead is purely coincidental.



Editor: Frederick Williams, Alanna Boutin
Book Cover Designer: Davida Baldwin, Oddball Designs
Typesetting: Carla M. Dean, U Can Mark My Word

Printed in the United States of America

First Edition

ISBN#: 13-digit: 978-0-9826499-0-9
10-digit: 0982649908

Library of Congress Control Number: 2010921947

Published by: Golden Ink Publishing

Visit our website at: www.goldeninkpublishing.com

# Dedications

This book is dedicated to all those who struggled and worked tirelessly for many years fighting an unyielding system to change a racist 100–1 crack law.

This book is also dedicated to my soldiers in the system. We haven't forgotten about you. Keep ya' head up.

—And—

To Christopher Barefield—godfather to my firstborn, my best friend, my son, my brother, my soldier, my heart—there is a love between black men that can only come from God. I will carry you with me forever.

Acknowledgments

First and foremost, I want to thank the Almighty Creator. It would take a lifetime to list all of the blessings that have been bestowed upon me. I know that during the darkest times in my life, it was He Who carried me.

To my lovely wife, Jennifer; my beautiful daughter, Cheyenne; and my handsome sons, Curtis and Caleb.

To my mother, Gwen; my father, Charles; my sisters, Denise, Staci, Erin, Syidah; and my brother, Theron.

And a very special acknowledgment to my grandmother, Lillie.

To my aunts and uncles, Jo Ann, Joyce, Thomas, Billy, Herbert, Charles, Tot, Mildred, Ernestine, Tommy Faye, Florence, Clara Jo, Edna, and Bubba.

To my nieces and nephews, Cibon, Gregory, Elijah, Kennedy, Christian, Arbani, Janice, Devin, Samantha, Toni, Daphne, Ebony, Breanna, Amaya, Avante, Lachelle, Andrea, Malik, Omar, Antwondo, Terianna, Clarence, and Deja.

To my cousins, Nikki, Monnekka, Dwayne, Lisa, Dana, Sylvia, Steven, Ivory, Cheryl, Cynthia, Timothy, Christine, Darlene, Jimmy, Marsha, Pat, Lionel, Anthony, David, Sammy, Daniel, Marcus, Ronnie, Thomas, Bryan, Brandon, Crystal, Gail, Rodney, Romona, Pam, Cookie, Kelvin, Dewey, Temple, Miriam, Keisha, Halimah, Jameelah, Kameelah, Jamal, Jasmine, Messiah, Thad, and Comfort. To Natalie, Kim, Charles B, and LaDonna.

To my godmother, Janie.

To my mother-in-law, Betty; my father-in-law, Marshall; my brothers-in-law, Matthew, Andre, Sonny, Ronald, Marshall,and Marcus; and my sisters-in-law, Belinda, Lakesha, and Audrey.

To my friends, Tyshea Wagner, Jackie Webster, Sharonda Carter, Fred Carter, Ernie Lacour, Valerie Lacour, Mike Lacour, Terrance Spellmon, JV Green, Brian Green, Pat Gafford, Theron Duncan, Jerimiah Barefield, David Barefield, Stephen Walker, Wynell Clay,

Thomas Duncan, Gloria Sharp, Primas Jones, Nicole Sinson, Perron Stinson, Erica Hood, Kenny King, Stacey Wynn, Fresh Reggie William, Cornell Cleaver, Greg Palmer, Quentin Henry, Charles Deese, Dashawn Batts, Ray Matthis, Tyris Foster, Kathy Foster, Albert Gistard, Cedric Quigley, Ron Johnson, Dennis Ray, Stacey Robinson, Nick Clay, Jesse Brooks, Billy Pen, Kenneth MaCraken, Teke Beck, Joe Linton, Terry Williams, Donnell, Jason Leyva, Michelle Williams, Anthony Frisco, Wayman Goodley, Pat Patterson, Montez Bonner, Ron Wallace, April and Richard Kice, Silverine and family, Veno, James, and J.P.

To the LaCour family, the Spellmon family, the Williams family, the Washington family, and the Gafford family.

Special acknowledgments to: Professor Fred Williams and Brother Jamil.

A very special acknowledgment goes out to all of my fans. Thank you for your support and loyalty throughout the years. Peace, Love, and Blessings. If I missed anyone, it wasn't on purpose. It's just that I owe so much to so many.

# A Warrior's Poem

Captured and bound,
transported and chained,
gagging, wrenching,
kicking, scratching,
bleeding, whipped,
dragged, beaten,
branded, starved.
I fought and destroyed,
killing, hacking,
slicing, chopping,
spearing, and gouging.
Angered and salivating,
sweating, tired,
and bruised, I died…
Because I could not be a slave.
My freedom was my life.

—Caleb Alexander

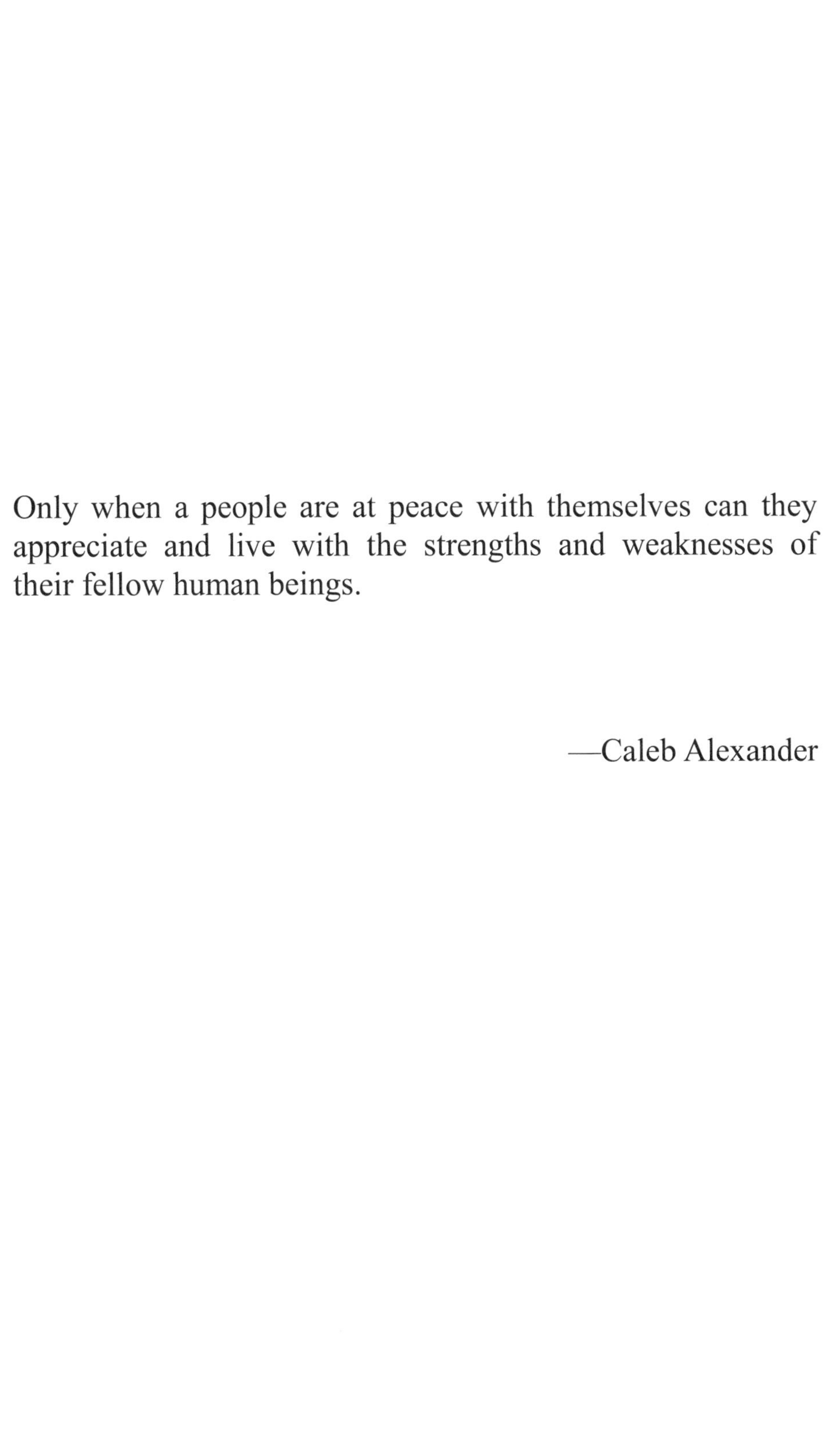

Only when a people are at peace with themselves can they appreciate and live with the strengths and weaknesses of their fellow human beings.

—Caleb Alexander

# Prologue

"*Craig's dead!*"

I recall those two words like it was yesterday. For years, I replayed them in my head over and over. Those two words changed my fucking life forever. Most people can't tell you when things changed. For most, there is no defining moment, no cataclysmic event, no psychological snap or click that signified their descent into hell. But for me, there was. For me, there were two fucking words that I can look back on and say, "*That* was it."

My moment came in nineteen eighty-six. My uncle was murdered while he and one of his friends were walking a couple of girls home from a party in the neighborhood. He wanted to make sure that they got home safe. They did—he didn't. A group of Mexicans rolled up on him and shot him and his friend for no other reason than because they could.

It was my first real understanding of power, my first real taste of senseless, wanton violence. It was the first time that death really hit home. Lesson learned. Life is not fair, and you can do anything you want to in life and get away with it. Fucked-up lessons for a kid to learn. But growing up in the 'hood, I would need those distorted and twisted perceptions, along with an ability to rationalize my brutal actions. That hardness in my heart allowed me to sleep comfortably at night after blowing a muthafucka's brains out.

My 'hood didn't become a real 'hood until after my generation came of age. It was my *fuck-the-world* generation that destroyed it, that turned it into one of the city's premiere dope spots, that turned it into one of the nation's most violent inner-city war zones. And I played a major part in making that shit happen.

My first body came at sixteen, my second shortly thereafter. I had my fourth and fifth confirmed kills before I reached eighteen. Popping a muthafucka a new asshole in the forehead meant nothing to me. I had no sense of purpose, no sense of community, no sense of brotherhood to other black men. I had no moral compass, and an extremely distorted perception of right and wrong. I could lift a gun and kill without hesitation or remorse. In fact, after blasting a muthafucka, I would usually go and hang out with the homies and have a good laugh about it.

My uncle's death robbed me of the last black male father figure/big brother figure in my life. After his death, I had no more male guidance. My grandmother had buried her husband only two years earlier, and my dad? Huh, locked up doing multiple life sentences up in New York for murder and armed robbery. According to my mother, not only was the son of a bitch a rolling stone, he was a hit man for whoever had some dough and a beef. He was true gangsta, and I had his blood coursing through my veins. I guess murder came easy to both of us.

My grandmother raised me. She did the best she could with what she had. And no, I ain't one of those muthafuckas who grew up in a dirt-poor household. I went to private school, Catholic school to be exact. And I made straight A's, did my homework, and scored off the charts on all of the national and state exams—at least until my uncle was murdered. After that, I became—wait, let me get the quote right.

In the words of the venerable Judge H. F. Hippo Garcia, I became a "gang-banging, dope-dealing, son of a bitch." The judge was pretty accurate. I banged harder than ten muthafuckas and sold more dope than twenty. And that got me caught up in the end. Slanging a lot of crack. But that was in the past. Now, I was on my way to a federal prison, the place where I would really become a fucking living, breathing, human nightmare.

# Chapter One

I had never seen so many guns in my life. The U.S. Marshal Service, the Travis County Sheriff's Department, the FBI, the United States Customs Agency, the ATF, the Texas Rangers, and the DEA were all there in record numbers. They surrounded the federal prisoner transport plane with a human circle that was armed to the teeth. They were ready for World War III.

That perimeter was encircled by a larger one that protected the transfer area, and *that* perimeter was surrounded by agents, deputies, and officers guarding the section of the airport that the Feds used as a loading area for their prisoner exchanges and transports. Staring at all of the security outside the window of my tiny U.S. Marshal van made me feel like John Fucking Gotti or somebody.

"*Díos Mío!*" my shackled buddy proclaimed, peering out the window. "What the fuck is going on out there?"

"That's how they do it," Enrique laughed. "You in the big leagues now, baby!"

Enrique, well … I call him Henry, was a friend of mine from the old neighborhood. We went to elementary, middle, and even high school together. We had known one another our entire life. We weren't on the same case together, but we had both gotten caught up about the same time. We walked into the federal pretrial detention center about three days apart.

I saw his arrest on the TV in my holding cell. He had thirteen dope houses that the Feds hit all at the same time. In fact, they hit Henry's house, his brother Herbert's house, his cousins' houses, his parents' house, and all of his underlings' houses simultaneously. In order to pull that shit off, they had to call in extra officers from all over Texas, and even use elements of the National Guard. Henry had us rolling with his story about waking up to a room filled with muthafuckas in camouflage uniforms pointing M-16s at him.

Henry was an old pro at prison. He had been down three times already. Twice in the state, and once in the Fed's. He had stripes already.

"Look up!" Henry told us. "See that helicopter up there?"

I peered into the sky and for the first time noticed a couple of slender, hovering silhouettes ominously circling the area.

"Those are Cobra attack helicopters from the National Guard," Henry explained. "Any shit goes down that those two hundred agents outside can't handle, those helicopters are going to tear our asses to shreds."

A U.S. marshal dressed in black paramilitary gear opened the door to our van.

"Climb out and line up as I call your name!" he barked, holding a large clipboard in his hand. "Alamendez, Alexander, Arias, Baustista, Carmona, Carver, Davis, Dominguez, Jackson, Johnson, Mendoza, Munoz, Rodriguez M., Rodriguez R., Salazar, Sanchez, Smith, Wallace, Washington, Zapata."

We stood in line with two agents holding riot guns standing just before us, while the Fed dressed in the black army gear read us the riot act.

"Any of you slimeball muthafuckas even think about getting outta line, we will drop you. Make no mistake, we will shoot first, and not even worry about asking a goddamned question later. You will do what I tell you to do, you will do it immediately, and you will do it without being asked a second time, is that understood?"

We all stared at the country muthafucka. What did he expect, a "Yes sir"? If so, he was in the wrong fucking profession. We were criminals, not soldiers, and we could give a fuck about his orders.

Next, a U.S. marshal in a flight uniform approached. "Listen up, scumbags, you're about to get on my plane. Once on my plane, you will remain shackled to one another, and you will be shackled to the floor of the aircraft. You need to go to the little girls' room, you raise your hand, and one of the marshals will take you to the potty.

"There are women prisoners on board. You do not talk to them, stare at them, whistle at them, or even lay eyes on any of them. And do not disrespect my female marshals. That will earn you an ass whipping.

And just in case any of you have any bright ideas, we are armed onboard. Don't believe what you see in the movies. I will shoot your ass in midflight."

He turned to the marshal holding the clipboard, "You may bring them aboard."

They herded us between two solid lines of federal agents as we were escorted up the steps and onto the plane. It was an older plane, no doubt seized from some big-time drug dealer or tax delinquent rich prick. The Feds had a slew of them that they used for their prisoner transport operations. They called this little decrepit fleet, "Con Air." Brilliant. I wonder what straitlaced, choked-tie muthafucka thought of that name. Real original, huh?

Once onboard the transport, I was able to get a better understanding of the security involved in this little operation. It was fanatical.

"Why the fuck they need so many muthafuckas to guard us?" I asked.

"No telling who's on this bitch with us," Henry answered. "The Feds be transporting some big-time muthafuckas, homie."

The answer made me peer around the cabin to see if I recognized anyone. Was some big-time Columbian head honcho on the bird with us? If so, was he going to end up in the same place where I was going, and would I have a chance to hook up with him? I had heard that they unload that shit for two or three thousand a key, whereas I was paying seventeen. Damn, that would be a lovely fucking hookup!

The marshals came by and shackled us to the floor of the plane, and then buckled us in before buckling themselves in for the ride. I peered out the window and watched as the armored vehicles, patrol cars, fed Tahoes, and Crown Vics pulled away from the aircraft. I had never been on a plane before, and admittedly, I was scared shitless. I was a 'hood nigga, and until then, my whole world had been confined to the 'hood. It was fucked-up that my first time in the friendly skies would be on a federal transport plane filled to the brim with murderers, dope dealers, tax evaders, and armed marshals ready to blow our brains out.

Before I knew it, we were taxiing down the runway and then lifting off into the wild blue yonder. And yeah, it *was* scary. The overhead bins shook and rattled, the interior lights flickered on and off, and the whole damn plane squeaked like an old Buick. Every time we hit an air pocket, the plane would drop like a rock and the wings looked as if they were about to snap right off. By the time we landed, it no longer mattered to me that I was heading into a federal transfer facility. I just wanted to be off of that flying death trap.

FEDERAL DETENTION AND TRANSFER CENTER—OKLAHOMA

FTC Oklahoma was one of the most modern prisons the world has ever seen. It was a prison with its very own airport. It had several runways, a control tower, and generally looked like a medium-sized airport, except this place had a massive steel and concrete prison rising out of the ground and was surrounded by razor wire and gun towers, with armed guards patrolling the perimeter in trucks.

The tripped out part about Oklahoma was that you go from the plane into the prison without your feet ever touching the ground. A conveyor transported us from the plane right into a holding cell for processing. No seeing the outside, no walking into the building and scoping out the facility—no nothing. You went from plane to processing cell, and from processing cell to your cell, all neat, efficient, and sterile.

My roommate, a Jamaican cat named Calvin, had been down for about six years and was being transferred to a federal prison in Florida. He had been at the transfer center for over two weeks already, waiting to catch a chain back East. At two weeks, he'd become an old head at the center, as most prisoners were in and out within a week. He knew all the tricks, the ins and outs of the center.

"Yo, you got lucky, my man!" Calvin said in a husky, baritone, Caribbean accent. "Everybody was trying to get transferred to this room."

I threw my bedroll onto the bed. "Why?"

"'Cause we got the best view!" he said excitedly.

Calvin walked to a narrow, gun-slit window and pointed across the courtyard. "See that building across from us? That's the women's side. At night, they put on a freak show for us. Nothing but horny, white pussy, bro."

I smiled and nodded. Something told me that I was in for some bullshit. I was right. Eight o'clock rolled around, and my cell became the gathering spot for every goddamned horny dog on the floor. They crowded in, peering through a window no bigger than one foot across, grabbing their dicks and imagining that they could actually see some pussy through another gun-slit window fifty yards away. I was glad when nine o'clock hit so they had to get the fuck out and back to their own cells. But then, I was left with horny dog supreme. My celly grabbed a chair, pulled it up in front of the window, and stripped down naked.

"What the fuck are you doing?" I asked.

"Sorry, dawg!" he grinned without shame. "I've been down a long time, and I got to get my freak on."

"Aww, man, what kinda bullshit is this?"

"This white bitch plays with her pussy for me every night," he explained.

"So you gonna sit there and jack off in the window?" I was new to the game, and this seemed like some real faggot-ass shit to me.

"No disrespect, man, but I gotta hit this bitch."

I shook my head and turned away from him, putting the pillow over my head as well. I hoped the muthafucka wasn't the type to start moaning and shouting and shit. Nasty, freaky son of a bitch.

My days in Oklahoma ran into one another. Wake up, eat, read, play chess, read, eat, read, play dominoes, play chess, eat, play dominoes, play chess, read, go to sleep. I also managed to get in a phone call every now and then. By the end of week one, I was ready to get the fuck outta there, and I didn't care where they were sending me. I just needed to hit a yard and feel the sun on my face.

My luck came on day eight. They called my name and told me that I was catching chain.

"Alexander!" the guard bellowed. "Chain."

"Yes!" I shouted.

"Know where you're going?" he asked.

I shook my head.

"Big Springs," he smiled.

"Is that in Texas?"

The guard nodded. "Have fun."

I didn't know what he meant at the time, but I certainly found out later. For the time being, I was just happy to be getting the hell out of Oklahoma. I had spent over a year in the county jail fighting my fed case. I just wanted to hit a yard and be able to walk more than thirty feet before hitting a steel wall.

The bus taking us back to Texas was a big armored son of a bitch the Feds used to transport prisoners. It had four inches of steel plate surrounding it, along with thick bulletproof windows, and a steel cage in the center. The prisoners sat inside of the steel cage. My seat was in the center of the cage next to the window. It brought back memories of trips to the zoo. Never again would I feel good about seeing animals in cages. No one and nothing was meant to be in a cage.

The bus trip to Lubbock County Jail took thirteen hours. It was the longest thirteen hours of my existence. Nothing but tumbleweeds and dry and dusty land rolled by my window. I thought tumbleweeds were something that went away with the Old West, but here they were, rolling by like giant bales of hay.

Every once in a while, a patch of green would appear, usually filled to the brim with cattle grazing on it. An oil well here and there, maybe a gas station, and occasionally a Dairy Queen would appear and break up the monotony. I was glad to unload for the night in Lubbock and stretch my legs. Once inside, I quickly came to the conclusion that I would have much rather stayed on the bus.

Lubbock County was the shit hole of shit holes. It was a jail that should have been used in Iraq. One night in there and those assholes would've told us everything they knew. It was a countrified torture chamber.

They put us all in one giant cell, where we slept on razor-thin mattresses spread out on the floor. The room was so packed that I could smell the next guy's breath when he faced me. The toilet was an open commode in the corner of the room. If you had to take a squat, it would be in full view of everyone. We ate cold bologna sandwiches and an orange for dinner. If we wanted water, there was a rusty old fountain next to the shitter. Bon appétit.

Next morning's breakfast was a tray of cold runny eggs, a slice of white bread, and carton of suspicious-looking milk. The eggs looked like they had been dipped in water, and the bread was equally soggy from having been set on top of the runny eggs. I passed my breakfast to Henry and chalked it up for the morning. After a year of county jail bullshit, I had grown used to going hungry some days.

The trip to Federal Correctional Institution (FCI) Big Spring was almost as shitty as the trip to Lubbock, except a lot shorter. We arrived at the yard close to lunchtime, which was good. I was more than ready to get my grub on. The bus pulled up to the entrance of the facility, and a bunch of prison guards greeted us with twelve gauges and M-16 assault rifles. No welcome speeches, no shit talking, just all business. We marched into the prison at 11:15 A.M. And that's when my life changed.

The guards rushed us through processing, gave us room assignments, a bedroll, some uniforms, and told us to drop our shit off and get to the chow hall. Walking through a prison yard during lunchtime was like walking down a fucking runway in Milan. Everyone's eyes are on you. Everything about you is being sized up. I put on the meanest mug I could conjure up and gritted on a couple of fools while walking through the yard. I had heard the stories. *No weakness.*

One of the muthafuckas behind me had been here before and apparently had quite a reputation. The muthafucka went from having a hardcore gangsta scowl, to switching and waving and greeting muthafuckas like he really was on a catwalk or runway. His shirt came up, the front was twisted in a knot, and a rubber band was quickly tied around his long hair. Whistles and howls flew through the yard. On the bus he was inmate Gomez, but on the yard, his ass was Renee.

I put my shit up in my room and headed for the chow hall. It was my first lesson on the yard. Henry, Manuel, a cat named Lubbock, and I sat together. Our meal lasted five minutes before we were approached.

"What's up, man?" he said, sliding up next to me. "My name's Pluck. Say, the brothers all sit over there on *that* side of the cafeteria."

I peered over him towards the section he referred to. Sure enough, all of the black faces in the cafeteria were sitting in that area.

"Yeah, this section belongs to the *esses*," he continued. "Y'all come on over here and sit."

I nodded, grabbed my tray, and followed him to the brothers' section. Manuel, Lubbock, and Henry followed. We found an empty table and sat down. No sooner had we resumed our meal before a couple of Mexicans approached Henry and Manuel.

"Hey, this is where the brothers sit. *We* sit over there. Where you from?"

"San Antonio," Henry told them.

"Hey, San Antone!" They hugged him. "What's up, hometown?"

"Where you from?" they asked Manuel.

"El Paso," he answered.

"Your people are over there on the *other* side," he was told.

One of the Mexicans lifted Henry's tray and nodded for him to follow. "C'mon, hometown, I'll introduce you to the homies and break shit down for you."

Henry turned to me. "I'll see you later, C. Hey, C is from the 'Tone, too."

I got nods and a couple of handshakes.

"Later, C," Henry repeated. We shook hands and embraced.

"*Hey*, your people are over there," Manuel was told more aggressively this time.

He rose, shook our hands, and grabbed his tray. "I see you fools later. I'ma go see what's up."

"All right, I'll holler," I told him.

As soon as they left, two brothers slid into the unoccupied seats. "Where you from, bro?"

"Satown," I said.

They turned to Lubbock. "What about you? Where you from?"

"Lubbock," he told them.

"Okay, you know Pree? He's over there. You got a couple a homies here." He extended his hand. "I'm Jackson."

"I'm Big Austin," the other one said.

We all shook hands.

"You got a couple a homeboys here, San Antone," he told me. "I think your homeboy Lou is on the weight pile. Slowpoke, too. You might catch Old School in here."

"What room are you in?" Jackson asked.

"Sunrise, one twenty," I told him.

"Okay, you right down the hall from me," Big Austin said. "I'll look out for you. Get you hooked up with some hygienes and shit."

"Cool, I appreciate it."

"What size shoe you wear?" Big Austin asked.

"Thirteen."

"I'll see what I can find," he said. "That way, you can get outta them hard-ass black shoes."

"All right," I nodded.

"We'll let you finish eating and shit. Get with me later," Austin said.

"Y'all ball?" Jackson asked.

Lubbock and I both nodded.

Jackson lit up. "Cool. We got some more ballers on the yard. We're balling after chow. You know where the gym is?"

I shook my head.

"Up there where y'all came in," Big Austin said, pointing. "I'll tell you what. Just follow somebody with a water jug. It's right up there next to the iron pile."

Handshakes were exchanged.

"I'll see you up there," I told them.

I was ready to ball. I was ready to run, to get some real exercise and stretch my legs. I ran through my hamburger and fries, then hit the compound. It was then when I realized what the hostility towards Manuel was. The Mexicans were divided like a muthafucka.

On one side of the yard, the Piasas and Border Brothers were lined up and ready to roll, while on the other side, the Texans were gathered up. The Aztecas, the M, and the Califas were huddled in their individual groups. The white boys and the brothers were also posted up and waiting for the show. I decided that I had better head for the area where the brothers hung out, and that's when it happened.

Hundreds of Mexicans charged one another with fists, sticks, pipes, shanks, and whatever else they could arm themselves with. And I got caught in the middle. I didn't want to make a mad dash for the brothers, because it would have made me look scared. So I calmly walked through the mêlée to where my people looked on in amusement.

The battle turned into a bloodbath. People were hacked, stabbed, and beaten, some to death. I saw one guy burst another guy's head open like a ripe watermelon, and another stick a guy with a shank so long it came out of his back. Men were stabbed in their heads, necks, and throats, as well as their stomachs and chests. The ground was saturated with bright red blood.

The guards did the best they could, but they were totally overwhelmed. Some guards fought valiantly, taking away weapons, protecting fallen inmates and trying to break up the mêlée. But for every guard I saw battling and saving a life, I saw one running or locking himself into a building or office. There were heroes, and there were cowards among both the gangs and the guards.

Bloodcurdling screams, Mexican battle yelps, the blaring emergency siren signaling that the guards had lost control of the prison, and the clanking of metal sounded through the air. Fires were started throughout the yard, creating an eerie cloud of black smoke that caused further confusion among the combatants and observers.

Confusion reigned on the yard. Black smoke made it difficult to see. I could hardly recognize him, but I did see Manuel fall. He rose and stumbled forward, searching for help. He was on the wrong side of the yard. His people were battling farther down the compound, as the battle lines had shifted dramatically. Blood poured from his neck and mouth. His khaki uniform was crimson red. I started toward him, but a brother grabbed me.

"This ain't our fight!" he shouted.

I broke away from him and ran out into the yard. Manuel spotted me and ran toward me. He collapsed in my arms.

"C!" he shouted. I heard the gurgling in his voice, and I knew it was bad.

"Manuel, hang on!" I shouted, lowering him to the ground. His blood covered my clothes. I took off my khaki shirt and pressed it up against his neck wound. It worked on TV sometimes, but TV never said that blood was so thick and sticky, and that the gurgling sound from his chest was so deep and haunting. It sounded like he was sticking his mouth in a tub of water and blowing bubbles.

I sat Manuel up slightly to keep him from choking on his own blood. He stuck his bloody hand inside his pocket and pulled out the same picture that he had showed me on the bus. His three-year-old daughter's face was covered in his blood.

"Hold on, Manuel!" I shouted. I peered around the yard, searching for a guard to help me. None could be found. "Just think about your daughter, Mannie! Remember her! Fight for her!"

He tried to shove the photo into my pockets but couldn't.

"You hang on to it, Mannie!" I shouted. I tried desperately to remember the little girl's name. Finally, it hit me. Anna Marie! Her name was Anna Marie! "Remember Anna Marie! Fight for Anna Marie!"

He coughed, and blood shot out of his mouth. It wasn't until I shifted slightly that I realized my pants were soaking wet. I peered down at the ground and saw that I was sitting in a pool of blood—

Manuel's blood. I tried desperately to plug the hole in his neck, but there was no way I could plug the other two dozen or so holes that were in his body.

Tears ran down my face, and I began to laugh and cry at the same time. "I only have ten fingers!" I shouted to no one in particular. I don't know if it was at that particular moment when the last bit of sanity that I had fled from my body. All I know was that I was laughing and crying at the same time, because I didn't have enough fingers to plug up all of the holes that they had put in him.

Manuel pressed his daughter's photo into my hand.

"Help me!" I shouted at the top of my lungs. "*Will somebody help me?*"

I balanced myself on my knees as I lifted his body up and began to rock him. He closed my hand around his daughter's picture, his eyes rolled back, and he died in my arms.

# Chapter Two

The fight had been between the Los Piasas, the Mexicans from across the border, their Border Brother allies who were Mexicans from the border area, and the Aztecas, who were Mexicans from the El Paso area, and their Texas allies, the Texicans. It turned out to be a pretty big battle, and despite being outnumbered three to one, the Aztecas managed to fight to a draw. In prison, a draw only meant that there would definitely be a part two. After both sides licked their wounds, recruited soldiers, made more weapons, and got their leaders out of the segregation unit, the battle would resume.

The war had taken the Feds by surprise, and the whole prison staff got all fucked-up about it. Several of their guards had gotten hurt, as well as a few staff. It took the goon squad over two hours to get the place back under control. The goon squad is our nickname for the Special Enforcement Riot Team, or SERT, for short. They're the assholes dressed in all-black paramilitary gear, carrying batons and shock shields, who come in, kick ass, and restore order. They are the lead elements who are followed by the rest of the prison guards and staff who are also suited and booted and ready to kick ass.

When the alarm goes off, so does every staff member's emergency pager, telling them to get their asses to the prison immediately. Some of the dipshits had just gotten off work, some had been dead asleep, some of them had been at their other jobs, while others had been out with their families. So having to pull the kids out of the movie theater or pull their dicks out of their wives made for some pretty pissed-off guards. They came in here deep, and they came in ready to beat the shit out of somebody. The first time you see them marching into the prison is the first time you understand the power of the Feds. The night of the riot, I watched from my window as they began to enter through the Control

Gate.

"Here they come!" I shouted to my celly.

The guards marched in, eight abreast, in lines four deep. I watched as platoon after platoon stomped into the prison, forming a snaking line that stretched from Control all the way down to the actual compound. It was a line of black-clad, booted, helmeted, pissed-off guards with batons and shields, ready to kick some ass. There were so many of them, each marching with such precision, that the ground shook with each of their steps. It taught me the value of shock and awe.

"Holy fuck!" I exclaimed.

"What is it?" my celly asked, peering over my shoulder.

"How many of them is it?" I asked.

"Too goddamned many," my celly said. He leapt into his bed and climbed beneath the covers.

The trash spread throughout the yard, and the burning embers and still-billowing smoke only served to make the guards look superhuman as they marched through the smoke and flames. Their faces were masked, and they all wore black body armor over their death-black uniforms. The black Kevlar helmets, black uniforms, and the preciseness of their movements made it seem as though I were watching a torchlight ceremony of the SS or Gestapo. I felt uneasy about the numbers and their intentions, to say the least.

The guards stormed the buildings, raced through the halls, and then came into each room individually and searched everyone. We were stripped down to our boxers, our belongings were searched, and we were checked for marks or bruises to see if any of us were involved. I don't know why I say "we." I was actually shoved aside and ignored, while my Hispanic cellies were checked and searched thoroughly. They knew that it was a Mexican thing, and that no blacks were involved.

The warden placed us on lockdown for the time being while they investigated and rounded up the leadership and main participants from the combatants. And how did they know who the combatants were? Well, for one, one of the guards had grabbed a camera and filmed the entire incident from a third-floor balcony, while a camera in the library aimed at the compound caught some of it, too.

But the biggest reason that they knew everything that went down was because there are way more snitches inside of the fucking joint than there are on the outside. The Feds had a way of fucking over snitches. They promise the muthafuckas the world to get them to tell on their codefendants, and then after all is said and done, they send those muthafuckas away, too. The Feds don't discriminate. They pass out equal opportunity dick for all to get fucked over. Best thing I can say about the Feds is that they fuck over the snitching bitches that tell on us, too.

My first night in the federal system, and we were locked down. The Feds had been nothing like I expected. What the fuck happened to the golf courses, the tennis courts, the swimming pools? Those things existed, but not for me, not for my class of prisoner. I learned that there were two fed systems.. There was one for senators, congressmen, big-time executives and investors—and one for everyone else. I was in the one reserved for everyone else. In fact, I had been sent to one of the worst ones reserved for everyone else. I was in a place where the Mexicans were battling for control of a poor-ass prison with no money in it.

After the guards had secured the joint and retreated to their stations down the hall, I rolled out of bed to take a leak. It had to have been about two in the morning. I stumbled into the bathroom and found more than I bargained for. I heard grunting, moaning, and groaning in the shitter stall.

Yeah, I was in shock. I leaned over and peered at the floor beneath the stall, and sure enough, there were four feet in there, all turned in the same direction. Needless to say, I backed out, went across the hall, and pissed. *Welcome to prison, son.*

After two days of cold sandwiches, we finally came off of lockdown. My stomach was touching my back, and they allowed us to hit the cafeteria for a hot meal before opening up the yard.

Staff was out in force, monitoring our every move. The SERT team stood in the middle of the yard ready to bust heads. Representatives from the regional office of the Bureau of Prisons were also on hand. They were undoubtedly the most useless muthafuckas to ever put on a tight-ass suit. They could look you in the eye and tell you everything that you wanted to hear, and then do the exact opposite. They were supposed to oversee the running of the prisons in their region, but in all actuality, they were a bunch of fucking enablers. They simply ran interference for the wardens, giving them a blank check to do anything that they wanted to do.

"Look at Fifth Ward, putting in his bid," Inglewood laughed. "He's on region's ass about a transfer."

"Leave the people alone, Fifth Ward!" Grave Digger shouted. "They ain't trying to hear that bullshit!"

Everyone within earshot laughed.

"What's up, San Antone?" Pluck asked. "You balling after count?"

"Hell, yeah!" I told him. "Being stuck up in that room for three days, I need some exercise."

"You working out with anybody?" Big Lou asked.

I shook my head.

"You can work out with me and Slow Poke," Big Lou said. "We can have us an all-San Antone car."

"Cool," I shrugged. Big Lou was the homeboy from San Antonio. He had been down about six already, and he had about six more to go. He was a beast on the weight pile, too. Homie was huge, and he promised to get me there.

I hadn't know him in the free world, I just knew *of* him. He had been a local high-school football star; one of the ones who get all the hype and all the newspaper clippings, and then just disappeared. Well, he actually left to go and play for Spike Dikes over at Texas Tech and things didn't work out.

He blew his knee out and returned home filled with broken dreams and broken pockets. His girl bounced after she realized that her dreams of being an NFL wife were gone. His mother constantly talked shit to him once the realization set in that he wouldn't be buying her that big old giant house on draft night. I even think his dog stepped out into the street and committed suicide. He was a good dude who had been dealt a shitty hand. Like all the rest of us.

Four o'clock count was one of those things you just had to experience to understand. It was a national stand-up count. Every single swinging dick and tit in the federal prison system had to stand by their bunk and be counted every single day at exactly four o'clock. This count they sent directly to Washington, D.C., as if some tight-suited muthafucka was going to call out the National Guard because Inmate Johnson wasn't standing by his bunk at four fucking o'clock. There was stupid, and there was ridiculous. This was both.

The guards came into the room, counted, and then moved onto the next room. After four o'clock stand-up count, they rang a buzzer indicating that count was clear and that we could go to chow.

There were two housing units on the yard: Sunrise and Sunset. Their names are self-explanatory. Both had three floors and housed roughly a thousand inmates each. Each had its own laundry rooms, TV rooms, and offices. Each building had a unit manager that oversaw several case managers, who, in turn, oversaw several counselors. We were like one big happy summer camp. *Except we killed each other.*

Which housing unit went to chow first was determined by the cleanliness of the housing units. An assistant warden, or someone he appointed, inspected the buildings once a week, and the cleanest building got to go to lunch and dinner fifteen minutes earlier than the other one. Can you believe the fucking prisoners took this shit seriously?

The Mexicans broke their necks waxing the floors, scrubbing the toilets and showers, and polishing the beds just to go to dinner first. It would be comic if it weren't so tragic. Most of the bullshit and tension stemmed from Mexicans complaining about niggas not cleaning up the right way. Plenty of bullshit had gotten jumped off behind that trivial-ass shit.

Dinnertime came and went. Today it was, well, let's just call it spaghetti. I had learned the art of holding my nose and just swallowing without tasting. One thing about prison food: if it didn't have any taste, then that was usually a *good* thing. Most of the food tasted like shit. It was cooked by prisoners with absolutely no previous culinary experience or skills whatsoever. The trick was to wolf it down and be done with it. It took some practice, but I had just done a year in the county jail fighting my case, so I was an old pro at eating shit.

The gym was the one good thing about the shit hole I had been sent to. Big Spring was an old Air Force base, and some of the facilities from the base had been kept by the prison. The runways went to the Big Spring airport, while the gym, the warehouses, and several other support buildings went to the Bureau of Prisons. Somehow, the assholes had maintained the gym in pristine condition. It had an indoor basketball court with genuine hardwood floors. The thing was better than my old high-school gym and comparable to the local college gym where we would go and ball some weekends. I was able to get my ball on.

I admit, I wasn't the most athletic nigga to ever step on a court, but

I had a shot like a Winchester rifle. My shit was deadly accurate. I could sit behind the three-point line and shoot a muthafucka's lights out. I could also create space for myself, and I had a hell of a handles. I was a beast in the low post, especially for someone who was only six one. I hated running up and down the court, and being in the county for a year and playing on that bullshit rooftop court didn't make things any better. I got winded quick and found myself lagging back sometimes. But it usually worked out for the best, because by the time I got down the court, I would get the ball and pull up for a three.

"You can't fade me, Little Rock!" I said, talking shit. "You can't handle this, baby." I put the ball on the floor and blew past him. Quickly, I swerved around Big Cali and laid the ball up.

"Come on, San Antone!" my homies clapped and cheered me on from the bleachers. "Show'em how we do it in the 'Tone!"

Next play, I ran down the court and pulled up. "*Swoosh*, all net, baby!"

By the time the night was almost over, I had forty-eight points, and we were blowing the other guys out by thirty. Not everyone enjoyed our show.

They had put a Hispanic cat named Julian on me. He was supposedly their best perimeter defender, and I had torched his ass for forty-eight. His help defense sucked, he didn't know how to take away the baseline, and he gave me way too much space whenever I was behind the arc. His own people started to jeer and ridicule him for his defense, and it had gotten to him. I went around him and laid the ball in for my fiftieth point.

"Foul, *cavron*!" Julian shouted.

"Man, ain't nobody fouled you," I said.

"That shit ain't funny! You been fouling me all fucking night, *pinche joto*."

"Fuck you, bitch!" I told him. "I ain't no punk."

"Fuck you, muthafucker!" he said, walking towards me.

I stood straight. He violated my space and put his hands up. I connected with a right, then a left, and another right. The second right dropped him and put him to sleep.

Mexicans vacated the bleachers, and so did the brothers. The gym staff and the guards who were watching the game got between everyone.

"You wanna go back on lockdown?" Officer Bryant shouted.

"Alexander! Get your ass over here!" Officer Tucker commanded. "You, too, Julian!"

Julian was just waking up.

Officer Tucker pointed me towards the exit. "To the SHU! You know where it is."

The SHU was short for Special Housing Unit, or what we called *The Hole*. It was the disciplinary housing unit where you're locked in a cell for twenty-three hours a day. Trays are brought to you. Commissary is brought to you. Books are brought to you. You get a shower every other day and recreation for one hour every day.

Something was seriously wrong with that picture. I wasn't going out to recreation if I couldn't shower afterwards. Some filthy muthafuckas didn't care. They could go out and sweat their asses off, then climb right back into their bunk and go to sleep. They were what we called Vikings. They were the filthy, funky muthafuckas that made the prison smell with an overbearing stench.

Well, I had been on the yard for four days, and so far I had been in the middle of a prison gang fight, had a friend die in my arms, got strip-searched by the goon squad, saw some punks fucking, led my basketball team to victory, whipped some ass, almost started a race riot, and already got sent to the hole. Not bad for my first week. Imagine how wonderful my first year would be.

I had violated just about every unwritten rule in prison the moment I stepped onto the yard. I hadn't heard from my girl in two weeks, I didn't know how my son was doing, and I was fucking up big time. My son was two weeks old when I got caught up. He was my life, my pride and joy. He represented all the good I had left in me. I plopped down in my bed, lay back, and pulled the bloody picture of Anna Marie from my pocket. By now, the family had heard the news. By now, Anna Marie had seen her mommy crying and had been told that her daddy was in heaven.

I didn't have a picture of my own son to look at. But one thing was for certain: I was going to make it back to him. No one was going to tell my baby that his daddy had gone to heaven. If I had to leave a trail of bodies a mile long, I was going to get back to my son. I was determined to hold him as a free man once again.

# Chapter Three

I did three weeks in the hole before the captain kicked me out. I was green, and he knew it. He liked my spunk and the fact that I kicked ass without having to go through a committee. No sit-downs, no shot callers, nothing but a quick combination to a muthafucka's nose and jaw.

The brothers talked things out with the Mexicans. They explained that I was new to the yard and didn't know the procedures. The Mexican shot callers let it pass. They had bigger fish to fry. They were fighting amongst themselves for supremacy, and even within most of the groups, there was infighting over leadership. They didn't have the time or inclination to fight the brothers right now. So I got out of the hole without even a talking to.

They gave me a new room assignment once I got out of special housing. I was sent to a balcony room, and it was like night and day from my old room. In my old hovel, I was the only brother; in my new pad, there were seven of us. Seven brothers and one cool-ass white boy.

The room next to ours had three more brothers, and the one on the other side of that one, six. Most of my new roommates were at work when I moved in, so I didn't get to meet them right away. But I did get to meet one of them. His name was Joe; he was a brother from H-Town. Cool as fuck. He had a seven piece, and he had been down two on it. He had got caught with a couple a keys of powder, and since he was black, they stuck it to him. Normally two keys of soft would get you twenty-four months in a camp—if you were white, that is. Brothers always got the long end of the sentencing stick when it came to handing out time.

My new job was in the library as a clerk. It was a sweet-ass job. It would give me time to sit back and chill, to read, write, and work on my case. All I had to do was sit behind a desk, check out books, pass out magazines and newspapers, and mind my own fucking business. It was beautiful.

"I'm here to turn these books in. I ordered them through the interlibrary loan system."

I peered up from my *USA Today*. He was tall, about six foot four, with a thin muscular frame and the most regal bearing I had ever encountered. He was African, Nigerian, to be exact, and he spoke in a very distinguished British accent.

"I can turn those in for you," I said, removing the books from my desk.

"You are new here?" he asked, extending his hand. "My name in Omene."

I shook his hand. "Christian. Everybody just calls me San Antone."

"Ah, you are from San Antonio?"

I nodded and examined some of the books that he turned in. "Yep."

"Very good books. I ordered them for a friend of mine to read."

"*From Superman to Man*?" I asked, peering up at him. "And *The Miseducation of The Negro. The Destruction of Black Civilization. The History of African Civilization. Nile Valley Civilization?*"

I had never heard of any of these books. They were as alien to me as the civilizations that they covered.

"Have you read any of them before?" Omene asked with a smile.

I shook my head.

"Oh, my!" he said, becoming very animated, "then you don't know what you're missing!"

"Yeah? They pretty good?"

"*Good?*" he asked, pursing his lips like a slick salesman easing in for the kill. "They are powerful beyond belief! These books are treasures. They are filled with the knowledge of self. They uncover the hidden history and greatness of your people."

"Of my people?" I lifted an eyebrow and leaned in. "Let me ask you a question."

"Certainly."

"What do Africans really think about blacks here in the states?"

I could tell that he was taken aback by my question. He paused, deliberated, and then smiled. It was a smile that I would come to know well. "You are our brothers and sisters. You must go to Africa, every person in the Diaspora must go to Africa and experience it for themselves. You will see; you will be treated like long-lost family. Like royalty, almost. You will be welcomed home with open arms."

"I heard that Africans really don't like blacks from America. They think we're all stupid and lazy and that we're all gangbangers."

He laughed. "Africans understand what they see on TV is not true. We do think you are crazy for not taking advantage of the tremendous educational opportunities America has to offer. But no, we do not think that you are all gangbangers."

He leaned in. "You see, Christian, we know the white man. He wants to keep us apart. So he puts out images in the media to influence people's perceptions of one another. Whenever they show Africa on TV, they only show the jungles, never the cities. And we do have cities in Africa. We do not live in the jungles."

I laughed, and so did he.

"If people believed everything that was shown on TV, then you would think that Africa was nothing but wild animals and people living in huts, and we would believe that all the white people here lived on South Fork Ranch, while all the black people lived in the ghetto like on *Good Times*."

Again I laughed.

"Many people's greatest fear is our unity. They fear our unity. Africa has tremendous resources, while here, African Americans have a tremendous amount of money and technological know-how. We want African Americans to come and invest in Africa. The white people are doing it, and they want to keep everyone else from going over there and investing, so they put out negative images in the media."

I nodded and lifted *African Civilizations*.

"No, don't start with that one." He lifted *Superman to Man*. "Here, start with this one. And then read *The Destruction of Black Civilization*. We'll work you into Dr. Diop's books. You're not ready for them yet."

"Why not?"

"Because once you get on that level, you'll be walking around here screaming at all of the white people, telling them to get out of your way," he said, laughing.

I did read *From Superman to Man*. It was the book that started me on my journey to becoming a man. A *real* man. A *black* man. I began to understand the heights from which my people had fallen, the depths to which we plunged, and the enormity of the tasks which we face to rehabilitate ourselves as a people. It was with this first book that I got a taste of history. Not the bullshit that we're fed in school, but *real* history, *hidden* history.

Reading Carter G. Woodson, Cheikh Anta Diop, Anthony T. Browder, Dr. Francis Welsing, Dr. Chancellor Williams, Basil Davidson, George Cox, John Henrik Clarke, Dr. Yosef Ben Jochanan, Roger Bastide, G. K. Osei, Walter Rodney, J. A. Rogers, Randall Robinson, Rudolph Windsor, and so many others would teach me that I was part of a twenty thousand-year-old history. That I was so much more than America's definition of me, that I could surpass the boundaries of those perceptions, that I was a child of history and a citizen of the world. They taught me that I was so much more than a mere "nigga."

Eventually those books would instill in me a kinship with other people of African descent and give me a freedom that no prison could contain and no judge could take away. I would become connected to the universe and to God and to man in ways that few others would understand. My mind would explode like the beginning of time, and my possibilities would become as infinite as the stars in God's universe. But that would be later. Much later. Right now, I was still a "nigga" with all that that title entailed.

Lunchtime came quickly. My love for my new job and my conversation with Omene made the morning disappear fast. I found myself wolfing down my food and then heading for the telephone gazebo to call home and check on my folks. My grandmother was home.

"Hey, baby!"

"Hey, sweetie," I said. "How are you doing?"

"We're doing find, baby," she replied. "How are you doing?"

"I'm doing great; getting into the swing of things. They got me working in the library."

"Oh, well, that's good. Are you eating?"

"Yeah, I just came from lunch."

"What did you eat?"

"Fried chicken, mashed potatoes and gravy, some corn, a roll, some cake. It was pretty good."

"Hey, that does sound pretty good!"

I laughed. "It was all right. Not better than yours, though."

"Is that what you want when you come home?"

"Yeah, some fried chicken and dirty rice."

"You got it! The lawyer says that it won't be long."

"Yeah? I tried to call him earlier, and they said he was in court. Whenever I call him, he's either in court or out of town. Next time you talk to him, tell him I need my trial transcripts."

"Okay. Trial transcripts, I'm writing it down right now, so I won't forget."

"Tell everybody I said hi."

"I will. Everybody be asking me how you doing. Reverend Bouldin asks about you all the time."

"Oh, yeah? How's he doing?"

"He's doing good. He prays for you every Sunday. He prays for you, and Ethel's grandson, and Phoebe's grandsons, and Ellie's grandchillins, and Lucille's grandchurin, and …" She paused. "Hmmm, now that I think about it, I guess I'm lucky. I only got one grandchild in jail."

"Tell reverend that I said thanks."

"I will, baby."

"I'll call you on Wednesday."

"Okay, baby. You take care of yourself."

"I will."

"I love you."

"I love you, too."

I hung up the phone and sat down on the bench inside of the stall. I had to process what my grandmother had just told me. She felt lucky because she had only *one* grandchild in prison. She felt *lucky*?

I closed my eyes and leaned my head back against the wall. *What had I put her through? What had I put my family through? What was happening to us, to all of us?* My steps toward consciousness were now a quick stride. For the first time in my life, I began to question my actions. I began to see a bigger picture. For the first time in my life, I began to think in terms of "we" instead of "me." What the fuck had happened to us as a people? How did we get like this? We weren't a race of fuckin' criminals, were we? My grandmother felt *lucky* because she had only *one* grandchild in prison? That statement would haunt me for the rest of my life. I knew it would, as soon as it had been spoken.

Usually talking to my grandmother gave me a boost, but the conversation today shattered my spirits. A day that started off on a high quickly turned into a drag. Then it got even worse.

"Alexander, report to the lieutenant's office!" the dorm officer shouted.

I climbed out of bed, laced up my shoes, and headed for the lieutenant's office.

"They told me to ask for the special investigations lieutenant," I said, entering into the office.

"What'cha need?"

"I'm Inmate Alexander. They told me to report here—"

"He's mine," a slim, muscular lieutenant said, walking into the main office. He had a short box haircut and a ramrod-straight demeanor. He looked like he was ex-military, but even more importantly, he looked like a complete asshole.

"Alexander?" he asked, staring me up and down.

"Yeah?"

"Follow me," he said, exiting the office.

"Where we going?" I asked, trying to keep up.

"Warden's office. Some people want to see you."

"See me? About what?"

He shook his head. "Don't know. But it can't be good."

We walked into the warden's temple, and I followed him into a conference room. Two suited gentlemen stood and extended their hands.

"Alexander?"

I nodded and exchanged handshakes.

"I'm Special Agent Riley, and this is Special Agent Danforth. We wanted to ask you a couple of questions." Riley waved his hand towards an empty chair. "Have a seat."

"You're not in any trouble," Danforth reassured me.

"Do you know Ramon Sifuentes?" Riley asked.

I nodded cautiously.

"Tell us about him," Riley continued.

"Don't know much about him," I said. "Didn't hang out with him much."

"You were one of his closest friends," Riley declared.

I shook my head.

"He trusted you?" Danforth asked.

I shrugged.

"He ever bring any stereo equipment around you?" Riley asked.

I shrugged, "Not that I recall."

"Not that you recall?" Danforth repeated. "You don't remember him bringing any stolen DJ equipment around you?"

I shook my head.

Riley pulled out a piece of paper and read from it. "And you told him to get that fucking equipment out of your house. You didn't want to have anything to do with that shit."

It hit me in the stomach. The muthafuckas had quoted me word for word. Ramon had killed a DJ, and he and his partner and stolen their equipment. He brought the equipment to my crib, and once I found out what he had done, I told him to get the shit away from me. I also cut his ass loose. We were all murderers, but he was out of control.

"You told him that he had twenty minutes to get his shit and go, or else," Riley continued. "Any of this refresh your memory?"

I shook my head.

"Should I continue reading?" Riley asked.

"Do you know Penelope Rodriguez?" Danforth asked.

I shook my head.

"She was one of Ramon's girlfriends," he offered.

Oh, shit, not the girlfriends. Every time that fucking Ramon started ranting and raving about how much one of his girlfriends had pissed him off, she would disappear. We joked that he had buried them in his backyard. It was one of those jokes that wasn't really a joke, but more like a really good guess. Yes, Ramon was a psycho muthafucka.

"Why so quiet?" Riley asked.

"I have nothing to say," I told him.

"Did he kill his girlfriend?" Danforth asked.

"I never met his girlfriend," I answered.

"That wasn't the question," Riley said.

"FBI investigating a murder case?" I asked.

"Missing persons case," Danforth corrected me. "Kidnapping is within our jurisdiction."

I nodded. I had forgotten about that.

"Did he kill them?" Riley asked.

"*Them*?" I asked.

"Melinda, Jackie, Penelope … did he kill them?" Riley asked.

"I don't know. Have you asked him?"

"We don't have to. We got everything we need," Danforth smiled. "We just need you to confirm some things for us."

"So, you really don't need me."

"You need us," Danforth smiled. "We can speak to the U.S. attorney on your behalf."

"Get your sentenced reduced for cooperating," Riley chimed in.

I exhaled.

"Fill in the blanks," Riley said. He pressed record on a cassette player and slid it in front of me.

"Do I need an attorney?" I asked.

"No," Danforth shook his head. "We're not investigating you. We just need you to help us out with Ramon."

"I didn't know Ramon that well. I don't know anything he did, I never met his girlfriends, and I don't know anything about any stereo equipment. I'm sorry, whoever told you these things has lied to you." I stood.

Their faces went from a frown to a deep scowl. "You're willing to stay in prison for this guy? You barely know him," Danforth shouted.

"You can go home to your wife and son," Riley added.

"Eventually, I'm going to do that anyway. Funny thing about the Feds. They can lock me up, but they can't eat me. These doors are gonna open up for me one day, gentlemen. In the meantime, do your own fucking job." I turned and walked out of the building.

They had kept me in there past the four o'clock count. I raced to the chow hall, ate some dinner, walked the track, and then headed back to my room for a shower and some relaxation. I got the shower, but relaxation was out of the question.

"San Antone, what you know about these dominoes?" Gravedigger asked.

Digger was old school, a forty-something cat from sunny South Dallas. He looked like he was a smoker in the free world, and I really do think that he was. Funny thing about the Feds, they'll lock up a base head just as quick as they'll lock up a baller. There were a lot of cats in the joint for rocks, especially from small towns where the county turned all of the drug cases over to the feds for prosecution. I think Digger got caught up because of his record. He had been to the state quite a few times, and I think this time, they turned his case over to the big boys.

I leapt off my bunk and took a seat at the domino table. My other celly, Billy, was already at the table. He was one of those cases that I described before. Small-town cat caught with a couple of ounces. Billy was the crazy one in the room. He loved wrestling and liked to come back to the room and put the first one he came across in a headlock. He was a big dude, about two hundred and thirty pounds, and he was mixed. Black dad, white mom, confusing childhood—you know the story.

My other roommate grabbed the last seat. His name was Charles, and he was from Belize. He was a wild-looking cat with a wandering eye that was a different color from his good one. He would be looking at you, and it would look as though he were staring off into the corner somewhere. He was also a ticking time bomb, waiting to explode. Mexicans were filtrating into his country in droves and changing its dynamics. He absolutely *hated* Mexicans.

Gravedigger wired his radio to some larger speakers and tuned it into a black station that came on only at night. Al Green crackled through the speakers.

The room quickly filled with other brothers. Black N Mild smoked wafted through the air. The hooch was circulated, and the domino game quickly got crunk.

"Ella, Bella, and Stella!" Billy shouted.

"Brinkhouse!" Gravedigger shouted, slamming down his domino.

I slammed double five on the table and stood. "Dirty thirty!"

We laughed and drank and smoked and partied through the night. For the first time in a long time, prison didn't feel like prison. It was like kicking it in the 'hood with the fellas.

Some of the homies started grooving to the jams on the radio. Not dancing with one another, but just grooving by themselves, letting the old school take them back to a happier time and a happier place.

*"Driftin' on a memory, ain't no place I'd rather be than with you …"*

The Isley's took us there. They turned this scraggly collection of dope peddlers, bank robbers, and dope fiends into family. They eased our pain, and they turned a raggedy-ass prison room into a home away from home. Room 205 was an oasis in a sea of shit.

Months flew by, and we were in our own little world on that balcony. So much so that none of us sensed the winds of change. We simply woke up one morning to a new fucking reality. Our numbers on the yard had gone down substantially while the Mexicans had gone up. We woke up from our delusion to find ourselves outnumbered eight to one. The winds had definitely changed. Even the soothing voice of the Isley Brothers wouldn't be able to assuage the sounds of the howling winds screeching at us. A storm was brewing.

# Chapter Four

My days continued to run together. I spent them working in the library during the days and working out and walking the track in the evenings. It was during my job in the daytime that I met my boy, Ghirt.

"Bad boys," I said, handing him the book that he had ordered through our interlibrary loan system. We called it the ILL. Basically, if we didn't have a book that you wanted in our library, you could look in a catalog and order it. It would be loaned to us from the nearest library that had it in stock. It was a beautiful system, and one that would definitely come in handy for me.

"You don't know the half of it," Ghirt replied.

"I think I do," I answered.

The book we referred to was one written about the Waffen SS. These were the elite Nazi Party soldiers during World War II. They started off as Hitler's personal bodyguards and grew into an organization of millions. They were the most feared, the most dedicated, the most murderous soldiers during that war.

Ghirt pulled out another book. This one was on Himmler, the head of the SS. "What you know about him?"

"Chicken farmer," I smiled, which he had been before the war.

"Fanatical killer, fierce organizer, and the second-most feared man in all of Nazi Germany," Ghirt declared.

I shook my head. "Naaaah, I think Goering was the second-most feared. After all, he was the Deputy Riech Marshal."

"You're crazy," Ghirt countered. "A summons from Himmler was feared way more than a summons from Goering's fat ass."

We both laughed. And this was the beginning of a friendship that would change my life forever. Ghirt and I would talk about World War II, World War I, the Korean War, the Vietnam War, the Cold War, and every other war that had ever been fought. We talked about men and machines, organization and equipment, strategy and tactics. We talked about great battles and ancient empires. We ordered books, shared them, and quickly became inseparable. If a straight man could have a kindred soul, then this was mine. It was as if we were twin brothers that had been separated at birth.

I had developed my love of all weapons and war and history as a kid while lying at the foot of my grandfather's bed and watching old war movies with him. The Internet had expanded my horizons even further. I admit I loved playing Risk, and Civilizations, and Colonization, and Masters of Orion, and many other strategy and conquest games on my computer in between hustling. Crazy, right?

Ghirt was a military brat. He had been into warfare and weapons and military tactics and strategy since he could walk. He earned a black belt in karate and was a master at small unit tactics. He was also a master at weapons. I was great at the strategic shit, and he was an expert at the tactical shit. Together, we were unstoppable.

Slowly, our military conversations developed a radical tilt towards them and were mixed with our talks with Omene about Africa and about our history and ancestors. Slowly, we found ourselves in the chapel, searching for something else, something more. We both began to study Islam and the teachings of the black Hebrews. We also began to order books on African history from the interlibrary loan. For all of our lives, America had told us that we weren't shit. It was sad that we had to go to prison in order to learn different.

Slowly, we began to develop a sense that we were a part of something greater than ourselves; part of a people whose existence spanned from the very beginning of time to the present. Reading books by Chancellor Williams, J. A. Rogers, Anthony T. Browder, Chiekh Anta Diop, Francis Welsing, and Haki Madhubuti taught us more than we could have ever imagined. We were slowly becoming radicals within the walls of our confines. But becoming a black nationalist while surrounded by other races of people was a dangerous thing. In fact, we were ticking time bombs.

"Hey, brother, I need you to sign this petition," August said.

Big August was a brother from H-Town. H-Town is Houston, for the uninitiated. Brother August stood at six-three and had a five hundred-pound bench press. Yes, I said *five hundred.* And I'm not talking none of that hit-the-weight-one-time-shit. This brother could hit it anywhere between six to eight times, depending on how he felt that day.

I sat there and watched this man lift weights so heavy that the fucking squat bar that he had the weights on was bent nearly to the point of snapping. Nobody in prison wanted to fuck with Brother August. And few knew what I knew. The brother's mind was as sharp as he was strong.

"We sending this petition to region," August explained. "This is the first step. They got to acknowledge the petition. The next step is that we file our grievance in court. The conditions that they have us living under are inhumane. When they doing construction like this on a joint, they supposed to shut the joint down and transfer us. This is some bullshit. And then, they done turned this place into a damn immigration facility. I don't mind, but if they want this to be an immigration joint, they need to get us outta here."

And they basically had. The prison was surrounded by several immigration holding facilities, and the INS had a court at one of the holding facilities. So all the Mexicans in this region who were in the Feds but who were facing a deportation charge or who had to go to court for an immigration violation had been sent to the prison. The Feds thought that it would save them time and money and transportation costs, and it probably did, but they thought little about the consequences of having so many Mexican nationals all in one prison. At least until the shit blew up in their faces.

I signed Brother August's petition. In fact, I signed my name as big as John Fucking Hancock's, hoping that it would get me into trouble. I was quickly developing an I-don't-give-a-fuck-attitude toward *the man.* I began to view the white man as my natural enemy.

That evening, Ghirt, Omene, and two other African brothers, Wilson and Odukko, and I made our way through the chow line. As usual, the subject of the day was Africa.

"We have rubber, natural rubber that comes from the rubber tree," Odukko said. "Why don't African Americans come and put up factories to make tennis shoes? We have good quality leather, and the cost to set up a factory would be cheaper than in the Philippines. I don't understand why African Americans won't come and invest in Africa. The white man is there. He is getting rich off all of the gold and diamonds and oil. But African Americans won't come and invest in the land of their ancestors. We would much rather conduct business with you than with the whites."

Odukko was from Nigeria. He was an Igbo, and he was a Pan-Africanist to the fullest. He was in the Feds, like most Africans, for financial fraud involving a credit card scam. You can say whatever you want to about Nigerians, but I had yet to meet a stupid one.

"Yes," Wilson agreed. "Africa is a treasure trove of resources. It is quite unfortunate that blacks here in America do not invest in Africa."

"Africa needs to get its house in order if it wants outside investment," Ghirt said.

"But how can Africa get its house in order without outside investment?" Omene asked. "Turn to the World Bank? The IMF? We have had enough of that. We have had enough of others telling us how to run our economies. If there is to be a solution, it must come from us."

He was right. A people must find their own way. A people must find their own solutions. When being shot at, do you depend on the kindness of the person shooting at you to stop, or do you take matters into your own hands?

I pondered our dinnertime discussion about Africa, about the economy, about the World Bank, the IMF, the French, the dictators, the endemic and systematic corruption and what it would take to find a workable solution. Slowly, I was becoming more aware of my people and our place in the world. My mind was slowly beginning to crawl out of its prison and awaken. I was beginning to think about the bigger picture and not just my 'hood. I was slowly beginning to become something very dangerous to other people. I was slowly beginning to become a conscious Black Man.

"Is selling crack wrong or just illegal?" I asked Mr. Hall one day while walking the track together. Hall was a late forty-something brother from Oakland, California. He was raised on the tales of the Black Panther Party. He was one of the ultra smooth, soulful, pro-black brothers. I could just see him in the free world wearing a dashiki and sporting an Afro.

"Huh?" he asked.

"I mean, what if a person was selling dope but doing good things with the money?" I asked. "Let's say a youngster, maybe sixteen or seventeen, was hustling to keep his family inside of their home and to pay the lights and water. What if he was using the money to buy school clothes for his little brother and sister? Would that be wrong?"

"Well, if he's sixteen or seventeen, then he can go and get a job," Hall observed.

"But what if he couldn't because of a juvenile record? What if all he knew was the streets?"

Hall shook his head. "*Somebody* would hire him. He could go and work at McDonald's or somewhere."

"He didn't finish high school," I added. "He dropped out to support his little brother and sister."

"Where are the parents?" Hall asked.

"Pops in prison, Moms strung out. Dude just doing his best to keep food on the table for the youngsters."

Hall peered into the distance as we rounded the walking track and thought carefully about the scenario that I had just outlined.

"Is that wrong?" I pressed. "I mean, yeah, the white folks say that it's illegal, but is it *wrong*? If you've taken away every opportunity for someone, labeled them a criminal, they can't get a job, and all they want to do is put food on the table and buy school clothes for their little brother and sister. I mean, dude ain't out there trying to buy cars, and rims, and jewelry, and shit."

Hall continued around the track in silence for several moments before peering over toward me. "So, what do *you* think about the situation?"

I shrugged. "I think that it depends on what you're doing with the money. If you using the money to do something good, like keep your little brother out of trouble and send him to school, then ain't nothing wrong with it."

Hall nodded. "Back in the day, the Europeans took slaves in the name of Christianizing them for the salvation of their souls. They took an evil like slavery and justified it by using the same rationale. They were turning heathens into Christians. And they, too, believed that the end justified the means."

"So you think it's wrong?" I asked.

"It's not only illegal, but it's immoral," Hall said forcefully. "Do you understand what people have done in the name of crack cocaine? Women have sold their bodies, stole from their mothers, their *children*, just to get a hit. Crack has destroyed entire neighborhoods, entire communities. It has devastated the black community. And for what?"

Hall held out his hand with his palms turned up as if showing me a bunch of miniscule items. "For trinkets! Fancy cars, jewelry, expensive clothes … *trinkets!* We are still selling out one another. Back in history, Africans would capture one another and sell each other into slavery to the white man. What did they receive in exchange for selling out their brothers? A few fire sticks, some mirrors, some fake medicine, a few shiny beads … *trinkets!* And we're still selling out one another for trinkets!

"Let me tell you something about crack cocaine. It has been more destructive than any other drug in our history. And you know why? Because it was *targeted* at our women. The white man introduced heroin into the black community and strung out all the black men. But you know what they found? That black children were still able to go on and be successful and become educated as long as they had the mother inside the home.

"So they had to change up the drug and introduce something that would hook the black woman. And that's what crack has done. It has taken the black woman out of the home. And now look at us. *Look at us!* Kids are out on the streets killing, at home starving, or in the cemetery pushing up daisies. The white man learned the secret a long time ago. Target the black woman and you destroy the black family. Why? Because the hand that rocks the cradle rules the world."

That night lying in bed, I thought long and hard about what Mr. Hall had said. Crack had destroyed my people, and I had taken part in that destruction. I had taken part in *his* destruction. Mr. Hall had fallen victim to the drug as well. He told me stories about his years as an addict and how prison helped him to get clean. For the first time in my life, I met a crack addict that I actually respected. For the first time in my life, I actually viewed a crackhead as a real person and not just a subhuman with a few dollars in their hand. It was a strange feeling.

When I first fell, I had fantasies about meeting a bomb-ass connection and going home and getting keys for five grand from the border. Those dreams died on the track that day. Lying in bed, I began to see their faces. All of them. All of the people I had served.

Neighbors, friends, relatives. I had traded dope for sex. I had traded dope for backbreaking labor. I had run roughshod over people and treated other human beings like dirt. I had sold crack to my best friend's father. The conversation played over and over inside of my head, like I had just spoken the words.

*"My dad wants to holler at you, fool," D-Low told me.*

*"What about?"*

*"You got something?"*

*"Yeah, in the car. Why?"*

*"Him and his girlfriend is in the bedroom fiending."*

*"Damn," I said, thinking about the money. "You cool with this?"*

*"You might as well make the money," D-Low told me.*

I could see his eyes clearly now. My nigga was a soldier, but there was definitely liquid in his eyes. I only saw money then. But now, his face haunted me. I should have refused. I should have grabbed my keys, and me and my boy should have gotten out of there and went and blown some kill. Instead, I killed a little piece of him when I sold dope to his father.

I turned over in my bed trying to escape the faces and the stories behind them. I had done so much wrong in the name of money. That night, I realized that crack not only affected the lives of the people who used it, but the people who sold it. The quick money that it brought passed on its vile addiction to both parties. In the free world, I had become addicted to selling crack—addicted to hustling, to hiding it, to cooking it, to having it in my hands, to spending the proceeds, to carrying the guns, to fucking the bitches. And now that the faces haunted me, I realized that I, too, was a recovering addict.

# Chapter Five

I met Henry the next day. He, too, was changing as the months went by. He now wore dark sunglasses all the time, and his hair was slicked back on his head. He wore only the top button on his shirt fastened and now sported a tattoo on his neck. His accent was considerably more pronounced, and he asked that I call him Enrique instead of Henry. He had risen within the ranks and was now a sergeant for his people. We met in secret behind the gym at the weight pile.

"What's the word, homes?" Enrique asked.

"Same shit," I answered. "How you making it?"

"Shit, I'ma soldier, homes. I'm gonna survive anywhere."

I smiled. He was trying to act hard, and it was just the two of us around. "How's your family? You heard from your girl?"

Enrique shook his head. "Sancho got her. He's keeping her real busy." He laughed, but I could tell that he was hurting. He and Marisa had been together since middle school. They had two kids together.

"And how's Lil Henry and Lil Ernesto doing?" I asked.

He shrugged. "Shit, hell if I know. That bitch don't write no letters, she don't send no pictures. My sister said that she seen her in Wal-Mart, and my fucking kids looked all raggedy and shit. I'ma kill that bitch when I get outta here, homes."

"Let her make it, man," I told him. "Hell, she's just doing what everybody else's girl is doing."

"Your girl kicking it with Sancho, too?" he asked.

"Man, my girl *been* kicking it with Sancho. I don't think I was out of the city before she started partying."

It made him feel better. I got a smile from him. Sancho was the Mexican version of Jody, that mystical fucking boyfriend that creeps in and lays pipe while you're away.

"So what's your lawyer saying, San Antone?" he asked.

"Man, that muthafucka ain't saying shit!" I said. "Last time I talked to him, he was still talking the same old bullshit. 'Bad warrant. We gonna win the appeal.' All of that bullshit."

Enrique nodded.

"So, who you been working out with?" I asked. "We got us a San Antonio car, if you want to roll with us."

He shook his head. "You know I can't do that, homes."

"Why not?"

"'Cause I got to stick with my people."

"Aww, you done fell into that bullshit?" I asked.

"Shit, that's the way it is in the pen."

"We ain't in the pen," I reminded him. "We in the Feds."

"We in prison, homie. You got to stick with your people when you in the joint, San Antone."

"That's what I'm trying to do. You my people, right?"

"You know what I'm saying. Mexicans got to stick with Mexicans, blacks with the blacks, and the whites with the whites."

"Damn, I thought we was better than that."

"Shit, I ain't trying to get jumped, homes."

"Damn, for fucking with ya hometown?" I asked, just picking at him. I already knew what the deal was. He knew that I was just acting lame.

"You know what it is already, hometown. I see you kicking with your people."

I laughed. "We got anymore homies here from the 'Tone?"

"Yeah, a bunch," he smiled broadly. "I'm calling the shots for the hometown."

"Oh, yeah?"

He nodded proudly. "You have any problems with any Mexicans, you come to me."

"Well, well, congratulations. My fucking homeboy's a shot caller."

We shook hands and smiled at one another. I gathered my shit, ready to head to the lower yard. They were about to call ten-minute move on the loudspeaker. Movement was done every hour, five minutes before the hour, and lasted until five minutes after. It was only during the ten-minute move that a person could go in or out of the dorm or travel from the upper to the lower yard, or vice versa.

"Oh, yeah, what's the deal with the fucking costume, Henry?" I asked. "You look like a fucking *'American Me'* reject."

He smiled and lifted his middle finger.

I headed to the lower yard to see what was happening. There were domino games going on beneath the gazebos in the center of the yard. I pulled up and called next.

"You don't want none a this, San Antone!" Grave Digger shouted, slamming down his bones.

"Yeah, you don't wanna step off into this here fire!" Dupriest shouted before slamming his domino down for twenty points. "Bolt the house down!"

"I got next," I reminded them. "I'ma run over here to the phone room and make a quick call."

"You better hurry back!" Duck said. "I'm skinning these niggaz' asses up over here!"

I hurried to the phone room, which sat in the middle of the yard. I wanted to call my girl and see how she was doing. As I passed by my man Prentice's booth, he was falling and I quickly caught him.

"Say, you all right, fool?"

His mouth was open and tears began to stream down his face. At first I thought it was a seizure until his voice caught up with his intentions, and he screamed.

I frantically checked his body for stab wounds, thinking that this fool had been done up. There were none. "What's wrong, dude?"

"My son!" he shouted in between his heavy crying. "My son ..."

Deep down I knew it was bad. "What's the matter?" I grabbed the phone in the booth where he had been talking and lifted it to my ear. A woman was crying hysterically on the other side.

"What's the matter with Prentice?"

"Our baby!" she screamed. "He accidentally shot himself! He's dead!"

I dropped the telephone, dropped back down to my knees, and I grabbed my homeboy. There was nothing soft about me, and nothing soft about him. His son was three years old, and so was mine. That phone call could have just as well been mine.

"He's dead!" Prentice cried.

"It's gonna be all right, man," I told him. "It's gonna be all right." I sat there rocking him in my arms on the floor of the phone booth while staring up at the ceiling and secretly asking God *why*. I know that we're not supposed to question and that we're supposed to have faith in His plans for us. But to me, right then and there, it was all a bunch of bullshit. It was all fucked-up. Why would a God who was supposed to be such a good God take a three-year-old baby? I didn't understand, and so there was no way for me to try to rationalize to this man God's reason for letting it happen.

I had fought with God many times in my life. I had been a disobedient child, arguing, questioning, even cursing. I had challenged my Father many times in my life, but with this one? I was so mad at The Man Upstairs that I didn't want to speak to Him anymore. I was beyond angry at Him. How could He take children? God and I had battled a lot in my lifetime, because my life had been so hard. I knew that I deserved every shitty thing that happened to me, because I had been the scum of the earth. But not a child. An innocent, three-year-old child?

I think I was so angry with God because my boy was three. If He was willing to let something like that happen to Prentice's three year old, then He would let it happen to my son. That scared me more than anything.

"What's the matter with Pree, San Antone?" Grave Digger asked, as he and several others made their way inside of the phone room.

"His baby, man. He lost his baby."

"Awww, naw," Grave Digger said. "Man, that's fucked-up."

"I'ma kill that muthafucka!" Prentice whispered.

"Who? What happened?" I asked.

"My son, he went under the bed, and he got hold a that nigga's gun," Pree explained.

"What nigga?" Duck asked.

"That bitch-ass nigga she fuckin' with," Prentice said.

"*What?*" Grave Digger lifted the telephone receiver. "Hello? Yeah. You let this nigga come up into your house and put a gun under the bed? Knowing you got little churin' runnin' around? Bitch, you deserve to die, and so do that nigga. And if I ever come across either of you two low-down, no-good muthafuckas, you gonna be smelling some grave dirt." And then he slammed the telephone down.

I don't know what it was about him doing that, but it changed everything in that telephone room. It made us all realize that whatever happened, we weren't going to go through it alone. No matter how bad things turned in our lives, we had each other.

The death of that baby fucked me up real bad. I wasn't in the mood for any dominos. I needed to unwind, to clear my head, to withdraw for a moment. I headed for the library.

The prison library had turned into my personal getaway. It was my place of solace in a mad and crazy world. The shelves of books lining the walls were like the thick stones of a medieval fortress. They helped keep out the monsters.

Inside of the library, I picked up Adam Smith's *The Wealth of Nations*. We had a collection of classic novels in the library, and I had taken to reading them whenever I dropped by the library on the spur of the moment and had nothing else to read. This is where I first read Herodotus, Locke, Rousseau, Tolstoy, Mann, Melville, and most of the other classics. It helped me to understand and converse with the white folks on topics that interested them. Educating myself in the classics and being able to speak intelligently about them would no doubt come in handy in the future.

"You sleep in the room next to Juarez, huh?"

I looked up to see who was talking to me. It was this Blood nigga from California. A big, swole-ass, gang-banging muthafucka who was down for selling illegal firearms. His name was Leo.

"Yeah," I said, wondering what this fool wanted.

"It be a lot of muthafuckas in and out of that room at night, I know."

Juarez was the biggest gump on the yard. And for the uninitiated, a gump is a punk. He stood six foot three and had more cum flowing through him than the Hover Dam had water.

"Man, I don't know," I said, dismissing him. "I don't be paying no attention to that bullshit."

"How can you not pay any attention," he laughed. "She needs a turnstile at her door."

First of all, calling a *he*, a *she* was something I didn't get into. The muthafucka had balls, so *he* was dude. It was these accepting, down-low, punk-ass niggaz that rolled with that shit. My alarm started going off about this dude and his whole line of questioning.

"Man, I just mind my own business," I told him. "I'm just here to do my time."

"So punks don't really faze you?" he asked with a gay-ass smile.

"Man, I've had friends die in my arms," I told him. "Nothing fazes me."

"Hmmmph. Well, I just wanna let you know that a closed mouth don't get fed."

"What?" I asked.

"I said, a closed mouth don't get fed," he repeated, giving me another gay-ass smile.

I was seated behind the library desk where the clerks sit. The nighttime clerk was off bullshitting, so I had copped the spot for some privacy. I peered around behind the desk and found what I was searching for. Our window squeegie. It had a long handle on it with a sponge and plastic blade at the end of it. I lifted it and clocked this fool upside his head with it.

He was a huge, muscle-bound meathead, but I didn't give a fuck. He came on to me, so I had to throw down. I had to make my manhood unquestionable to everyone on the yard. In prison, if you give one inch, they don't just take a mile, they take *everything*. I was determined to walk out of that place a man and still be able to look my son in the eye.

I leapt over the counter and continued to pummel that son of a bitch with my squeegie. I wasn't going to give him a chance to recover. He had twenty-one inch guns and a four hundred-pound bench press. I swung that fucking stick like I was Babe Ruth.

By the time the guards arrived, I had beaten the asshole to a pulp. They handcuffed me and dragged me up to Special Housing. That night, while lying in my bunk in the hole, I heard the alarms in the compound go off. My friend Prentice had been discovered in the shower, where he had hung himself.

# Chapter Six

I got out of the hole two weeks later. I did fourteen days in Special Housing; I hadn't seen the sun nor been able to walk more than fourteen feet in the last two weeks. My legs were wobbly, and the sun wreaked havoc on my eyes.

As usual, the powers that be assigned me to a new room on the yard. I packed my belongings, went through the compound to the lower half of the yard, and carted them upstairs to my new room. It was there where I met Young Gangsta.

Gangsta was just barely eighteen. He had been locked up in jail since he was fifteen for a murder charge and a federal drug charge. The Feds tried him first, so he got to go to the Feds first. It was the way most people preferred it. That way, the federal sentence got to eat up a big chunk of the state sentence, if not all of it. Most would rather do their time in a federal joint than on some gladiator farm in the state.

Gangsta had gotten caught up for less than an ounce. Can you believe that shit? A fed case for less than an ounce? Turns out that the Podunk West Texas counties had decided to turn over all crack cocaine cases to the feds. They were serious about handing out some time for fucking with dope. And so, we had black men locked up in the Feds for rocks. Yeah, I'm talking twenty dollar pieces. The worst case that I had heard of so far was my man Lefty. He was a dope fiend who got caught with a twenty-dollar rock that he had just scored. That single piece of crack rock cost him ten years of his life in a fucked-up fed joint. Imagine that.

"What's up, fool?" Gansta asked, extending his hand.

"What's up, man?" I replied, clasping his hand.

"Not like that, old lame-ass nigga!" Gangsta shouted. He slapped my hand twice and snapped his fingers.

"Okaaaaaay," I said, turning and tossing my shit onto the bed.

"Hold up, I put in a cop-out for that bunk!" Gangsta protested.

I shrugged. "Well, they gave it to me."

"Awww, that's fucked-up!" Gangsta declared. "I've been trying to get that bunk for a week and a half."

"A week and a half?" I asked, smiling. "You been on the yard for an entire week and a half, and you mean they ain't gave you a bottom bunk yet? *Damn*, what's wrong with these people?"

"Okay, smart-ass."

I smiled, and he smiled, and instantly, I knew two things. One, my time had just gotten a lot more lively, and two, if I didn't take this kid under my wing, he'd be dead in a month.

"Where you from?" I asked.

"Odessa."

Odessa was in West Texas. Right down the road from the joint we were in. Most of the blacks on the yard were from West Texas: Midland, Odessa, Amarillo, and Lubbock. The latter two cities were considered the Panhandle, while the first two were located in what was called the Permian Basin. They were both far removed from civilization as far as most people were concerned. Once you passed San Antonio, civilization ceased until you got to El Paso. Some would even exclude San Antonio and El Paso. And by some, I mean Houston and Dallas fools. But that's another story entirely.

"Where you from?"

"San Antonio," I told him.

"San Antone!" he shouted. "How 'bout them Spurs?"

I laughed. He was crazy and wild, filled with all of the energy and brashness that youth brought. I was a little older in years, but decades older in wisdom, outlook, and bearing. I had been in prison for more than a year, and locked up for damn-near three. Prison had a way of aging a person rapidly.

Young Gangster would eventually find that out. He had a ten-year sentence in the state, and a six-year sentence in the Feds. He had murdered another kid for a dollar. Yes, I said *one dollar*.

Gangsta was fifteen; the kid he killed was eighteen. The eighteen year old had been whipping his ass and taking his dope money from him on a regular basis. Gangsta had gotten tired of it, lured the kid back to his crib with the promise of more money, and then shot his stupid ass. Why he would go back to this kid's house after picking on him and taking his money for so long is beyond me. Anyway, the state came down hard on the youngster. He ended up pleading out to ten. Same bullshit story, he got a court-appointed attorney, who herded him through the justice system while taking the path of least resistance. So in essence, there were two victims that day. No change that—there were a lot of victims that day. Both kids left behind families.

Young Gangsta left behind a little sister in a community where the fucking predators are circling by the time the girls turn thirteen. That small-town shit made me sick to my stomach. With him gone, she would be pregnant by the age of fourteen, on welfare by fifteen, and hulled out by eighteen.

Gangsta's mother had been killed when he was around four or five. She had been shot. That left him, his little sister, and his brother, to live with their grandmother on the roughest, poorest side of town in Odessa. He was destined to come to prison.

"Man, throw that shit in ya locker, San Antone, and let's go eat!" Gangsta shouted.

I nodded. I threw most of my shit into the locker, put my lock on it, and headed out the door.

In the cafeteria we met up with my boys, Ghirt and Omene, and walked through the line together.

"Ghirt, this is my celly, Young Gangsta," I said, introducing them.

"Ghirt, what's up, baby?" Gangsta said loudly. He slapped Ghirt's hand and snapped, "Aww, old lame-ass nigga!"

Ghirt turned toward me, and I shook my head. "He's crazy. That's just the way he is until he takes his medicine."

"Aww, fuck you, old black-ass nigga!" Gangsta replied.

My time had definitely gotten livelier.

"Hey, Officer, can I have some more eggs?" Omene shouted to the guard standing behind the prisoners serving the food.

"Hey, you got a problem with what I give you, you talk to *me*!" the convict serving the eggs told him.

"Talk to you?" Omene asked. "Talk to you for what? You can't do anything for me."

"You got a problem with the food, you talk to *me*!" the Mexican repeated.

"Man, you can have my eggs," Ghirt told him.

"You're an inmate just like me," Omene said, tugging at his shirt. "You can't give me shit."

"Fuck you!" the server told him. "You got a fucking problem with me, we can handle this shit."

"I'm here!" Omene told him. "I wasn't even talking to your ass, I was talking to the police. You should mind your own damn business."

I grabbed Omene and pushed him on through the line. It wasn't even worth it. Besides, I would straighten that shit out later. The egg server was a Califa; a California Mexican. Usually they divided themselves in prison between *norteño*, who were from the north, and *sureño*, who were from the south. But being so far from home, they all stuck together and called themselves Califas. You could tell them by the tattoos they wore on the back of their bald heads.

I was going to get with them tonight, because they were going to do a tat for me in one of their rooms. They had the hottest talent on the yard right now, as far as tatting goes. I had seen a dragon that they put on my boy, and I wanted a similar one. The bitch was bad. The dragon would start on my back, and go over my shoulder down to my chest. It was going to cost me three hundred bucks.

I showered and went to the room that night. They were fucking professionals. They had lookouts spaced throughout the halls. We would know as soon as the guard left his desk, or as soon as one tried to enter the building. They had a system of whistles to let each other know exactly where the guards were and which direction they were going in. They could even tell which guard by the tone, pitch, and different variations in the whistle. It was a valuable lesson. Just because someone may or may not speak English, never underestimate their intelligence.

My painful-ass tattoo went on. They fashioned tattoo guns using guitar string, tape, ink pens, and used the motor from the hair clippers in the barbershop. The ink was real tattoo ink, straight from the free world. We all know how they got it. Like all the other illegal shit, it came from guards on the take.

We took breaks in between counts. The guards counted at ten P.M., midnight, two A.M., and five A.M. We finished sometime around six that morning. I climbed in the shower, went to eat breakfast, and then headed for bed and slept until two o'clock that afternoon, then rose, got dressed, and headed upstairs to see what Omene was up to. When I got there, the guards were packing his stuff.

"What's up with my boy?" I asked.

The guard stopped and turned toward me. "He got jumped."

"*Jumped?*" The first thing that came to mind were the Mexicans. "When?"

"Earlier today," the guard said. "They made him check into the hole."

"What?" I turned and headed down the hall and found Tuck. "Omene got jumped?"

"Yeah, that was fucked-up."

"Fucked-up?"

"Them niggaz was wrong for that shit."

"*Niggaz?*" I was shocked. "He got jumped by some niggaz?"

Tuck pushed me into a nearby room. "Unc and Magic and them youngsters."

"*What?*" Unc and Magic and them were from California. I guess they were supposed to be Big G's enforcers. Big G was from Cali too. Somehow, someway, these stupid-ass youngsters from West Texas had allowed a nigga from Cali to represent us. In other words, California niggas was shot calling in a prison in Texas.

I had argued the point until I was blue in the face, but to no avail. Those stupid-ass youngsters had been reared on Boyz N The Hood, and so their small-time country asses had elected these fake-ass, gang-banging muthafuckas to represent us. And now, this had happened. I rushed to the BET room, which was the TV room for the blacks, and found a meeting going on. I jumped right in.

"What's happened to Omene?" I asked.

"That's what we were in here discussing," Big G said. "Come on in and pull up a chair."

"I'd rather stand," I said, locking eyes with him. "What happened?"

"It was something that we had to do," Bone stated. He was a youngster, one of the country-ass idiots from West Texas who stared at the California brothers like they were movie stars.

"What do you mean it had to be done?" I asked.

"Things on the yard have changed," Magic added. "We have to be more organized and more disciplined. They came to us with a gripe and asked us to take care of our people."

"A gripe?" I asked. "What gripe?"

"They say that Omene disrespected them in the kitchen," Big G explained. "So, we had to take care of him. When we go to them, they take care of their people."

"That's the way *they* do things, not us!" I shouted. "They're a bunch of fucking followers with shot callers and lieutenants and shit! That's not us!"

My speaking out had given others the courage to do the same.

"Yeah, man, that was some fucked-up shit," Cat Daddy told them. "And even if y'all felt that it had to be done, you don't do that boy like that. Y'all broke both that man's jaws, busted both his lips, knocked his teeth out, broke his nose, fucked up his ribs and shit!"

Uproar shot throughout the room.

Big G lifted his hands to regain order. "Okay, it was a little excessive. I take responsibility for that."

"They don't even do they own people like that!" Duck shouted.

"Okay, okay, I understand your point. Next time—"

"—Next time?" Duck stood up and headed for the door, followed by several others. "Shouldn't be no next time."

"Look, we gotta organize," Magic said.

"This ain't how you organize," I said. "You did him like that?"

"What we could do from now on is just hit in the body," Big G said, trying to salvage the meeting. "If some of our people need to be disciplined, we'll get some guys around the same size, and we'll just hit him in the body."

"Bullshit!" I said. "Ain't nobody hitting me. That's for them Mexicans. We should be protecting one another. And I was there when that bullshit went down. He didn't disrespect nobody. He told that muthafucka that he wasn't talking to him, that's all. This shit wasn't about no disrespect. This is that California shit. Them is ya boys from California, *that's* why that shit happened. And y'all know Omene is from Nigeria, and he ain't got no backup. We could have told them Califa muthafuckas to go to hell. It ain't but thirty of them on the yard. We could have held our boy down. This is some old West Coast-ass shit!"

Magic and I exchanged fierce glances, as did the other California boys and the West Texas youngsters. I knew they wanted to kill me.

"Let me tell all you muthafuckas something," I said. "I ain't down for this bullshit; I ain't down for nobody putting they hands on me. Any of you muthafuckas touch me, I'ma kill you. It's just that plain and simple. I'm killing every muthafucka there, and I'm killing the muthafuckas who gave the order."

That speech I gave sent plenty of dudes over to my side. But for the most part, the cats who followed me were older heads. Late twenties on up. They still had the eighteen to twenty-five set. They had the gladiators.

Omene had been my brother, my older brother. He had taught me much about my people, my African heritage, and my place in the world. Most of what I knew about Africa, I learned from him. I had begun to emulate him. If ever there were a man whom I wanted to be like, whom I respected, it was he. He brought out so much more in me. It was around him when I felt like so much more than a just a "nigga." And now, he was gone. He had been taken from me by some ignorant-ass fools and an equally ignorant system of prison justice.

The fools that beat the shit out of him were taken to the hole. They would be getting out while he would be transferred. And me? I would become lost. I sat down and wrote a letter to my father, and then went out and sat on the balcony with Ghirt and Young Gangsta. It seemed as though it were just the three of us against the world.

# Chapter Seven

The following week I got a letter back from my dad. I had started writing to him since my own incarceration. It proved to be the wisest decision I ever made. He had been locked up since the late seventies, and it seemed as though he had read every book ever published. He was like Lex Luthor or Professor Xavier from the X-Men. He could see shit or know what a muthafucka was thinking before it even happened. Prison had turned his mind into much more than just a fucking razor; it was a weapon of mass destruction. Pops' intelligence and wisdom was more than just penetrating, it was scary. Having his mind on my side gave me the advantage in prison.

My father and I had decided that no excuses and no apologies were necessary. He and I were not going to live in the past. We weren't going to go through that whole "Why weren't you there for me?" type of bullshit. He was who he was, and I was who I was. Fathers who disappointed their sons came with sons who disappointed their fathers. Had he been around, would my life have been different? More likely than not, yes. My life was hard. His absence made me become a man that much earlier in life. And becoming a man earlier in life helped me deal with the bullshit that I was going through now. Would I thank him for that? Of course not. No apologies also came without thank-yous.

I opened my dad's letter after mail call to find his responses to my earlier queries. I had told him about the Omene situation and about the situation going on with the Mexicans and with the brothers. He told me to hold fast, to remain steady in my convictions. He told me that it was better to live my life as a lion for one day than to live a whole lifetime as a sheep. That quote struck me deeply, and it stayed with me forever.

I would carry that quote with me in all decisions that I made, in everything that I did or advised others to do. Be a lion. Be courageous, be aggressive, be the hunter and not the hunted. Stand and live on your feet, not on your knees. I watched as the brothers gave in time after time to the demands of the Mexican shot callers and thought about my father's statement over and over. We were living on our knees. Although outnumbered ten to one, we still should have roared and went out like lions. But I was outnumbered, outvoted, and outgunned.

I went to the Jamaicans and Haitians on the yard. The Jamaicans were down, and so were the Haitians. The fact that I spoke French and could talk with them in French won my Haitian brothers over. And being that Omene was West African, I felt that securing the support of the African brothers would be easy. I was wrong.

"What do you mean, 'no'?" I asked.

"I don't want to get involved," Okumbar said flatly.

"Omene was our brother!" I protested. "*Omo eya!*" ('Mother's son!')

Olusegun shook his head. "But he is gone. Now, we must survive. Alexander, we are few."

"I just want to do my time," Malaika added.

I thought that he would have been my ally. I turned to Malaika. "Eusi, we must stand up for our own. If we don't fight for ourselves, then who will? We have to protect ourselves!"

"What you are talking about is suicide," Alex scowled. "Going up against the brothers?"

I shook my head. "No, not all the brothers; just those leaders who would beat us. Those who would break our ribs, bust our noses, split our lips, because they fear what the Mexicans would do. They are cowards. They beat their own people to save their own skins. If not for Omene, then do it for yourselves."

"You're trying to revolt against the leaders, Alexander," Alex smiled. "That's admirable, but I'm too old to believe in revolutions, son."

And with that, Alex rose and walked off. The rest of the Africans followed him. And with that, my hopes of avenging my friend's brutal beating faded away. Every number that we could muster counted. But without the strength that the Africans provided, my plan was a no-go.

The evening provided me some consolation. Omene had managed to sneak me a letter out of the hole.

The note was short. He said that he wouldn't be returning to the compound, and he gave me the address of his cousin in California. The note also gave me some instructions. I could hear his erudite, high-pitched, British/Nigerian accent as I read it.

> *"Keep on the search for the knowledge of self. Pass on what you learn to the people. The Great Creator of our ancestors will bless you, if only you pay your duty to Him. Now, you owe Him the teaching of His people."*

I folded that note and put it away. And I read it often, especially when my clouds hung low. *Keep on the search for the knowledge of self.* It was something that I would continue to do. I needed to find myself, to find my purpose.

Oftentimes, Omene would tell me that the Creator had a plan for each of us. And that all we could do was prepare ourselves to be His instruments. The Almighty had a plan for me. The more I came to understand the greatness of my friend, the more that I came to understand that it was his ability to make every individual feel worthy. It was his African upbringing. In Africa, every human life was precious, every soul, sacred. The message that was sent to me, through Omene, was that despite my current condition, despite what I had done in the past, I was still worthy. I was still an instrument of the Almighty. Omene gave me hope.

My search for knowledge of self led me to evening prayers in the chapel. My brothers were inside of the chapel making *salat*. I joined them in submission to the Almighty. And for the first time in my life, I opened up a Koran. I wanted to know more about God. I had read the Old Testament and the New Testament. And now my curiosity had taken me in this direction. Learning one book, or two books, or two aspects of God, was like learning only two-thirds of God. I wanted to know the third aspect.

"*A Saalam Alaikum*, my brother."

"*Alaikum As-Saalam*."

I split my time learning Islam between the Sunnis, The Nation, and The Sufis. It was an experience, to say the least. The Sunnis and The Nation battled over Muslims and converts. The Sunnis claimed that The Nation wasn't real Muslims. The Nation claimed that they were the only real Muslims for black people to join. They spent fifty percent of their time disparaging one another and the other fifty percent worshiping Allah. The Sufis were much more laid-back and much more spiritual. They were more in tune with Allah, with Allah's creations, and with finding an inner peace. Needless to say, I spent more time with them than with the other two. Ghirt disagreed with all of them.

"It's not for us!" Ghirt protested.

"And you think Christianity is?" I asked.

"That ain't either!" Ghirt argued. "We had a religion and knowledge of God before any of them. Moses was an Egyptian priest, right?"

"Yeah?"

"He learned his teachings in the temples, right?"

"Yeah."

"And he taught those teachings to the slaves, which was against the law," Ghirt said, pressing forward. "He went on the run with the slaves. And what was the first thing that they did when he went up on the mountain and left them alone? They went back to their old religion and built a golden calf to worship the Egyptian god Hathor. The Hebrews learned religion from Egypt. This one-God concept came from Akhenaton. The Ten Commandments are right there inside of the Egyptian temple and Pyramids for everyone to see."

I nodded. "The Forty-Two Negative Confessions."

"You know all of this, so why are you tripping?" Ghirt continued. "The Madonna and Child? The Virgin Birth? That's Isis and Osiris. The Trinity? That's Tefnut! 'From one I made myself into three!' All of it comes from Ancient Egypt! From our people! Christianity comes from Judaism, Islam from Christianity, so why would you pick Islam? Look at what they are doing to Africans in the Sudan! The Arab word for African is slave. You're trading in one slave master's religion for another!"

"Ghirt, I'm learning," I told him. "I'm just learning. I want to find peace. Islam is peace. I can get in my corner, kneel down, and submit myself to God. It feels right. It feels humbling."

"Look at your skin, black man!" Ghirt smiled. "'Ye are gods!' We are the Children of the Sun. God's Chosen. We are the first! The fathers and mothers of all humanity. Humble yourself before God, but humble yourself to the God that created you first. '*I come from the base of the*

*River Nile. I come from the mountains where the God Hapti dwells.*'

"Where did Egypt come from? From the base of the Nile. From the soft silts of Ethiopia. Where did the people of Egypt come from? Egypt was a colony of Ethiopia. Where did their God come from? From the base of the River Nile, where Hapti dwells. African man, African god."

Ghirt was more radical than me. He was militant. He submitted only to an African god. And he was co-opting Young Gangsta more and more as the days went by. We had taken the youngster under our wings. I would take him with me to watch the minister speak on videotape, while Ghirt would take him jogging with him in the evenings. I taught inner peace and submission to the will of Allah. Ghirt taught African superiority and talked of a coming international race war. My Islam and Ghirt's radicalism all came to a collision one weekend while watching a tape of the minister. It was one of the most profound things that I had ever heard anyone say. The minister said, "A man isn't a real man if he cannot protect the women who gave birth to his race."

That statement stayed with me forever. It haunted me. *A man is not a real man if he cannot protect the women who gave birth to his race.* It made me think about my people and our position in this world. My thoughts frightened me.

Here in America, we were truly at the mercy of the United States government. What if one day they woke up and decided that they were tired of us? What if they woke up one morning and said, "Get all of your dope peddling, gang-banging asses out of here!" Certainly that wasn't all of us, but it was their perception of us.

We were welfare queens, pimps, dope dealers, crack babies, gangbangers, etc. ... The Mexicans were taking all of the menial jobs, the jobs that they didn't want. We weren't educating ourselves and trying to take over the high-tech jobs. Besides, most of those were being outsourced to India and China. So where did that leave us? What could we do if such a nightmare scenario occurred? We couldn't protect our women. And Africa fared no better.

Not one African nation had a military that was worth anything. They couldn't defend their countries against a well-armed Cub Scout pack. How do you live in a world at the mercy of another people? How do you live in an America that doesn't want you, that views you as a criminal, a leach, a dreg?

"If we were really a part of this country, we wouldn't have needed a Twenty-Fourth Amendment to the Constitution, now, would we?" Ghirt asked when I brought the subject up.

"There will never be two Americas," I replied. "Never."

"We don't need there to be," Ghirt said. "We need to invest and make Africa into a United States of Africa, with all of the first-world comforts of the West."

"And you want all of us to move over there, huh, Marcus Garvey?"

"Wasn't a bad idea."

"And then we can divide ourselves into Returnees and Aborigines, and go to war with one another."

"Why would that happen?" Ghirt asked. "If it was a first-world nation with an economy that benefited everyone?"

"Because if there's more than one of us in a room, we'll find a way to disagree," I said with a smile.

"You're getting cynical in your old age," Ghirt returned.

"My old age?"

"Today's your birthday, right?"

I thought about it for several moments. "Yeah, it is."

Ghirt patted me on my shoulder. "Congratulations. You made another one."

I nodded and stared out over the yard. Like all the rest of the days, my birthdays had begun to run together. Birthdays on a prison yard meant little. And the only way you could tell it was a holiday was by the food they served.

"How old are you?" Ghirt asked.

I shrugged. I had been in prison for more than four years, dealing with Mexicans, tension on the yard, prison politics, stupid-ass guards, bullshit-ass lawyers, and all the rest of the drama and hysterics that prison entailed.

"I think I'ma get another tat," I told Ghirt.

"What this time?"

"A sun," I said. "And I'ma have 'em fix up my black panther tattoo on my arm."

"A sun?" Ghirt asked. "Why a sun?"

"Because, like you said, I'm a child of the Sun. Original black man!"

Ghirt held out his hand, and I clasped it. “And don’t ever forget it.”

# Chapter Eight

The bus pulled up to the front gate, and in through Control walked the most beautiful fucking thing I ever saw. Out of a chain of about seventy-eight people, sixty of them were black, ten were white boys, and only eight were Mexicans. I almost wanted to write a fucking love letter to the regional designator. That muthafucka had sent us a miracle. He had damn near doubled our numbers in one swoop.

And even more wonderful, fifteen out of the sixty were from San Antonio. I had homeboys from my hometown. Lots of them. Plus, we got three from Austin, ten from West Texas, six from the Panhandle, two from New York, two from Jersey, one from the ATL, and the rest from all over. The only bad thing about it was that sixty new brothers meant sixty care packages. Soap, shampoo, shower shoes, deodorant, toothpaste, toothbrushes. All that shit added up.

The newbies made it down the yard and into the housing units. I would meet them later. Right then I had more important matters to attend to. I had to call my girl.

"Hello?"

"Hey, baby," I said softly. "How you doing?"

"Hanging in there."

"Hanging in there? What's the matter?"

"Nothing. Just trying to make ends meet."

"I know it's tough. But I'll be back before you know it. And everything will be all right."

"What did the lawyer say?"

"I don't know," I answered. "Has my momma talked to him lately?"

"I don't know. You want me to call her and see?"

"Yeah, you check up on that for me. How's little Christian?"

"Bad as hell. He got into the baby shampoo and rubbed it all in his eyes. I had to wash it out and rush him to the emergency room."

"What did they say?"

"His eyes will be irritated for a couple of days. If they still red and bothering him after three days, then bring him back in."

"*Damn*. How'd he get into that?"

"He just climbed onto the sink and got into it."

"Wasn't nobody watching him?"

"Yes, I was watching him. But damn, I can't watch him every second of the day!"

"Why not? It's called parenting."

"Then maybe *you* should try it!"

And just like that, she hung up the phone in my face. I stood there inside the phone room trying to calm myself. I couldn't call her right back. The phone system was designed so that we had to wait fifteen minutes before we could place another phone call. Why? Who knew? Some supergenius in the Bureau of Prisons just sits around and thinks this stupid shit up. *What can we do to irritate a muthafucka? How about not letting him make phone calls back to back?*

*Brilliant, you're promoted just for thinking that stupid shit up!*

I gripped the handset tightly and then placed it back on the hook. What the fuck was she doing that she couldn't watch the baby? All kinds of wicked shit went through my head. Was she fucking some nigga? Was she cooking? Was she fucking some nigga? Was she sleeping? Was she fucking some nigga? Was she washing clothes? *Was she fucking some nigga?*

My agitation disturbed my fucking Spidey senses so much that I couldn't sense the tension on the yard. Usually it was something that I could feel. The atmosphere felt thick, heavy, almost like a thick South Texas swamp humidity. It was so thick that you could almost slice it. I walked into the kitchen, went through the chow line in a daze, and sat down at a table alone.

"Hey, San Antone!" Duck called out. "You got some homeboys here!"

I nodded and waved my hand. "I'll get with them in a minute."

What I hadn't realized is that the eight Mexicans that had hit the yard with all those brothers earlier were Califas. Eight Califas, two of them from another fed joint, a fed joint where they had whipped one of the Border Brothers that was now at this prison. It started with the quickness of a match strike.

The Border Brother struck the Califa across the back of his head with his serving tray, sending blood splattering halfway across the room. A second Califa was also struck by a serving tray, getting the war started. The problem with the Border Brothers' plan was that they had forgotten that all of the Califas worked in the kitchen; including in the back of the kitchen, inside of the butcher shop.

The lazy-ass kitchen guards on duty were supposed to lock the butchers inside of the butcher shop. They were also supposed to keep the locker that contained the butcher knives locked at all times. They had done neither. Califas poured from the kitchen area with knives of all lengths and widths. The kitchen quickly turned into a bloodbath.

*"Attention on the compound! Attention on the compound!"* the PA system blared. *"All inmates return to your housing units immediately! All inmates return to your housing units! Compound is closed! I repeat, the compound is closed!"*

I watched one Border Brother get his arm completely severed from the forearm down. I watched as Califa after Califa poured into the kitchen and chopped and hacked everything in their path. Border Brother after Border Brother fell and ran, or stood and died. Their calls for help shot through the cafeteria.

*"Piasa! Piasa!"*

*Piasa* meant "countrymen." The Border Brothers were the frontline soldiers for the Piasas, which was what the Mexican nationals called themselves. But the call to arms for their countrymen went unanswered. Most of the Mexicans were gathered at the doors, trying to get the hell out of the cafeteria.

Finally, one of the guards with some sense opened up the cafeteria doors and allowed the Border Brothers and the Piasas to escape onto the yard while containing the Califas in the cafeteria. The battle had been as one-sided as any the yard had yet to see.

The Border Brothers' plans to attack the Califas in the kitchen had been the dumbest plan in the history of prison warfare. The Califas had access to knives, and pipes, and brooms, and mops, and everything that the kitchen could provide. The Border Brothers thought that their numbers would be more than enough to crush the Cali boys. Many of them ended up paying for that assumption with their lives.

The yard was shut down, and the Califas were disarmed and marched up to the Special Housing Unit. This would be the last time any of them would be allowed onto the yard for many, many years. Although they had been the victims, it was easier to transfer thirty than it was to transfer four hundred. The numbers had taught everyone a valuable lesson: they didn't matter.

Ghirt and I knew that inside of closed confines, the numbers could be mitigated. The Spartans had held off the entire Persian army at Thermopylae. Surely we could hold off a few hundred Mexicans in a dorm, a kitchen, or a library. Ghirt immediately went to work creating battle plans to do just such a thing. If the brothers could rally to one area, or even better—one floor—we could hold off the majority while some of us destroyed the ones caught on the floor with us—piecemeal.

The second lesson from that battle was that iron weapons were critical: weapons that did damage, and weapons that gave us the longer reach. Young Gangster found the perfect solution to that problem one day.

"Check this out, C," he whispered. He lay down on his bed and pointed to the metal underbrace that supported the center of the bunk on top. "Check out the welds."

I did, and they were tiny. "We could get some of the brothers in the plumbing shop to cut the bars to the point where they're about to break. And when it's about to go down, we could just kick them or pull them off."

"I'll get on it," Gangsta nodded.

"Not for everybody," I told him. "Just for the people we trust. And tell them to keep it a secret and don't even pass it on to their partners."

Young Gangsta nodded and headed out the door.

That night, I met with Duck, Ghirt, and Young Gangsta. Duck opened up his gym bag and showed me a bag full of iron. Some sharpened, some not.

"Where in the hell did that come from?" I asked.

"Welding shop," Duck smiled.

"That place is wide open," Ghirt added.

"The bedpost," I said out loud. "Sharpen all of these, and get whatever else you can, and then have some of the brothers in the welding shop, HVAC, or wherever, solder them inside of the hollow metal bedposts in the rooms where our people are."

Duck nodded.

"Good work, Duck," I said, patting him on his shoulder. I peered in the bag once again and selected a sixteen-inch piece of steel that was already sharpened. "I'll hang on to this one." I stuck the shank inside of my khakis.

The Border Brothers had attacked a group without provocation, without notifying us so that we could keep our people out of the way, without even giving the Califas a chance to handle their own people in-house. They had violated all the rules of prison warfare, and had changed the face of prison warfare inside of our joint for good. The Califas had been caught off guard, but fortunately for them, they had the kitchen weapons to fall back on.

We would not be so fortunate, but we were going to be ready. I had about thirty soldiers following me. I now had a responsibility to them to make sure they returned home to their families. I was young and in charge of people's lives. For the first time in my life, I had real responsibility. For the first time in my life, I had to step up and be a real man. Too bad it took the life-and-death situation of being in prison to transform me. Be that as it may, I had been transformed.

I made a silent covenant that no one under my charge would leave in a body bag. We were all going to make it out of this place alive. I was determined to get these husbands back home to their wives, these sons back home to their mothers, these fathers back home to their children.

"Duck?"

"What's up, San Antone?"

"Make sure you bury some of the weapons up on the rec yard, too."

# Chapter Nine

"Yo, C," Young Gangsta shook his head and then lowered his gaze toward the ground. "Man, my people tripping. Man, my grandmother's sick, my sister is out in the street fucking with some old-ass nigga, and my brother is out there not giving a fuck. Man, C, I can't even think about my grandmother not being there when I get outta this shit."

I gave him a friendly punch in the shoulder. "Man, Gangsta, don't even trip. Ya grandmother is tough, dude. How many kids and grandkids she done raised?"

"A whole helluva lot," he smiled.

"See? Man, she's gonna be there when you get out. She's gonna have that big-ass feast on the table for you. All ya kinfolks is gonna be there. It's gonna be all luv, baby boy."

He shook his head. "Man, my little sister ... She ain't nuthin' but sixteen, and she fucking with some old-ass nigga 'bout thirty or something."

"She getting stretched out, huh?" I asked with a smile.

He punched me in my shoulder. "Nigga, fuck you! That shit ain't funny!"

"What?" I smiled. "I'm just saying a nigga putting that old meat in her life, huh?"

He couldn't help but laugh. "Fuck you, old bitch-ass nigga!"

"I'm just saying you wouldn't let me put my Mack game down on her, and now she getting hit in every hole but her eye sockets, and you wanna cry now."

He started swinging, and I kept backing up, laughing. His anger turned back to laughter. "Fuck you, C! See? That's what I'm talking about. A nigga come and confide in you, and you wanna play games and shit!"

"Nigga, do I look like muthafucking Dear Abbey to you?" I asked. "I'm your muthafuckin' road dawg, no doubt. But *damn*, baby boy, we gonna keep it gangster. She's sixteen. She out there experiencing shit, rebelling, and this old-ass nigga done spit game in her ear. She ain't trying to hear shit. That honey that nigga spit in her ear ain't gonna let her hear shit. You just gotta ride it out. Get at that nigga when you raise up."

He nodded. "*Damn*, and that bitch-ass nigga know that if I was out there, he'd be sitting in a shallow grave somewhere."

I nodded.

"And my punk-ass brother, he ain't doing shit. Man, he's a hoe!"

"Have you got at that nigga and told him to check up on y'all sister?" I asked.

He shook his head. "Man, he ain't worried about nobody but himself. He ain't like no regular nigga anyway."

"What you mean?"

"He's like into punk rock and shit. He's a weird-ass muthafucka. He be dying his hair purple and shit."

"Aww, hell! What the fuck wrong with him?"

"Man, C, if me and this nigga didn't look alike, I'd swear he wasn't my brother."

"Just get at him and tell him to go and check up on your grandmother."

He nodded. "I'ma try to get in touch with my cousin and see if he can find that nigga. I'ma see if he'll come down here and visit me, so I can holler at him."

"That'll work," I told him. I grabbed my thermos off the bed. "I'ma run up here to the yard and holler at this fool Henry real quick."

"Ya boy from San Antone?"

I nodded. "I talked to my people today. They told me that his old man got hit. I'ma go and rap with him and see if he's all right."

"*Damn*. Got hit by who?"

"Mexican Mafia. Free-world beef. Youngster rolled up on him with a gauge and popped him. He's in the hospital right now."

"Damn, that's fucked up."

"I'll holler."

I headed to the upper yard where Henry was exercising. Setting my thermos down next to his, I climbed onto the treadmill next to the one he was using, then programmed mine for a medium speed and started walking.

Henry held out his hand, and I clasped it. "*Qué pasa*, hometown?"

"*Nada, hermano*," I replied. "*Cómo estás*?"

"*Muy bien, gracias. Cómo estás usted*?"

"You already asked me that," I said with a smile.

"*Y tu familia*?" he asked.

"They're good. How's your family holding up?"

He nodded. "They good, homes."

"Naaa, what's the *real* deal?" I asked. "How's moms holding up?"

He nodded. "What can I say? She's tough. She'll make it."

"And Big Enrique? What's the latest news on him?"

"He's gonna make it. He's still in intensive care, but the doctors say he's gonna pull through."

"That's good news." I said. "Anything I can do?"

He shook his head.

"How are you holding up?" I asked. "You know you can come and talk to me anytime. You're still my homeboy from the street. Forget about all of this prison bullshit and all the fucking politics. Hey, man, I'm here if you need me."

"Thanks, hometown." Again, we shook hands.

"What's the family gonna do about the hit?" I asked.

"They ain't gotta do nothing. It was an unsanctioned hit on a lieutenant. That dude's already dead."

"*Damn*." I was genuinely shocked. "You guys move fast."

"We handle business."

"Rival crew?"

He nodded.

"Somebody's got some money coming," I smiled. The Mafia was definitely going to tax the other crew and give the money to Big Henry. Maybe a garage, a restaurant, or a big-ass shipment of dope. Big Henry was about to reap a quick windfall for his injuries.

"And rank," Henry smiled. "They gonna give him some more rank."

"Damn. When you talk to him, tell him I said congratulations."

"I will," Henry smiled. "Hell, ya boy gonna get some rank outta this too!"

"You?"

Henry nodded and started dancing on his treadmill.

"Congratulations, I guess," I said. "You seem a little too happy about all of this."

"What can I say? I ain't shoot him."

I shook my head. "You're a cold-blooded mutherfucker, Henry, you know that?"

"Hey, it ain't my fault he got popped."

"Naw, you just gonna come up off of it, though. Damn, I betcha the bloodstains on the ground ain't even dried up yet."

"Hey, we all got our crosses to bear, San Antone."

"Some smaller than others," I said, nodding toward the small gold crucifix he was wearing around his neck.

"You're a righteous muthafucka nowadays, huh?"

"You celebrating the rank you gonna get 'cause your pops' up in intensive care is not for me to judge, Henry. Your people feel that you deserve it, then wear it proudly."

"I'm getting rank, 'cause I been helping to run things around here. I'm getting rank, 'cause I ain't a snitch, 'cause my dad ain't a snitch, and 'cause my dad is a lieutenant out on the streets. Also, look around you, hometown. San Antone is getting deep around here. Did you think that they were just bringing in brothers from San Antonio? They bringing me soldiers too. San Antonio is the deepest *clicka* on the yard. More soldiers, the more rank I get. So yeah, I'ma wear it proudly."

"I'm just glad you stopped slicking your hair back and stopped trying to dress up like a fucking greaser."

He smiled.

Another bus arrived that day. I got ten more soldiers from San Antonio. I also got a godsend. I got Goodes and G-Man. Goodes was from Midland, while G-Man was from Odessa. They both had been in the system for five years, and they were well respected in the joint and on the streets. They were O.G.s from West Texas, just what was needed to get the West Texas youngsters under control. And they intended to do just that.

Goodes was the more reasonable of the two. They were both sharp, but Goodes was the quiet thinker, while G was more outspoken. Goodes was the con runner, the penitentiary hustler. He loved gambling. Spades, Dominoes, Tonk, Black Jack, Rummi, whatever. He was a straight-hustling, cheating, underhanded muthafucka, and I came to love him to death. I lost plenty of money to his con man ass, but like the saying goes: You get me once, shame on you. You get me twice, shame on me. I let the muthafucka get me.

G-Man was loud, boisterous, braggadocios, and had the personality of a cheese grater. He rubbed everyone the wrong way. But he especially hated California dudes. It was what was needed at the time, and so we made fast friends. Alley Cat summoned me to my first meeting with them.

"What's up, brother man?" I said, greeting each in turn.

"C, tell'em what's going on around here," Alley Cat said.

"Man, your people," I started off. "Them youngsters from Midland and Odessa. Man, they following them dudes from Cali and looking at them cats like they movie stars or something. They actually let some Cali cats become shot callers at a Texas prison."

Goodes shook his head. "Man, they don't know no better."

"They country ass, ain't never been out the 'hood," G-Man said in his country West Texas accent. "They looking at them niggaz like some real muthafuckin' gangbangers and shit. They done seen *Colors* and *Menace To Society*, and they looking at these niggaz like they something special. Me, I don't need no muthafuckin' gang. I can't stand no muthafuckin' gang members. They's cowards. They gotta roll in packs, the drive-by shooting muthafuckas."

"G, calm down," Goodes told him. "Hey, we gonna get them together and talk to them. Then, we gonna holler at all the homeboys from Texas and let'em know what the deal is. Cat, you get everybody together."

That meeting was to take place later. A more pressing one was to take place first. It was about David Prince, former grand wizard of the Ku Klux Klan. Prince had managed to land himself in prison for federal tax evasion. *Our prison.* And the most fucked-up thing about it? As some kind of sick-ass joke, they put him in the bunk over *me*. Yeah, the former grand wizard was my bunk mate.

The Mexicans had decided that it was a black problem. They would roll with whatever we decided. The brothers didn't know what they wanted to do. Most wanted to whip his ass, with a few wanting to kill him. The officers on the yard obviously wanted him dead, as that was the sole purpose for putting him on the yard in general population, and specifically for putting him on the bunk over me.

I had, over time, developed a reputation for being a devout racist. In fact, the guards and Mexicans and whites all thought that I was the most racist thing ever created. They mistook my pro-black, nationalistic ideals for being racist. I wasn't a racist per se. I wasn't of the school that I had to be *against* someone to be *for* my own people. I just wasn't concerned about anyone *but* my people. I do admit that I didn't talk to many outside of my own race, but that was because of a lack of common interest. And as far as the guards were concerned, I didn't talk to them like they were shit because they were white. I talked to them like shit because they were guards.

Prince moved in above me, and he had obviously been forewarned by some of the whites about my reputation. To them, I was Eldridge Cleaver, Malcom X, Medgar Evers, Geronimo Pratt, Huey Newton, Bunchy Carter, and Bobby Seal all rolled into one. My Black Panther tattoo, my deep angry scowl, and the Koran displayed prominently on my bed didn't help matters either. Prince would jump in fear every time I moved. He just knew that it was coming.

"Don't touch him," I said, walking into the meeting.

All the brothers turned in my direction.

"Why not, San Antone?" Duck asked.

"What for?" I asked. "Beat his ass, and then what? What would it matter? How would it benefit us?"

"It'll just feel good whipping his ass!" Memphis shouted.

"Yeah. Can you imagine how many brothers this man is responsible for lynching?" Duck asked.

Duck was from East Texas. The Klan, and racial issues, were still very much a reality in his world. He saw the opportunity for payback.

"That ain't this dude's type of Klan," I explained. "Cats like him ain't out there marching and carrying signs and shit. Cats like him traded in they white robes for black ones a long time ago."

"That's why we should really get dead in his ass!" Dupriest shouted.

I laughed and shook my head. "Let's see what he talking about. He looks like a scared old man. Ain't no points for doing this dude. If he's still with that bullshit, I'll be the first to go on him. Hey, y'all know me. I ain't got no problem doing a white boy. But this cat …" I shook my head.

And the brothers did know me. If *I*, the überracist, was giving Prince a pass, then there must be something to what I was saying. The anger bled from the room, and Prince never knew how close he had come to dying.

Why I decided to spare Prince was something I've never been able to truly reconcile within myself. Prison was our world, and in it, he was as helpless as a newborn baby. The free world belonged to him and his racist ilk. I wanted us to be able to compete with him in his world and not just be able to brutalize him in ours. If we had done him in, then everything that he had ever said about us would have been justified.

I wanted us to be better—better than him, better than his followers, better than what he stood for. I wanted us to show the world that in a situation where we were on top, in a situation where the white man was at our mercy, we could be more than animals, more than predators. When the black man held the cards, we could live and let live. I didn't want to dominate Prince in our world, I wanted to get out and compete with him in his.

"Hey, Prince," I said to him one day.

"Yes sir?" he answered nervously.

"Let there be no bullshit between us. No barriers, no fences, no walls. Let's talk openly and honestly with one another, okay?"

He stared into my eyes and nodded. "Deal."

"Nobody's going to fuck you up in here, so you can relax."

"Thank you."

"So, you were the chief pointy head, huh?"

He laughed. "I was young."

"And now?"

"I'm old."

"What the fuck were you doing in the Ukraine?"

"I was teaching. That country is what America was sixty years ago. It's actually freer than this country."

"And whiter," I smiled. "You ain't fooling nobody with that 'freer' shit. The Ukraine is lily-white. No blacks, no Mexicans, just tons of blond-headed, blue-eyed wenches."

Again he laughed.

"What are you reading?"

"This work, by this Canadian professor," he explained. "He has this theory about human physiology. He's saying that the Asian man is superior mentally, while the black man is superior physically, and the white man is in the middle."

"So, the white man can just trick the black man and beat the shit out of the Asian man to get what he wants, huh?"

This time, he laughed heartily.

"Pseudo scientist this time, huh? Prince, you haven't changed. You're still an undercover racist son of a bitch. But you know what? That's okay with me, because I'm a racist son of a bitch, too. And as long as you know where I stand, and as long as I know where you stand, then we can deal with each other straight-up."

He stared at me and nodded.

"There's a book called *Enemies: The Clash of Races*," I continued. "It's coming. And we're going to decide our issues then. But in the meantime, your folks better wise-up and start arming and developing Africa."

"Why is that?" he asked, lifting an eyebrow.

"Because you got a billion Chinese eyeballing a resource-rich Siberia. They're going to go north, and American boys and European boys are going to be dying in Siberia. You're going to need our help when the Asians unify and decide that they're tired of playing second fiddle. Europe's birthrates are declining, the Asians' are increasing, and they are going to need some *Lebensraum*, to borrow a term from our German friends. You're going to need us."

I lay down in my bunk, and Prince leaned over in his so that he could face me. He realized that he wasn't just talking to some dumb-ass nigga. Our conversations flowed freely from that point on. We talked about everything. Race, religion, politics, world affairs, the whole enchilada. We developed a mutual respect for one another's viewpoints. I saw the world through his eyes, and sometimes I was able to make him see the world through mine.

I got the opportunity to get inside the mind of a former grand wizard. What did white America want? What were they afraid of? What did they really think about black people? I learned the answers to these questions and more. It was as if my mortal enemy had opened up his strategic playbook and let me take notes. I was becoming more dangerous with each passing day. My mind was becoming a weapon.

# Chapter Ten

I kept my nose in the law books. I had a shit-hole attorney in the free world, but I wanted to know exactly what was going on. Besides, once he finished fucking over me, I would have to file a 2255 Appeal, showing the courts how badly he fucked over me in trial and on appeal.

It was while researching for my own case that I suddenly realized that I had become one of the residential jailhouse lawyers. Guys began to come up to me asking me to help them out with their cases. I would look over their materials and tell them what to do next or write letters for them or help them with their Bureau of Prisons appeals and complaints. After a while, I got pretty sharp at it. This is how I hooked up with Stacey and Fresh Reg.

Fresh Reggie, or Reg, as we called him, was a cat that fell outta Lubbock. Cool cat, always cracking jokes and high capping on fools. It was cats like Fresh Reg that made the time fly by. You could be in the most depressed mood in the world, but when dude came around, you knew he was going to make you laugh. Reg had a twenty-year sentence on his back. I did his case for him and helped him get it down to thirteen years. It was one of the greatest moments of my life.

Helping Brother Reg and refusing to take any money for doing it felt good. It helped me to understand what being a man was really about. My father had told me that the true measure of a man was how he treated someone who could do absolutely nothing for him. Reg really couldn't pay me; he worked in the prison factory, but he needed his bread to take care of *him*. Besides, even if he could have paid me, I wouldn't have taken it. He was a brother.

Helping Fresh out raised my standing amongst the Lubbock, Amarillo, and West Texas brothers. In fact, it raised my standing amongst the brothers in general. Getting legal help in prison cost money. It was one of the age-old penitentiary hustles brothers used to get money to eat. And here I was, doing it on the strength that he was a brother. I had shown them that I wasn't just talking the talk, but walking the walk. When I talked about unity and getting down for one another, I wasn't just talk. Brothers respected that.

I pretty much did the same for Stacey. He was a brother out of Ft. Worth, who got caught up in a conspiracy. They really fucked over my man. His lawyer checked himself out of a mental institution each day to go and represent my man in trial. Don't laugh, I'm serious. And the crazy part about it was that on appeal, his trial judge said that he still received *effective* counsel. Ain't that a bitch?

I helped Stacey file his papers and put together his appeal, and again, I didn't charge. I never thought much about it until later. But helping those brothers without charging them wasn't just about being for my brothers, it was about being for The Man Upstairs. For the first time in my life, I was a part of something positive that was greater than myself. It reminded me of a saying that I read in a book by Hazrat Khan. To paraphrase, it basically asked, what can man do for God? The greatest thing that man can do for God is to treat His children with dignity, respect, and kindness. In serving one another, we are serving God. Those words were deep and stayed with me forever.

My service to God, however, didn't extend to the rest of the yard. Outside the law library, I was still the same old asshole. Outside of the law library, I wasn't really serving the brothers, I was serving the Indians. I know it sounds fucked-up, and even stereotypical, but they were some drinking muthafuckas and some of my best customers. Me and Young Gangsta had set up a hooch factory. *Hooch* is prison liquor.

We made hooch by getting a plastic bag, filling it with sugar, orange slices, and orange juice we bought from the kitchen workers. We would add a little water, a little bit of yeast, which also came from the kitchen, and then tie the plastic bag up and hide it in the ceiling. Every two days, we would open the bag and let the air out, and then tie it back up and let it ferment. After about a week or two, it would be ready. We would sell a jug full of hooch for two books of stamps.

Stamps were the currency and lifeblood of a prison. Stamps weren't contraband, so you could have as many of them in your possession as you like. Also, muthafuckas in prison always needed stamps to write home. If the commissary was selling theirs for $6.50, you could sell yours for $5.50 and make a killing. The thing about books of stamps is that you could also send them home, where they could be redeemed at the post office for cash. We usually sold ours to the Asians, who needed them to run the gambling tables in the recreation room. Young Gangster and I were penitentiary balling.

Young Gansta and I also sold fiend books. Fiend books, also known as "Jack Books," were dirty magazines. We would buy them from dudes leaving the yard and going home or getting transferred. The Feds had forbidden any new pornographic material from coming into their institutions. They would confiscate magazines from prisoners who went to the hole, and they were supposed to destroy the confiscated material. Well, we bought magazines from the guards, too. And if not from them, from the dudes whose job it was to take the trash out to the compactor. We had the prison wired. Any *Black Tails*, or *Asian Beauties*, or whatever that were found, were ours. We paid top dollar, and got top dollar. We had hundreds and hundreds of books of stamps apiece.

Young Gangsta and I had amassed enough commissary and clothing to occupy half a dozen lockers. We kept our stuff in other people's lockers and empty lockers nearby our own room. We had all sizes of brand-new tennis shoes, all sizes of jogging suits, shower shoes, dozens of bars of soap, bottles and bottles of shampoo, packs and packs of razors, all kinds of shit. We made these lockers our "Texas lockers." Anytime a brother from Texas arrived on the yard, he'd be taken care of until his property arrived.

More brothers from Texas did arrive. We got a bus in that day, and two brothers who would change the course of history arrived on that bus. One was Anthony Michael Webber, and the other was Charlemagne Tamfu. They would become two of my most trusted advisors in the months and years to come. And they would become legends in their own right.

Webber was a short, skinny dude, who came to us from Leavenworth, Kansas. He had been in the Air Force and had been convicted and court-marshaled. After his military contract expired, he was transferred from the military prison to federal prison to serve out the remainder of his sentence. Webber was a technocrat. He was nerdy and dictatorial; he had been an Air Force computer scientist and engineer. He had a mind like a steel trap. He was brilliant in everything, and he would become my greatest organizer. I could give him an order and not worry about it being carried out. He would make sure that it was done—and done right.

Tamfu, on the other hand, was completely different. He was intelligent, but he wasn't a technocrat. His father had been the head of the Cameroon Foreign Intelligence Service. He was the son of a powerful African father and a rich white American mother. He had traveled Europe, Asia, and the Americas extensively. He spoke several languages, and he had an ego the size of the Rocky Mountains. The crazy-ass fool even referred to himself in *third person* sometimes.

Tamfu was pro-African, but first and foremost, he was pro-Tamfu, and pro-making money. Tamfu became one of my right-hand men for several reasons. Despite the fact that he was a megalomaniac who suffered with delusions of grandeur, he was efficient. He, like Webber, could be counted on to handle whatever task was assigned to him. Webber, Tamfu, Ghirt, and Young Gangster were the generals that would follow my orders blindly. Our coming together changed the federal prison system forever.

The meeting we had to attend that evening was held in the BET room, which again, was the black TV room. I walked in to find G-Man, Goodes, and Alley Cat standing up front, with everyone else seated or standing around the room. They had posted soldiers at the door and had soldiers watching for the guards. I already liked what I saw. G-Man and Goodes were from the pen, and they were experienced. The fellows in the TV room were giving them their undivided attention.

"Can't no nigga from Texas go to they muthafuckin' state and try to run shit," G-Man said. "So how the fuck you stupid-ass niggas gonna let them come to Texas and try to run shit?"

The youngsters from West Texas lowered their heads. It was then when I realized that I was dealing with a bunch of sheep. They were followers.

"I'll call out to the free world, and I'll tell ya mommas, and ya brothers, and ya cousins, and shit, that y'all in here being a bunch of followers behind some California-ass niggas," G-Man continued. "How ya like that?"

I peered around the room waiting for someone to buck. His threat to call their parents and big brothers actually had some of them scared. I wasn't sure how things worked in West Texas, but apparently telling a grown man's momma was still an effective tactic.

Magic and Unc and Big G tried to walk into the room, but their entrance was blocked by a couple of really big West Texas boys.

"What's up?" Magic asked, lifting his arms into the air.

"We havin' a meeting," Goodes told them.

"We can't come to the meeting?" Big G asked.

"We'll get with y'all later," G-Man told them. "Right now, we talking to our people."

I loved it.

"We ain't y'all people?" Magic asked.

"This is a *Texas* meeting," Alley Cat told them.

I was in heaven.

The three of them stalked off, fuming.

We finished our Texas meeting, and then had a private meeting.

"You shot caller for the blacks now," Goodes told me.

"No way in hell," I told him.

"You been on the yard longer than any of us," G-Man said. "And most of the brothers here are from Texas. And San Antonio has the deepest Texas car, so you it."

"Ain't no way in hell!" I repeated.

"Man, we need you, C," Alley Cat interjected. "You the smartest one outta all us. You like Pinky and the Brain."

And the name stuck. Goodes would always call me Pinky and the Brain.

"Man, I'm trying to work on my case. I ain't got time for this shit," I said. "Man, you deal with all the petty bullshit. Muthafuckas ain't cleaned they room, muthafuckas keeping the light on too late at night, muthafuckas shaking the bed at night jacking off. Man, I ain't got time for all the petty-ass bullshit."

"You run the San Antone car," Goodes told me.

I nodded. I could do that. Taking care of my homeboys was something that just came natural anyway.

"He runs the Texas car," Alley Cat told them.

"Look, G-Man, you steer the car," I told him. "Goodes, you got shotgun. Me, I'm in the backseat. I'll run the Texas boys and keep'em in line. But you got the car. You the shot caller."

"Somebody gotta do it," Goodes said, smiling. He patted G-Man on his shoulder.

"Yeah, but why it got to be me?" G-Man asked.

"'Cause we love you," Goodes said, hugging him.

"Fuck you!" G-Man laughed.

And just like that, he had been put in charge of the lives of hundreds of people. We were kids in our early twenties and deciding life and death for hundreds of people on a prison yard.

"I'ma go let them California muthafuckas know that they ain't in charge no mo'," Alley Cat said with a smile.

I laughed. "Tell Big G that I said hi."

Alley Cat laughed. Everyone knew that Big G and I hated one another with a passion. "Will do."

# Chapter Eleven

We weren't on the job long before our first test came. An older cat that we called Old School touched up a Mexican on the basketball court. They got into it over a foul call, and the Mexican ran up on Old School and put his dukes up. The rules on that were pretty simple: somebody runs up on you with they dukes up, do what you gotta do. And Old School did what he had to do. He dropped dude within seconds. Old School was from the old state penitentiary set. He could squabble for real. Dude found that out the wrong way and paid for it with a broken nose, a busted lip, and some missing teeth. *After* he woke up, that is.

It embarrassed the Piasas that their man had been dropped so quickly. They felt their honor was on the line. And so they lined up on one side of the yard, with us on the other. They demanded that Old School be punished for hitting their dude first. Our point was that dude ran up on Old School with his dukes up. And so we found ourselves facing off with one another, about to set the yard ablaze with a full-blown race riot.

Enrique and two of his lieutenants walked to the gazebo in the center of the yard, and he seated himself. G-Man, Goodes, and I walked to the gazebo and seated ourselves across from them.

"San Antone, man, stay out of this," Henry said.

"C'mon, man, how the fuck can I stay outta this?" I asked.

"My people ain't gonna touch you, hometown. You get up, walk away, and go and chill in your room. They won't touch you. My orders."

I shook my head. "I can't do that, hometown."

He turned to G-Man. "So, what we gonna do?"

"What do you wanna do?" G-Man asked.

Henry waved his hand around the yard. "Man, its four hundred against forty. Y'all can't win."

Goodes laughed. "Ten to one. I got my ten."

"I got mine," G-Man added.

"Use your heads, man," Henry advised. "You can't win. Ain't no sense in tearing up the yard, getting muthafuckas killed and shit over some bullshit. We'll be on lockdown for a week or more over this stupid-ass shit."

"If you know that it's stupid, then why are we here?" I asked.

"The people want justice," he said, turning back to his four hundred-plus soldiers.

Henry now ran the Border Brothers, which means he was in charge of the Piasa's frontline soldiers. He answered to one man, and one man only—the leader of the Piasas. He had gotten a big fucking promotion.

"We want justice," Goodes told him.

"Good, then you'll do what's right," Henry told him. "The rules are the rules. My man didn't hit first."

"He ran up on our dude," Goodes reminded him.

"And if he would have swung first, then Old School had every right to defend himself. Plus, our man would have gotten punished."

"So, you telling me that our people gotta get hit first before they can defend themselves?" G-Man asked.

"So, your people get to get a free lick in?" Goodes asked.

"I'm not saying that," Henry told them. "I'm saying that we agreed that whoever throws the first punch has to be punished. The rules are rules. My dude is saying that he was going to do nothing but talk shit."

"With his fist balled?" Goodes asked. "He put his fist up."

"But he didn't swing," Enrique countered. "Rules are rules."

"So what do you want?" G-Man asked.

"He needs to be disciplined. And I want two of my men to witness it."

"This is some bullshit!" I said. "You ain't gonna agree to this shit, are you?"

G-Man nodded at Henry.

I rose and stormed off.

G-Man and Goodes got up and approached Old School. They ordered him to wait for them in the BET room.

"What's up?" Ghirt asked.

"They sold him out, just like that," I said.

*"What?"*

I shook my head. "This is some bullshit."

G-Man and Goodes sent a group of youngsters into the BET room to touch up Old School while the two Mexican delegates watched. They all got a rude awakening. Old School touched up all five of the soldiers that they sent to discipline him, and touched them all up *real* good. It was the first time the Mexicans had ever witnessed blacks fighting one another close up. The ferocity and power of the battle scared them. They ran from the TV room.

Being that Old School disciplined his discipliners, there was only one thing left to do. Someone slipped a note to a guard and got him sent to the hole. The whole thing had been a fucking fiasco. I'll never forget the look on Old School's face as he was being carted out the housing unit in handcuffs. He looked at me and shook his head. He was disappointed in us—we had failed him.

"San Antone!" Old School called out to me as the guards were walking him up the yard. "Y'all said we could defend ourselves, San Antone!"

After the Old School fiasco, I made a promise to myself that nothing like this would ever happen again. Win, lose, or draw, it wasn't happening again. Never again would we sell out our own over a technicality. Old School was in the right. We should have gone to war for him. I was beginning to rethink this shot caller thing. Maybe I should have taken the job.

Another bus pulled in later on that day, and more blacks arrived on the yard. On this bus was my baby momma's new boyfriend. Ain't that a bitch? My baby momma's Sancho was now on the same yard with me.

"You gonna kill this fool?" Ghirt asked.

"Man, let me do it for you," Young Gangsta said. "You can go to the library and that way, you'll have an alibi, and I'll slice a smile across this fool's neck."

I shook my head.

"Man, let me kill him!" Young Gangsta pleaded.

Again I shook my head.

Ghirt opened his shirt, showing me a long, sharpened shank. "If you wanna do it yourself, you can use my piece. I'll get somebody to lure the fool to the TV room."

I laughed. "I'm not gonna kill him."

"C'mon, C," Young Gangsta said. "I know you better than that."

"Why would I kill him?" I asked. "He can't do no more than what she let him do, right?"

"Still, do it for the homies," Gangsta pleaded. "For the first time in history, we got one of these slick-ass niggaz up in here with us. You gotta do this fool. For every nigga that ever had his girl run up on while he was locked up, you gotta kill him!"

"He's from San Antonio," I told them. "I'ma at least talk to the dude and see if he's an asshole."

Ghirt whistled, and some of my San Antone homeboys wrapped their arms around David and walked him across the yard to where I was standing. He knew what was happening, and he was scared as hell. Apparently my girl had told the fool what yard I was on, and upon seeing my name tag, he looked as though he wanted to shit himself.

"Your name David?" I asked, leaning against the doorway. The entire prison yard had stopped and started watching us. Prison was a small world, and everyone knew what was going on.

"Yeah." He lifted his hands and plea-bargained. "Say, man, I don't want no trouble. I just wanna do my time and go home."

"I'm sure you do," I told him. "So, you know my girl, huh?"

"Man, I met her through my cousin," he explained. "My cousin was fucking with her cousin, and that's how we hooked up. I ain't did nothing but take her to the movies one time."

"*Really?*"

He lifted his hand. "My right hand to God."

"Man, don't worry about that shit," I told him. "We in here, we gotta get each other's back. We ain't tripping about no women and shit. You understand?"

He nodded. "Man, I never touched her."

"Put it out of your mind," I said firmly. "In here, we're brothers. In here, San Antone got each other's back. We leave free-world shit in the free world. Understand?"

He nodded.

"Go and let Gangsta hook you up with hygiene products and shower shoes and shit."

"Thanks, man." he said, swallowing hard.

"C'mon, follow me," Young Gangsta told him.

David and Gangsta headed down the hall.

Ghirt looked at me and smiled. "You want me to go do him?"

I shook my head. "I meant what I said. I ain't got no beef with dude. Go and get Webber, and tell him that we need to meet up in the library. We got more homeboys from San Antonio, and it's time we formed the squad like we've been talking about doing."

"A Zero Squad?"

I nodded.

"But first, I'ma have to get with G-Man and Goodes and see what they think."

"And if they don't approve of it?"

"Fuck'em," I shrugged. "We do it anyway. I just want to see if I can get their support behind it first. Send somebody to let them know that I want to meet with them."

Ghirt nodded, and he was off.

My next meeting wasn't the one I planned. It was an impromptu meeting with Enrique. I was in the restroom washing my hands when about a dozen Border Brothers walked into the room.

"San Antone!" Enrique shouted. "*Qué pasa, carnal*?"

"Same shit, different day," I told him. "How are things going on your end?"

"Beautiful," he replied. "Fucking beautiful."

"How's the old man?"

"Alive. Mad, bitter, but alive."

"Alive is good," I said flatly. "How's moms?"

Henry nodded towards his soldiers, and they exited the restroom with a quickness.

"Do me a favor, San Antone," he started. "I know we cool and all, but like, asking about my family might give the wrong impression."

"An impression like what? Like I know you from the free world, and I care about what happens to your family? Damn, you're right. People might actually think that we're all human beings in here."

"I'm number two to the old man now," Enrique told me.

"Congratulations."

"Yeah, thanks to you guys."

"Thanks to us?"

"My people see that I was able to get results," Enrique said with a smile. "I was able to get you to back down, whip one of your own, and then get him sent to the hole. You guys made me look like King Fucking Kong."

Enrique laughed, and I had to smile. We must've looked like cowardly pieces of shit in their eyes.

"I can't believe that you didn't take my offer, San Antone."

"What offer was that?" I asked.

"I told you to stay the fuck out of it."

"You and I both know that I wasn't going to do that," I told him. "I have to be a soldier for my people, like you have to be a soldier for yours."

Henry waved his finger. "Uh-uh. See? That's where you're wrong. I'm not a soldier, I'm a *general.*"

"Well, I'll have to remember that, Pancho Villa."

He laughed. "Except this time, we're all locked inside of the Alamo together."

"Results will still be the same," I said.

"We're going to win."

"Maybe. But they'll be a lot of dead Mexicans lying around."

"Not if your people don't all fight together."

"We're together," I countered.

"Are you sure about that, San Antone?" he asked, lifting an eyebrow. "Sure enough to bet your life on it?"

"What are you getting at, Henry?"

"You didn't notice Northside and all of the California brothers standing off to the side?"

I thought back to that day, and he was right. Those assholes were standing off to the side together.

"What about them?" I asked.

Enrique leaned forward and spoke into my ear. "They sold you out, hometown. They came to us and made a separate peace. They say they ain't rolling with y'all, and that they got their own shot caller. They would've stood off to the side and watched the rest of you get slaughtered that day, homes. When I tell you to go to your room and stay out of it, it's for your own good."

I don't know what had me angrier—this peacock son of a bitch standing in front of me smiling, or those sorry-ass muthafuckas betraying us.

"That was it, hometown," Enrique said, smiling and backing out of the restroom with his hands in the air. "I can't do no more for you. No more freebies, no more warnings, no more nothing. We gonna have to start acting like we in prison, homes. You and yours against me and mines." And he disappeared around the corner.

My meeting with G-Man and Goodes was postponed until the following day, which was just as well. I was tired. Not so much physically as mentally. I headed for my bunk, where Prince was seated and reading through a bunch of papers.

"What's all this?" I asked.

"My mail."

"Your mail? You keep all of your mail?"

"No, this is just from today."

He had lots of mail spread all over his bed and mine. Envelope after envelope, card after card, and box after box were piled on top of one another.

"All of this is just from *today*?" I asked incredulously.

He nodded and patted a spot on my bed next to him. "Here, sit down and have a look."

Curious, I took the seat and began rifling through his correspondence. Sure as shit, it was all from today. He had yellow money slips attached to about half of the envelopes, telling me that he had received a ton of money that day.

"Is this from family?" I asked.

"Nope," he smiled. "Don't know these people from Adam."

"And they just *send* you money?"

Again he smiled. "It's great to be me."

I began to read through some of the cards and letters, and I quickly came to realize that they were all from supporters and fans of the same ideology. Many of them urged him to continue on in the struggle against the Zionists. Some were not so polite. Some talked of their God-given mission against the niggers and the Jews. Some letters had Swastika letterheads; others had various Ku Klux Klan names and symbols. They were White Knights, Grand Freedom Riders, Southern Patriots, and various kinds of bullshit.

What disturbed me the most was that there were *so many* of them. This was mail from one day, and he got the same amount *every* day, the entire time we were there together. Hundreds of pieces of mail per day, translated into thousands per month, and over ten thousand pieces of racist mail per year. That meant that there existed thousands of them out there—lurking, waiting, plotting, warring against a population who had been lulled into thinking that they had overcome.

Prince's letters frightened me more than anything, because my child was out there with these people. He was an unprotected cub in a jungle filled with bloodthirsty animals that hated him because of the color of his skin. And the most insane thing about it is that they were teaching their children to hate.

Prison politics were small time; the real battle lay outside of the walls. I was determined more than ever to return to my child—to protect him from the monsters of this world.

"Here, check this out," Prince told me, handing me a black book.

"What's this?" I asked.

"My book."

"You wrote a book?"

He smiled and nodded. "Yeah."

I opened the book and flipped through the pages. I came across a section on Dr. King and paused.

"His real name was Michael King," Prince said. "He didn't change it to Martin Luther until much later in life."

I closed the book.

"You're more of a Malcom X-kinda guy, aren't you?" Prince asked.

"I didn't know they were different."

"C'mon, we said that we weren't going to bullshit one another," Prince replied. "You know, and I know, what the real deal is. I've heard you talking to your friends. You know that you have to build your race into a strong people."

I nodded.

"Michael King was against all of that," Prince continued. "What do you think was the most detrimental thing to ever happen to the black community?"

"You people," I laughed. "The first time my ancestors saw your damn ships off the coast of Africa, they should have put so many arrows in those muthafuckas that they looked like floating porcupines."

Prince threw his head back in laughter. "I agree. But once that was done, what do you think was the most devastating thing to ever happen to the black community in the United States?"

"Besides slavery?"

"Integration," he said, flatly. "Integration destroyed the black community."

"Is that why your people hated Dr. King so much?"

"Your people should have hated him. He set your people back a thousand years, not mine."

"Why do you say that?"

"Think about this," he said, leaning in. "After segregation was repealed and blacks were able to live amongst whites, what do you think happened? All of the professionals in the black community fled the community. All of the business owners, doctors, lawyers, and other professionals, all of the civic leaders, teachers, and other intellectuals, moved out of the community.

"So guess what happened then? There were no leaders left within the community. People who held the community to high standards were gone. Lawns started being overgrown, homes started going into disrepair. And since the people who could organize were no longer in the community, guess where the city's priority went? They weren't going to have anyone calling, or organizing, or protesting if the streets weren't repaired or if the trash wasn't picked up every week. Integration was the worst thing that could have happened to the black community. Where do you think all of the money that left the community went? It went to white-owned businesses outside of the black community."

I rose and started removing Prince's mail from my bed. He realized that I wanted to lie down, and he, too, began to pull his mail off my bed and place it on his own. When he was finished, he hopped up into his bunk while I lay down in mine.

Either prison was really getting to me, or he had a valid point. I know that integration was not bad and that forced segregation was evil, but *did* integration play a part in the decline of the black community?

The day had been too much for me mentally. I rolled over and fell sound asleep.

# Chapter Twelve

My own letters came the following day. To my surprise, I received one from my father. I had written to the old man and told him about the Old School incident. He wrote me back and told me to be strong. He also kept it real with me and told me that I should have stepped up and been the shot caller for the brothers. He said that it was partly my fault that it had happened. "Real men find a way," he said. The most poignant part of his letter was a quote that he passed on. It was, "An army of lambs led by a lion is infinitely more powerful than an army of lions led by a lamb."

I read his quote a number of times and thought about our situation on the yard. We were outnumbered more than eight to one in sheer numbers, and five to one if you count just those young enough to get down in a major way. In reality, the average brother could whip the average Mexican hands-down. We were bigger than them. Physiologically, we were taller, stronger, heavier, and just all-around bigger. We were the lions, but we were being led by a lamb. No way we should have sold Old School out. No fucking way.

One the other side of things, they were followers. Lambs, to be exact, but they were being led by Henry, a lion for sure. I had grown up with him, and he could squabble with the best of us. He had never run or backed down from a fight. He definitely had the heart of a lion. We had to reverse the situation. I would have to take my lions, and I would have to give them lions to lead them into battle. Lions being led by lions would be the ultimate combination. I was off to see G-Man and Goodes for precisely that reason. We met at the chapel and strolled around it leisurely.

"I want to form a hit squad," I told them.

"A hit squad?" G-Man lifted an eyebrow.

"We need some soldiers that stay ready so that they won't have to get ready," I told him in prison-speak. "We need some fireman with boots on or by the bed so that they are ready to rock and roll at a moment's notice."

"That's not a bad idea," Goodes said.

I knew that I would be able to count on Goodes. He was a guerilla for real, a straight-up soldier. If G-Man was our president, then Goodes could be considered our secretary of war.

G-Man nodded. "So who gets control of them?"

"What do you mean, 'control'?" I asked, already knowing what he was getting at.

"I mean, do they follow my orders, or are they San Antone soldiers? What?"

"G-Man, you represent us," I reassured him. "You represent us as best you see fit. When you tell me, I'll give my team the go, and we go."

It was what he wanted to hear.

"How many do you think you can get?" Goodes asked.

I smiled and shrugged. "I don't know."

"They need to be reliable, San Antone," G-Man warned. "And they need to be loyal to us. And they need to be some real go-getters."

"Nothing but young fire pissers," I assured him.

"We need to keep it quiet," Goodes added.

"Of course," I nodded.

"Well, you get it together," G-Man said. "You be in charge of it. But you gotta keep'em in line. They're your soldiers, so you're responsible for 'em if they start acting stupid."

I nodded. "I got'em."

"Did you talk to your San Antone homeboy?" G-Man asked.

"Which one?"

"Enrique."

I nodded. "I seen that fool yesterday."

"You know them niggaz sold us out, San Antone," Goodes said angrily.

"Man, tell'em," G-Man said, tapping my chest. "We need to use our heads. Just running up on them niggaz and smashing ain't gonna mean shit in the long run."

"Yeah, but I'll feel better about it!" Goodes scowled. "And them punk-ass niggaz a get the message."

"I say, let'em get out there on they own," G-Man suggested. "And the first time one of them gets into it, they gonna run back over here asking if we got they back. And I'm gonna turn they ass right around and escort they asses right outta my room. 'Naw, this is how y'all wanted it,' I'ma tell'em. Let them Border Brothers skin they ass right up."

I laughed. The two of them were like brothers. G-Man was the tall, bright-skinned one, while Goodes was the black-ass, short, stocky one. They disagreed on everything, but couldn't do without one another. They were like yin and yang; together, they balanced one another perfectly.

"I think that we should plan our course of action carefully," I suggested. "We should start preparing ourselves to move on these dudes, but in the meantime, we'll do like G said and feed'em with a long-handle spoon. I'ma get our soldiers ready."

"No Cali dudes," Goodes advised.

"Fuck no!" I said, in full agreement. "I don't know what the fuck is wrong with them dudes. Everybody else is riding together—the South, the East Coast, the Midwest brothers, the Caribbean and African brothers—everybody. Those dudes are on some old space alien type'a shit."

G-Man and Goodes laughed.

"I'll holler at y'all later," I said, lifting a black power fist into the air as I walked off.

I met Ghirt, Webber, and Tamfu in the library the next morning and gave them the news.

"Our Zero Squadron has been approved," I told them.

A quick celebration ensued amongst the four of us. What the formation of our squad meant was that no other brother would be subjected to the brutal beating Omene received or be sold up the river like Old School. No longer would we be subjected to just talk. We would now have the means to put our thoughts into action.

"This is how we are going to do this," I started off. "Ghirt, you're in charge of training. Everything from weight lifting, to martial arts, to weapons training, to PT. Webber, you will handle the education and indoctrination. We are creating an elite fighting force. Frontline soldiers for our people."

"And what am I to do?" Tamfu asked.

"Intelligence," I told him. "You're in charge of intelligence, counterintelligence, psy-ops, my personal bodyguard, special assignments, etc...."

"I'm in charge of bullshit?"

"You're second in command," I told him. He was happy with that. "Young Gangsta will be in charge of recruiting and finances. He knows how to hustle and make money to equip our people. Ghirt, you also handle weapons acquisition and storage."

Ghirt nodded.

"Any ideas as to who our first recruits will be?" Tamfu asked.

Ghirt and I looked at one another and laughed. We had quietly built up a secret army since the Omene thing. Now that we were sanctioned, they could come out in the open.

"We have a few prospects," Ghirt told him.

"We have enough warm-ups in the lockers to give to any recruits that don't have any," I told them. "Same thing with the tennis shoes."

"No tennis shoes," Ghirt said.

"Why not?"

"Boots," he smiled. "We all wear our black work boots."

I smiled. "Our big black boots, huh?"

Ghirt nodded. "I want them to hear us coming from miles around."

"Why would you want your enemy to hear you coming?" Tamfu asked.

"Psychological warfare," Ghirt explained. "The Germans had this thing called the Stuka dive bombers. They put sirens on them so that they would squeal like crazy when they went to dive. The Allied soldiers were more scared of the damn sirens than they were of the bombs. When the other prisoners hear those boots stomping and running down the hall, I want it to have that same effect. I want a muthafucka to huddle beneath they covers and pray that we ain't coming for them."

We all laughed.

"Okay, boots," I told them. "Any other suggestions?"

"We need a name," Tamfu told us.

"Guerilla Unit," Ghirt said adamantly.

"Naw," I said shaking my head. "I don't want nobody to get us confused with the Black Gorilla Family. We got a couple of them on the yard."

"The Terror Squad," Webber said.

"Nigga, we ain't rappers and shit," I said laughing.

"How about the Panthers?" Ghirt asked.

Webber shrugged.

"I don't know about that," Tamfu told him. "That's too nineteen sixties for me."

"What's the name that they used to call the Pharoah's bodyguards in ancient Egypt?" Webber asked.

"Okay, I think I got it," I told them.

They all turned and stared at me.

"In South Africa, they have the ANC, which is the African National Congress," I explained. "Well, the ANC is the political arm, but they also have a military arm. It's called The Umkhonto We Sizwe. It means, 'Spear of the Nation.'"

Slowly, nods went around our circle.

"We're going to be a weapon for our people, right?" I asked. "We're going to be their tip of the spear, right?"

"I like it!" Tamfu declared.

"It's catchy," Webber conceded. "Let's go with that."

Ghirt nodded and extended his hand. I clasped it. "*Spear of the Nation!*"

"The UMK is the African acronym for it. The Umkhonto We Sizwe. It'll throw the white folks off like a muthafucka."

We all laughed.

"UMK!" Webber cheered.

"UMK!" Tamfu joined in.

Ghirt and I smiled and nodded at one another. No one in the room understood what had just happened. None of us understood the monster that we had just given birth to. We had just given birth to what would become the most violent prison gang in the history of the United States. *The Umkhonto We Sizwe*.

More prisoners arrived by bus that day. The thing about prison is that people come, and people go. And in this prison, the turnaround was faster than in others. Most of the Mexican nationals in the prison had short sentences. Eighteen months for illegal reentry was a popular one. Twenty-one months for being a drug mule. Nine months for immigration violation. It was the brothers with the crack sentences who called the place home. All of the other muthafuckas were just visiting.

I got more San Antonio soldiers from the bus that day. More Texas soldiers arrived from Houston and Dallas, and what really seemed crazy was that we got a bunch of brothers from the East Coast, which was unusual. They had shipped those brothers pretty far from home.

It was in this bunch that I got the men who would eventually return to the East Coast and start Umkhonto chapters in those prisons. They were my future generals and prison commanders. There was Shorty, from Pink House; Scotty from Atlanta; Jersey, from … well, Jersey. There was Chuck and Wise, my D.C. boys, and there was Prince from Harlem. They were all conscious brothers, and they all fell up into the UMK without any second thoughts. These would be the seeds that would scatter throughout the system and create the monster that would become the Umkhonto.

The Feds always wanted to know how Umkhonto spread through the system like an uncontrolled wildfire. Well, they did it. They put us together in a place where we had to come together. Black men coming together for one another, standing up for one another, believing in one another. Believing in something greater than themselves was a powerful narcotic. We sparked a seed of consciousness within one another that Willie Lynch thought that he had destroyed. We were black men united and willing to kill or die for one another. We were America's nightmare.

I got my new soldiers settled in and returned to my own bunk to find a surprise. I had a new neighbor in the bunk next to me. I laughed my ass off.

His name was Pedro. He was a Border Brother, and his job was to kill me when things jumped off between us and them. I doubt that they had gotten wind of Umkhonto, but who knows.

They had an excellent spy apparatus operating on the yard. Stupid-ass niggas talked, thinking that someone around them might not understand English. Truth be told, most of the Spanish speakers on the yard spoke better English than most of the brothers. It was just a game that they played. By pretending not to speak English, they could sit and listen to the loose tongues all around them. It also gave them time to think and answer. It also meant that if brothers wanted to communicate, they would have to go and grab another Hispanic that spoke both English and Spanish, which meant that another Hispanic would be around to hear the conversation and go get help if necessary.

It was slick, and they used it to their advantage. But that's the way things were in prison. Everyone maneuvered for an advantageous position on the others. Prison politics were more vicious and trifling than anything under the sun.

My future killer—Pedro—was a big dude for a Mexican. He was about my height, six foot one, and stocky. He lifted weights, worked out every day, and ran around the track. He pretended that he spoke only a little English, and in his case, I imagined it to be true. In all likelihood, they probably hadn't found out about Umkhonto, so Pedro being assigned to me indicated they now knew that I was number three on the yard. Either that or they figured that I was the puppet master, pulling G-Man and Goodes' strings. Either way, in their eyes, I was high enough in rank to warrant an assassin. I had been promoted by the Mexicans. It was laughable.

What wasn't laughable was that the order to assign a hit man to me could have only come from one place—my friend Henry. What this told me was that one of my oldest and closest childhood friends no longer considered me to be a friend. It hurt a little; I can't lie. Henry was willing to kill me.

Pedro opened his locker and began to search his shelves frantically. He had cleaned off his locker door and had pictures of his family laid out on his bed. It wasn't difficult to guess what he was looking for. I reached into my locker and pulled out a tube of free toothpaste they issue at laundry once a week.

"Amigo," I said, holding the toothpaste out to him.

"*Gracias!*" he said, taking the toothpaste from me. He immediately began smoothing out some of the paste on the back of his pictures and then pasting them to his locker.

"*Tu familia*?" I asked.

"*Si!*" he smiled, and pointed at each picture, telling me who the individuals were. "*Mi esposa, mi hijo, mi hija, una otra hija, and mi novia*."

"*Tu novia!*" I said, laughing. "You're going to hang your girlfriend's picture next to your wife's?"

"She's family," he said in broken English.

We clasped hands and laughed heartily.

"*Ta loco!*" I told him.

For a guy who was assigned to kill me, he was pretty cool.

# Chapter Thirteen

Umkhonto grew quickly. Webber and Tamfu had organized it well. Ghirt got a job in the recreation department so that he could be on the rec yard for most of the day. He organized PT classes and secretly taught martial arts, armed, and unarmed combat to our soldiers inside the cover of the gym.

Webber had classes up and running within days. He taught from the books, *Enemies: The Clash of Races, The Isis Papers, We The Black Jews, The Destruction of Black Civilization, From Superman To Man, The Debt, Nile Valley Civilizations, Before The Mayflower, African Civilizations*, and from his own notes. He used the classrooms in the library in the evening. They pretended to be watching videos on ancient civilizations, but were really being indoctrinated into Umkhonto.

Our recruiting, training, and indoctrination program went off like clockwork. We rolled smoothly for a couple of months with no hitches. And then, the Feds got wind of what was really going on.

I don't know if it was because of a hating muthafucka who couldn't join our organization or one of their resident snitches that sold us out. One thing about the Feds, though, snitches are everywhere. Those itty-bitty time muthafuckas don't stop being rats once they get inside of the system. They keep on being rats. By whatever means they found out, one thing was for certain. I now had the fucking SIS lieutenant on my ass.

SIS stands for Special Investigations Service. It's like the Bureau of Prison's own private FBI service. They had an SIS lieutenant or two at each of its prisons. Their job was to investigate anything and everything out of whack. In my situation, they skipped giving the case to the gang lieutenant and had me investigated by the SIS off the top. He was a punk-ass bitch with a little-man complex.

"Inmate Alexander, what's going on today?" SIS asked.

"Just being a model prisoner," I answered.

"Oh, yeah?" he asked. "How you doing that?"

"Just waking up and going to sleep, and waking up and going to sleep."

"Funny," he said without cracking a smile, "what's this I hear about a terrorist organization in my prison?"

"Congratulations. You finally made warden, huh?" I said with a smile.

"I ain't no fucking warden, and this here is still *my* prison." He spit on the ground. "Wardens come and go, but I'll be here day after day, busting a muthafucka's balls."

I nodded.

"So what is this Umkhonto shit?" he asked.

"A what?"

"Some Umkhonto shit. You're a South African terrorist?"

"I'm from San Antonio, not South Africa. Now, I may have ancestors from South Africa, but at this point, it's just a hunch. But something inside just tells me that I'ma bad Zulu muthafucka."

I finally got a smile out of him.

"Is that why you bringing this terrorist shit into my prison?"

"I ain't brought shit into prison but a bad attitude and a lot of hostility."

"Word on the yard is that you boys are forming up some kinda terrorist group." He spat on the ground once again. "Let me let you in on something. After 9/11, the government ain't playing about this terrorism shit. I got a long list of son of a bitches on a watch list, and I ain't got time to deal with no bullshit. Now, you need to be a good, red-blooded American, cut your bullshit, and let me watch the son of a bitches that I really need to be watching.

"Alexander, I know you ain't no troublemaker. You been in some fights and shit, but that's just from muthafuckas disrespecting you. You ain't no terrorist, son, and you don't want your name affiliated with any of that bullshit. You'll be on a watch list for the rest of your natural born life, and that's just trouble that you don't want."

I nodded. "I promise you, Lieutenant, I ain't no terrorist, and I ain't trying to be one."

"Well, that's good. You wanna be a part of something, hell, join the

Texas Boys, the BGF, something that we know about. Don't start up something with some weird names and some ties to some South African terrorist group. Hell, you had me up all night on my computer researching this shit, trying to find out what it is. Go with something we're comfortable with. Man, we're just Podunk, country-ass rednecks out here. We don't know nothing about no damn Umkhonto Kente shit. I'm just telling you this so you can keep on doing your time the same way you been doing it, which is low-key."

I nodded. "Thanks for the advice, Lieu. And you have my word, I'm not a terrorist."

"Well, does this thing have anything to do with the Muslims?"

I shrugged. "You got me. I've never heard of what you're talking about."

"Well, why'd your name come up?"

He was a country-ass redneck, and I knew exactly how to get him off of me. I reverted to my deepest Texas accent. "I know one thing; two things for sure. I know that Jesus was blamed for a bunch of shit He didn't do. You got people that swim across that border and don't understand a lick of English. This is Texas, Lieu. God's country. And instead of learning the language, they don't even bother, which is why they get everything all twisted up when they run back and snitch. The Benedict Arnold muthafuckas have no reason even being over here in the good ole U.S. of A. Sure as Dixie shit, I ain't no terrorist."

The lieutenant looked as though he had tears in his eyes. He rested his hand on my shoulders. "I knew the son of a bitches were probably lying. You're a good inmate, Alexander. Don't you worry about a damn thing. The next time somebody comes up to me with this bullshit, I'ma tell'em to get the fuck outta my office."

The lieutenant stalked off to the kitchen to stand guard. I was sure that I wouldn't catch anymore shit from him for a while. I had hit him hard by invoking the redneck trinity: God, Texas, and the Confederacy. Invoke those three, and you're considered a good nigger who really understands what life's all about.

I headed into the housing unit and was walking down the hall when I passed by Unc. Again, we said nothing to one another, and I acted as though he didn't exist. I was still raw about what they did to Omene.

"You got a problem with me?" he asked.

I stopped and turned toward him. "Who *me*?"

"Yeah. You walk around the yard huffing and puffing and not saying shit to me. I just wanted to know if we had a problem."

He had a pair of nuts on him that was for sure. I couldn't believe that this cat had the nerve to ask me if I had a problem with him. "I do have a problem with you. I have a problem with what you did to my boy Omene."

"Man, you still tripping over that bullshit?" He waved his hand, dismissing my statement. "Look, if that's really bothering you and you feel like you gotta get it off ya chest, then handle ya business. We not broads. All of this walking about not speaking to one another, that's broad type'a shit."

I wasn't saying nothing to them cats, because I didn't want to kill one of 'em. I was just that angry. I knew that once I started, it would take an act of Congress to get me off somebody's ass. "What are you saying? You trying to dance?"

He threw his hands up. "It's whatever."

I hit that fool three times before his hands came back down. Everything that I had been holding in, I released on him. The fight that we had was the kind where you are trying to destroy something. I lost all consciousness, all control, all links to humanity; my only objective was to hit as hard as I could until I could hit no more. The only thing that was going to stop me would be fatigue or death.

I don't remember him striking me. In fact, I don't really think he did. After my eighth or ninth punch, he just went into hedgehog mode and balled up. I kept moving forward, swinging as hard as I could until he fell backwards. And then it became a kicking festival.

I kicked him continuously, striking head, stomach, chest, back, arms, ass, and hands when they got in the way. I kicked and stomped as hard and as brutally as I possibly could. The whole time he lay curled up the only thing going through my mind was—*is this how they did my friend?*

I kicked that son of a bitch until three or four guys pulled me off him. I shouted, and yelled, and clawed, and pawed, trying to get back to him. I was pulled out of the unit and practically carried over to the library, where I was handed off to my people.

"What the fuck is going on?" Webber asked.

"I just got into it with Unc," I told him.

"Did they jump you?" Tamfu asked.

I shook my head. "Naw, it was one-on-one. I had to beat that muthafucka's ass."

Webber snapped his fingers and a chair was brought to me. "I just sent some guys looking for you."

"For what?" I asked, swallowing hard. I was still a little out of breath.

"We got a problem with the Muslims," Webber told me.

"What problem?"

"Your homeboy, Can't-get-right," Tamfu said with a smile. "He's been tripping."

I shook my head. I was tired, and I needed a breather if we were about to go at it with my Muslim brothers. I spied Shaw waiting in the corner, and I waved for him to come over. One of my soldiers handed me a water jug filled with cool ice water.

"*As-Salaam Alaikum*," I said, holding up my hand.

"*Alaikum Salaam*," Shaw said, clasping my hand.

"What can I do for my brother?" I asked, still trying to catch my breath.

"Are we still brothers?" he asked.

"As far as I know," I replied. "Why do you ask?"

"I heard you been reading Chancellor Williams' book," he said.

"We judging? We are questioning? O how powerful we have become to be able to stand in the steed of Allah."

He bowed slightly. "Forgive me. What I hear troubles me greatly."

"Put your fears to rest," I told him. "I make *salat* five times a day."

"Hmmm, let's not beat around the bush," he said. "It was bad enough that you're a Sufi, as if your powers and beliefs in mysticism are going to save you from the hellfires. But now, you've turned completely away from your brothers. You don't even attend *jumu'ah* any more. You spouting black consciousness and talking about how the African is the original man, and how a black Pharoah was the first to proclaim that there is but one true God. That's blasphemy!"

"What is the Arabic word for African?" I asked. "Answer that. And then tell me what the Arabic word for slave is?"

Shaw was from Iran. Though his native language was Farsi, he was also fluent in Arabic. Color bled into his face, and he turned ruby-red. "I'm not Arab."

"Shiite, Sunni, Sufi, what difference does it make? You spout divisiveness, and yet, when I point out a contradiction, you become defensive. What can I do for you this evening, Brother Shaw?"

"Your homeboy Can't-get-right. He's running around spreading malicious rumors about one of my Muslim brothers. It needs to stop."

"Which brother, and what rumors?" I asked.

"He running around talking about he caught Brother Sharif with a punk."

"Brother Sharif?" I laughed. "Have you investigated the claim?"

"There is no need to," Shaw said dismissively. "I'm going to take the word of my brother over a *kaffir*."

"You and I both know that Brother Sharif is more than just suspect. He's a fucking booty bandit. So you come to me with this shit? What? What do you want me to do? So Can't-get-right is like a big fucking kid. He saw what he saw. If he saw Sharif fucking with a punk, then you need to get on Sharif's ass. Don't come to me, telling me to tell Can't-get-right to shut up. Don't cover up; beat the fuck up!"

"Beat who? That's the question. Can't-get-right? Are you giving us permission to discipline Can't-get-right?"

"Why does Can't-get-right need disciplining? He wasn't the one fucking with the punk; Sharif was. Whip *his* ass, and let him know that we don't play that bullshit! We ain't no punks; we're soldiers for Allah!"

"No, *we're* soldiers for Allah!" Shaw shouted back. "You, you're going to have to decide who you're with. Either you're with *us*, the Muslims, or you're with Umkhonto."

I leaned back in my seat and examined him. "Let's get this straight. You're telling me that I have to choose between being Muslim or being black?" I laughed in his face. "I was born black, so I can't help that. My father is a Muslim, his father is a Muslim, as was his father before him. So I don't think that I have too much of a choice in that matter either."

"Tell your boy to shut up and stop spreading rumors about our brother," Shaw said forcefully. "You shut him up, or *we'll* shut him up."

"You touch one hair on Can't-get-right's head, and that'll be the last time you pick your nose with that hand," I told him.

"You've decided," he said, walking off.

"Shaw!"

He stopped. "What?"

"We are who we protect," I said solemnly. "What do we stand up for? Do we stand up for what the Koran itself condemns?"

"I stand up for my Muslim brother," Shaw said, without turning to face me. "And obviously, you stand up for your black one."

There are a lot of things that I could say about Islam, but the most important thing that I can say is that the racism and bigotry against Africans comes from Arab nationalism, not from the religion itself. Islam is peace. And my particular sect, the Sufis, believed in inner and outer peace and balance with all of Allah's creations.

That Shaw was a racist son of a bitch was something that I knew long ago. It was Muslims like him that sought to divide and destroy my religion. He preached divisiveness and fostered hatred and resentment. To him, a black man could never be a true Muslim or be a true believer. To him, we were nothing more than converts. He had a Persian outlook on Islam.

And even crazier was that most Arabs took an even *more* racist outlook on things. To them, *he* was a convert, and we were even lower on the totem pole than the Persians. The Arab word for African and slave are one and the same. And inside, like so many other people of African origin, I fought an internal *jihad*. Was I African, or was I Muslim? In a world where the Arab Muslims still enslaved the African Sudanese, where were my loyalties? As an African, was it not my responsibility to protect the Sudanese Malkias, the black princesses, the descendants of Nubia, ancient Egypt, ancient Ethiopia and Kush? The women who gave birth to my race?

Shaw had thrown down the gauntlet. I never made *jumu'ah* again. When I made *salat,* it was in the corner, next to my bed. There, I prayed to an all-powerful Allah, an Allah of infinite wisdom, power, and mercy. An Allah who created the heavens and the earth, and all above, below, and in between. An Allah who loved all, and whose forgiveness was boundless. I prayed to Allah, who loved and created a beautiful garden called Al-Kebulan first. Alone, I was free to love my God above all others, and then love my people second. I was African. I would pray to my God *and* protect my people.

I awoke for 2 A.M. prayers to the sound of tennis shoes running through the halls. Shortly afterwards, I heard screams and shouting in nearby rooms. More footsteps. More rumbling. More screams.

I jumped out of bed and put on my tennis shoes. I slept in warm-up pants, and so I slipped on the top to the jogging suit and I was ready. Or nearly ready. I reached beneath my pillow and grabbed my shank.

The sounds of Mexicans yelping echoed throughout the halls. And soon, the call of "Piasa!" joined in. Ghirt and Webber rushed into my room.

"The Aztecas are hitting the Piasa's leadership and their main soldiers!" Ghirt shouted.

"Get everyone to the BET room!" I ordered. "Get a team, get armed, and go room to room and get all the brothers. Make sure they wake up and get to the BET room. And make sure that we don't miss anybody."

And they were off.

Pink House Shorty, New Jersey, Quick, and Big Austin ran into my room. They were Umkhonto, and they were armed to the teeth.

"You all right?" Shorty shouted.

I nodded. "Get all the brothers together! Assemble Umkhonto! And find G-Man and Goodes!"

"That's already taken care of!" Jersey shouted. "Umkhonto is assembling outside of the BET room."

"I got soldiers going room to room getting all the brothers!" Shorty said.

I nodded. "Good work."

"G-Man is already in the BET room," Big Austin told me. "Goodes is on the first floor helping check the rooms and getting all the brothers."

"See if G-Man needs anything!" I ordered and then turned to Young Gangsta, who was one of my cell mates. "Break out the weapons. I want everybody armed."

Gangsta nodded, and shot out of the room.

"It's bad," Shorty said, shaking his head. "Aztecas caught these fools completely off guard, yo! They smashed them dudes."

"There are bodies all over the unit," Big Austin said solemnly.

I shivered and nodded. "Get to the BET room and get with your units."

Shorty shook his head. "Yo, we here for you. We ain't leaving without you."

I nodded and headed out the door and down the hall. And they were right. The halls were filled with blood and several bodies. The moans from the wounded echoed loudly throughout the halls. Shorty brushed past me and took the point. As we past each room, he was on guard. He wanted to make sure that no one was hiding around corners, waiting to jump out and stab me. We came across a group of Mexican soldiers that were armed to the teeth. My soldiers raced past me with their weapons ready.

"Hey, it's cool!" one of the Mexicans shouted. "We're cool with the brothers!"

"You not in it!" another one declared.

"It's okay, guys," I told my dudes. "Let'em pass."

Shorty pushed me into a nearby room, and he and New Jersey stood in front of me while the Mexicans filed past us. When we arrived at the large ante room just outside of the BET room, it was crazy. I hadn't realized until that moment what we had done. Actually, what Ghirt had done. That damn fool had really created a fucking army. Forty soldiers all standing in precise columns snapped to attention, stomping their boots on the ground while doing so. It made a thunderous sound. Everyone's attention was on us.

I got goose bumps, and my heart welled up with pride. My Umkhonto We Sizwe were all dressed, armed, and standing at attention in perfect rows.

"What are your orders?" Ghirt asked.

I turned to G-Man. "Are all the brothers accounted for?"

"Yeah, this is everybody," G replied.

I nodded. "Has anybody heard anything from the other housing unit?" I peered out the window and across the yard. Through the other window, I could see the Umkhonto soldiers that lived in the other housing unit standing at attention just outside of their BET room. I wanted to turn to Ghirt, and Gangsta, and Webber, and Tamfu, and embrace them all.

"They got all the brothers in the BET room over there, sir!" Deonte shouted.

I nodded. It had worked. Everything that we planned had fucking worked. Our soldiers had stepped up and did what they had been trained to do. They went through the unit, got all the brothers up out of their sleep, and then got them to safety.

"Orders, sir?" Ghirt asked again.

"At ease," I said softly. And again they stomped and went into a parade rest position. Their precision stunned us all. The Umkhonto were disciplined, and every movement they made was precise, powerful, and even awe inspiring. They performed like an elite military drill team in grey warm-ups and work boots.

I walked into the BET room and lifted my hand to get everyone's attention. The place went silent immediately. "Everybody relax. I know it's the middle of the night, I know we're all tired, some of us a little nervous. But put your fears to rest. This fight is between the Mexicans, and it has nothing to do with us. They ain't going to bother us. What we're going to do is take over these four TV rooms. Go and grab a spot on the floor and get comfortable. We'll just ride it out here until the riot teams get control of the prison."

"Spread out in the TV rooms and get some sleep," G-Man told them.

I walked back into the hall where my Umkhonto had gathered. "I want a five-man team patrolling the first floor, and one on the third floor, making sure they ain't breaking into our lockers. I want a five-man team in this stairwell, and one in the other stairwell on the south side of the building. I want the rest of our men here guarding these TV rooms while the brothers get some rest."

Ghirt turned and issued orders. The Umkhonto broke up, with each man racing off to do his duty. G-Man approached from behind.

"Good work, C," he said, patting my shoulder.

"It's Ghirt's work," I said, giving my dude his props.

"Good work, Ghirt," G-Man told him.

"Did the Aztecas let anybody know they were going to pull this shit?" I asked.

G-Man shook his head. "They kept this shit to themselves. They knew the Border Brothers were going to hit them next, so they said 'fuck it,' and hit the Border Brothers first."

My thoughts turned to Henry, and I wondered if he survived. I peered out the window at the carnage going on outside. Fires were everywhere, and the Aztecas and Piasas were engaged in pitched battles in the middle of the yard. The guards that patrolled the perimeter of the prison in trucks had pulled over and started firing tear gas and plastic buckshot into the prison in an effort to break up the battle.

"Gangsta!" I said, turning and looking for my celly.

"What's up?"

"C'mere." When he came close, I whispered into his ear. "Tell the soldiers patrolling upstairs to peek into each of the rooms and see if Henry is dead or wounded."

Gangsta nodded and took off.

Henry wasn't among the dead or wounded that evening. Instead, he fought off his attackers and managed to rally enough of his soldiers to lead a counterattack. In fact, if it hadn't been for Henry, a lot more of his people would have died. He led his men in battle from the front, even after being stabbed more than six times. He was a hero to them, and they wouldn't forget his actions that night.

The battle raged until the morning hours, with Henry leading his Border Brothers against a united Azteca and EPT gang. The rest of the Border Brothers and Piasa leadership had been killed or severely wounded. And the few that weren't had hidden inside of the showers and locked themselves into bathroom stalls until the battles ended. They paid for that cowardice in the coming weeks by being brutally beaten by their soldiers.

The Aztecas and EPTs had taken the Piasas by surprise, but as the night went on, the sheer weight of the Piasas numbers—along with Henry's heroics—turned the tide of the battle. By the time it was all over, thirty Aztecas lay dead or severely wounded, with the remainder in the hole. The Border Brothers had been emaciated, but they could claim victory because they were still on the yard. They had lost the majority of their leadership and most of their main soldiers. They had more than a hundred dead or severely wounded, with another two hundred with some kind of stab wound, but they had survived.

The battle had taken the twelve guards on duty that night by complete surprise. In truth, it had scared the shit out of them. This was the third major battle in as many months, and the warden wanted to demonstrate his resolve this time. He put us on complete lockdown until further notice.

By day five, the peanut butter sandwiches three times a day had the entire yard starving. One peanut butter sandwich, one piece of fruit, and one small-ass juice box, three times daily, was what we were issued. Those of us with food in our lockers weren't really feeling the pinch. I had many lockers filled with food. I was snacking on some chips when I noticed Pedro watching my every bite like a starving, homeless dog.

"Amigo," I said, offering him some.

"*Gracias*!" he said, snatching my bag and wolfing down the chips.

I opened my locker, pulled out an unopened bag of chips and tossed them on his bed. I pulled out a couple of candy bars, some packs of Ramen noodles, and a container of drink mix, and tossed that on his bed as well. He looked at me like I was crazy.

"Alexander, I no have no money!" he said. His eyes were bucked out of his head as he examined all the food.

"Don't worry about it," I told him. "*Tú eres mi hermano, no*?"

I could see tears welling up in his eyes. I held out my hand, and he clasped it.

"You need anything, *hermano*," he said, with his voice breaking, "you tell me, okay?"

I nodded. "Okay."

The Umkhonto lockers stayed full for times like these, and we were passing food to all of the brothers in the unit through the guards. We were okay, and we had more than enough to ride out a lockdown for months.

Pedro was a Border Brother and was assigned to take me out in case of a war between the Piasas and the blacks. But over the last couple of months, I had gotten to know him and his family. He was a soldier for his people for sure, but beyond that, he was a father like me. He wanted a better life for himself and for his children. He loved Tejano music, he had a beautiful young wife, and three beautiful children. He wanted to go home and work as a carpenter building houses. He had dreams, and I had come to know those dreams. And so I shared my food with him. Even mortal enemies could break bread together, right?

# Chapter Fourteen

Henry was now the top dog for both the Piasas and the Border Brothers. His people caught the old man who ran the Piasas hiding in the shower. Ain't that a bitch? The old man was a real gangster when it came time to ordering hits, or ordering a muthafucka to get disciplined, or when it was time to send his people off to war. But when it came to getting his own ass skinned up, he hid like the bitch-ass coward he was.

Henry's promotion to the top made me happy. He deserved it. His actions the night of the battle with the Aztecas made me proud. Even though we didn't fuck with each other like that anymore, he was still my homeboy, and he showed everybody how we did it in the hometown. We don't fucking run! Two feet planted like some muthafuckin' trees, no matter what was coming our way.

We came off lockdown after two weeks. The yard opened up, and shit went back to being a regular old fucked-up prison. A lot of the Border Brothers got taken off the yard, and all of the Aztecas and EPTs were shipped off to other prisons. With all of those muthafuckas gone, along with all the Califas off the yard, shit actually became kinda peaceful for a minute. We were even able to start up a football league.

"All right, you go long," I told Gangsta. "Duck, you go out about twenty yards, and then cut right. Pree, you go out about ten yards and cut right. Ready ... break!"

We lined up in formation, and I called the snap. Young Gangsta flew down the field, beating his man by twenty yards. I lobbed the ball downfield, hitting him perfectly.

"Touchdown, bitches!" I shouted.

My team cheered, and so did the punks on the sidelines.

Prison punks cheering at a football game was something I could never get used to. They were men, and they wore homemade lipstick, tight, cut-off warm-ups as shorts, and had their T-shirts tied in the front. They had nicknames like Chocolate, Cinnamon, Caramel, and Coffee. Hell, Chocolate and Cinnamon even had tits!

I had been down long enough so I no longer looked at them like they were circus freaks, but still ... Grown men cheering, doing cartwheels and the splits, was a little disturbing to me. But apparently some of the brothers didn't feel that way.

My boy Mississippi Slim actually sent Caramel to the hospital one evening. The prison had to call an ambulance to come and transport him to a local emergency room. Apparently the prison nurses couldn't stop Caramel's rectal bleeding. Slim's booty-bandit ass had apparently worn the lining out that muthafucka. It was a disgusting thought. Two hairy-ass, grown-ass men cuddling up at night. And the sad part is that on Saturday and Sunday, Slim would be up in the visitation room hugging and kissing on his girl like he wasn't a booty lover. The even sadder part was that he wasn't the only one doing it.

Plenty of other brothers in the joint were on the down-low. But the Mexicans! I don't know if it was a cultural thing or if it was simply because we were locked up with the worst elements of their society, but they saw absolutely nothing wrong with fucking punks. Those muthafuckas would gather in the common showers and watch the punks take showers. They would lift the punks onto tables and clap and cheer while the Mexican punks did table dances and stripped. And the even crazier thing was we actually had to go to a meeting with the Mexicans about their punks. They were pissed, because some of their punks had actually gone black and didn't want to go back. Needless to say, I stayed out of that one. G-Man, Goodes, and Rock handled it.

Rock was a new brother to the yard, but wasn't new to the system. He had been bidding for a while. He had been down in Three Rivers with G-Man and Goodes, and he knew what was what. He was our age, and like us, prison had turned him old early. He was old-school mentality, but still young physically. He could toss it up with the best of them. Having him on the yard was a blessing. It meant that I could really step the fuck away from the day-to-day petty shit and let him, Goodes, and G handle that shit.

Unfortunately, Rock wasn't the only one with leadership potential to step onto the yard. We also got a loudmouthed muthafucka named

Weasel out of Oak Cliff. Oak Cliff was a predominantly black community located on the south side of Dallas, and blacks there had real economic and political power. It was an old community, and blacks coming out of there were different. They were loud, boisterous, braggadocios even. They were proud, strong black people. And Weasel had all of these qualities in him.

My problem with Weasel was that he was one of those brothers who thought that he knew every fucking thing—like we had been doing everything all wrong until *he* showed up. And now, he wanted us to toss him the reins. We built this shit, and we were standing on line protecting brothers, while he was still out in the free world selling nickels and dimes. And now, he wanted to lead us? It was laughable.

Weasel was from Texas, but he was from Dallas, Texas. There were ten brothers on the yard from Dallas. I had over eighty brothers from San Antonio, over thirty from Austin, and over two hundred whose federal numbers ended in 080 or 180. The significance of the last three digits of your prison number was that it signified where you were from. The number 080 meant that you were from the Western Judicial District of Texas. These were all my soldiers. He had ten, I had over two hundred, and *he* wanted to lead?

My biggest problem with Weasel was that he wanted to lead so that he could call himself a shot caller. With him, it wasn't about the brothers and keeping them safe, it was about his ego. Could he lead? Potentially. But he had to wait his turn and show the brothers what kinda cat he really was. You can't just show up on the yard and start making noise and expect us to toss you the keys to the car. You wanna drive—you have to *earn* that right.

G-Man had gotten moved into the other housing unit after the Azteca riot. This was a good thing, because Goodes, Rock, and I were all in the other building, and we needed someone in that other housing unit. The bad thing was that Weasel was in the other housing unit with him, and G-Man caught hell behind it. Weasel questioned his every decision, his every order, his every move, and worked diligently behind G-Man's back to build up support for his own bid for leadership. He even had the brothers rumbling under their voices about a dictatorship, saying that we hadn't held elections for leadership in years. He wanted an election because he thought that he could win. He was stupid.

Our football game ended once dusk came. It was just as well. We all had to rush back to the housing unit, shower, and change into our best prison uniforms. We had an outside choir coming into the chapel to perform that evening, a choir filled with females from a local black church. We wouldn't be able to touch, but we could damn sure look. Who knows, we might be able to get them to choose. They had brothers and cousins inside of the joint, and it wouldn't be hard for them to find out who we were if they wanted to choose.

"Are you going to the chapel, San Antone?" G-Man asked.

"Mos def," I told him.

"Man, wait 'til you see Money's sisters," he said laughing.

"I heard about them."

"Picture Money as a broad," G said.

We both stared at one another and laughed. "That won't be hard."

Money was suspect. He was too feminine not to be.

I showered, dressed, and arrived at the chapel to find it standing room only. But I was escorted to a front pew by some of the soldiers from Umkhonto. Yeah, it was beginning to feel weird. I no longer waited in line at commissary, or laundry, or the chow hall, or for the weekly movie at the visitation room. When I arrived at the library in the morning, the newspapers that I liked to read were waiting for me behind the library desk, and most of the time when I hit the yard, I was quickly surrounded by bodyguards. It was almost as if I had become a prisoner of Umkhonto instead of its founder.

"That's Money's sister right there," G-Man whispered.

"Damn, she is *bad*," I told him.

"She looks just like that nigga," Rock whispered.

"You comin' outta the closet tonight, Rock?" Goodes asked.

"I knew you was after Money," I added.

"I'm after *you*, San Antone," Rock said, placing his hand on my knee.

"Fuck you!" I told him, knocking his hand off.

We all broke into laughter.

The choir sang several songs for us all while we ogled their bodies and had some really nasty thoughts about what we would do to them if given the opportunity. And with that, our opportunity soon came.

*"Attention on the compound! Attention on the compound!"* the loudspeaker blared. *"All inmates return to your housing units! All inmates return to your housing units! The compound is closed! I repeat,*

*the compound is now closed!"*

"What the fuck?" G-Man asked, peering toward me.

I shrugged. And then the emergency siren went off.

Oakman, one of my Umkhonto soldiers from the ATL, ran into the chapel breathing heavily. "The Piasas and the Texicans just went to war!"

"Shit!" I shouted. More lockdown.

The choir members huddled together in fear.

I turned to the chaplain, who was frozen in fear himself. He had a chapel full of men, many of whom hadn't been with a woman in ten, twelve, even fifteen years. And he had a chapel full of fine-ass women in tight-ass skirts, standing on the stage.

"Umkhonto!" Ghirt stood and shouted. "Assemble outside!"

I rose. "Ghirt!"

He turned toward me. "Yeah?"

"Protect the choir!" I shouted. "Everybody but my soldiers, get back to the housing units. Get strapped and get to the BET rooms!"

The chapel cleared. My soldiers ran to the front of the chapel near the stage, lined up, and turned toward the crowd and locked arms. The women were safe behind them.

I would be questioned about my decision that day, but I wasn't an animal, and I wasn't about to let anyone violate my sisters.

Finally, the chaplain's ass tried to move into action. "I want everybody out! Everybody back to the housing units!"

"If you do that, then we'll be in the housing units, while the choir will be stuck up here on the upper yard without any protection, in a prison that you've lost control of," I told him.

"I'll lock the door when you're gone," he countered.

"And you think locking the door is going to keep the Piasas at bay?" I asked. "They are going to kill the Texicans, then come in here and kill you, rape them, and maybe even kill them so there won't be any witnesses!"

"What would you have me do?" he asked. "You want to leave some guys outside of the chapel to protect us?"

"I need my soldiers," I told him. "We need to get them out of here."

"How? It's a madhouse outside!"

I heard the boots stomping as my soldiers jogged to the chapel. Their thunderous stomps, interspersed with their commanders giving orders, sounded like joy to my ears. I clasped the chaplain's arm and led him to the door, where we peered outside of the chapel. I had two platoons outside of the chapel, each consisting of forty-eight armed men. They were lined up, fired up, and ready to go.

"We're going to escort them to the Control Gate and get them out of here," I told him.

"How do I know that I can trust you?" he asked.

I turned him around so that he could see my men lined up in front of the stage, locked arm in arm, protecting the choir. "We're already protecting them. Besides, we're you're only hope."

The chaplain nodded and lifted his walkie-talkie. "Control, this is Chaplain Davis. I'm escorting the visitors from the chapel out of the prison."

"Roger that," Control replied.

I turned and walked to where the choir members were gathered. "You're going to be all right. No one is going to bother you. They're having issue on the lower half of the compound, but we're on the upper part of the yard, so we're all right. What we're going to do is escort you to the entrance where you came in, and then they'll let you out of the front gate so you can get to your bus and get back home."

I nodded, and my soldiers in front of them made a hole for them to pass through.

"It's all right, folks," Chaplain Davis said.

We escorted them to the door where my Umkhonto was.

"I have one *iButho* in Sunrise Unit and another in Sunset," Ghirt told me.

*IButho* was our platoon level formation. It was the equivalent of a platoon. Four *iButhos* formed an *amaButho*, which was like a company. Four *amaButhos* formed an *iKhanda*, which was a battalion. Four *iKhandas* formed an *iMpi*, which was a regiment. Our organization was based on the old Zulu formations in Shaka's army. In places where you had a camp, a low-security prison, a medium-security prison, and a United States penitentiary, or USP, it wasn't unheard of to have an entire *iMpi* between the four of them.

My disciplined soldiers standing at attention outside of the chapel shocked most of the visitors.

"About face!" Ghirt commanded. The units stomped and made a precise turn.

The chaplain's mouth fell open, and he stared at me. I knew that I would have a lot of explaining to do once this was all over with.

"We're escorting our women to Control," I told them. "Protect them with your life."

"First platoon, forward!" Ghirt ordered. First platoon marched forward.

I waved for the visitors to follow behind them, and they did.

"Second platoon, forward!" Ghirt ordered.

First platoon was the advance guard, and second platoon acted as the rear guard, with the choir safely in between. We marched them up to the edge of the visiting room and stopped. The Control Building was only twenty yards away. They would be safe the rest of the way, and Control would not open the doors for them if any prisoners were nearby. I got hugs and thank-yous from nearly all of the women in the choir. We watched them march safely through the Control Gate, and then turned our attention toward the carnage taking place on the yard.

Again, our people were not in it as it was between the Mexicans. This time, the Piasas had initiated the war. They were feeling themselves after their win against the Aztecas. It was easy to see the handwriting on the wall. They had gotten rid of the Califas, the Aztecas, and now they were getting rid of the Texans. Texans, or Texicans, were a conglomeration of various Texas gangs and U.S.-born Hispanics. The Piasas despised the U.S. Hispanics almost as much as they despised us. They called them *plásticos*, or "plastic." In other words, they were "fake" Mexicans and Hispanics.

Getting rid of the U.S. Hispanics told us two things: the Piasas wanted total control of the yard, and we were next.

My Umkhonto and I walked back down to the lower yard, and everyone went into their respective housing unit to wait for the goon squad to come and restore order. Goodes walked into my room that night and sat on the edge of my bed.

"They did it again, San Antone."

"Who?" I asked, sitting up in bed. "What are you talking about?"

"Them California muthafuckas," Goodes said. "Didn't you see them out on the balconies with their headphones? All of the brothers were together in the BET room, and they out there separate."

"Fuck'em," I said, lying back down.

"No, you don't understand," Goodes told me. "They knew. They knew this shit was going down tonight, and they didn't tell none of us. That's why none of them was in the chapel."

"How did you find this out?" I asked.

"Henry sent a message apologizing for getting us all caught up in this shit. He said that he told Magic and Unc to tell us that it was going down tonight. But they only told their people."

My mind was made up—it was time for us to deal with these dudes.

"I'll take care of them," I told Goodes.

"We *all* gonna take care of them niggaz!" Goodes said.

"We'll get with G and Rock tomorrow and plan this shit."

"I wanna hit them niggaz tomorrow!" Goodes said. "No more talking, no more waiting, no more second, third, fourth, and fifth chances bullshit. They either with us or against us. And they done showed us that they're against us."

I lifted my hand into the air, and he clasped it.

"Tomorrow."

"Tomorrow."

# Chapter Fifteen

We went to war with the California brothers that next day. The yard was still on lockdown, which made things easier for us. Each unit was tasked to take care of the California cats in the rooms with them. That meant they were sitting ducks. They couldn't escape, they couldn't call for help, and they couldn't help each other.

Young Gangsta gave the signal by barking loudly throughout the hallway. Big Shreveport, Young Gangsta, my homeboy Shawn, and I ran into the room with Unc, Smoke, and Magic. I stole on Magic before he could get out of the bed.

Unc tried to get up and dance, but Big Shreveport yanked that fool up off the ground and threw him into the wall. Young Gangsta ran in on Smoke and commenced to whipping his ass. That left Shawn to freelance. He got in free shots at them fools, whenever he could. It was meant to be a lesson for those cats, not a boxing match, so the fight wasn't supposed to be fair.

Magic was about six-two, and he was in the four hundred club, which meant that fool had a four hundred pound-bench press. I wasn't in the four hundred club yet. I was pushing three eight-five, so tangling with that big, two hundred and fifty-pound monster was a job. I just couldn't let him get up. But even if he did, I had a plan for that, too. He was all up top with his. His upper body would make the ladies swoon, but if pulled off his pants, they would surely laugh at him. He didn't even have toothpicks for legs; they were so thin, they looked more like dental floss. It he managed to get up, I would take his legs out from under him and send him crashing to the ground. After that, it would be a stomp fest.

I punched Magic, and punched him hard and fast, landing as many face and head shots as I could. He tried to go blow for blow at first, sacrificing his face in order to get some blows in on mine. The problem was I had an iron jaw, and I could take more punches and pain that the above-average man could dish out. He couldn't. Pretty soon, his offense gave way to defense, and he began to try to cover his face, roll away, and kick.

Shawn grabbed one of Magic's legs, and I grabbed the other, and we pulled him out of his bed, sending him crashing to the floor. And then it became a kick fest. Big Shreveport handled Unc with ease, while Young Gangsta touched up Smoke real nice. Up and down the hall, all you could hear were the thuds and thumps of Cali dudes getting touched up. We whipped ass until they stopped moving and until we got tired of kicking. The order of the day was to break'em down real good, so that the message sunk in real deep.

"You punk-ass bitches wanna be on your own, huh?" I asked while kicking. "You wanna make separate treaties and leave us hanging during the riots and shit, huh? You bitch-ass niggaz either get with the program or get the fuck off the yard! That's it! No more fucking around with you niggaz! Next time we send a message, it'll be at two in the morning, and we ain't coming empty-handed, you got that?"

Magic had curled up in a ball on the floor, along with Unc. Smoke was curled up inside of a bunk with Young Gangsta still wailing on him.

"The man asked if you bitch-ass niggaz got the message?" Big Shreveport said.

"Yeah!" Smoke shouted.

"Okay!" Unc said weakly.

We turned and walked out of the room. I wish that I could say that I hated doing that to the brothers, but the fact was I didn't. It felt good. All of the bullshit that those assholes had put me through and the way they did my boy Omene had me waiting for the day when I could pay their asses back. Hopefully, they would get the message.

We came off of lockdown a little over a week later. The thing about the Feds is that each prison has a factory that produces shit for clients in the free world. Business is business, and the white folks ain't gonna let a muthafucka play with they money for too long. We could riot day in and day out, but the fact of the matter was the yard was gonna open, and that factory was going to run.

The federal prison factories were all organized into one huge billion-dollar corporation. The corporation was called UNICOR, Federal Prison Industries. They produced all kinds of high-dollar, free-world shit. I'm talking parts for jet fighters, parts for tanks, uniforms for the military, trucks for the border patrol, generators for the Air Force—you name it, they made it. The fucked-up part was that the prisoners got paid twenty-three cents an hour to work in the factories, while the corporation made millions.

People aren't hip to this, but there is a law stating that the government has to buy from UNICOR first if they need something and UNICOR makes it. So UNICOR has an in-built client for life. Also, UNICOR doesn't have to pay workers comp, workers insurance, Medicare contributions, social security contributions, nothing. The taxpayers foot the housing bill and the medical care bill, and the bill for feeding and clothing the prisoners, so UNICOR is *all* profit. And guess who the investors are? Only federal government employees can invest in UNICOR. Your senators, congressmen, justice department officials, bureau of prison officials, and cats like that.

A corporation's job is to expand. How does UNICOR expand? The powers that be have to build more prisons and put UNICOR factories in them. Do the powers that be *want* to build more prisons? Is there a reason for them wanting to create stiffer laws and penalties for breaking the law? I peeped the game after I had been there for a while. It wasn't about public safety—it was about fattening their pockets. More prisons meant more factories. And that meant they would need more prisoners to work in those factories. They simply moved the slaves from the open fields and hid them behind the fences. That's what the bullshit was all about.

Work call came, and the prison was back to normal. *Almost* back to normal, that is. The guards noticed the bruises on the California brothers and sent them to the infirmary. Some of them snitched, and the shit hit the fan for us.

The first one I saw handcuffed and being taken to the hole was G-Man. Ten minutes later, I saw Goodes, and about ten minutes after that, I saw Rock being handcuffed and taken away. I knew that I was next.

The hit on the California brothers decimated our leadership and scared the devil out of the rest of the brothers. We called an emergency meeting during lunchtime.

"I'ma hold down Sunrise Unit," Weasel started off. "C, you hold down Sunset. We'll meet daily to compare notes and discuss things. That way, I'll know what's going on in y'all unit, and you'll know what's going on in our unit. For the time being, we all just need to remain calm, and most of all, don't say nothing if they call you to the lieutenant's office for questioning."

"Hold on, hold on, *and you are*?" I asked. Some of the brothers snickered. I really didn't like this dude. "First of all, we have an order of succession, and you ain't in it. Any problems on the yard and the *esses* are going to come to me, and I'm going to handle it. Don't trip, don't worry about nothing, just keep ya mouths closed and don't snitch. They come to you, you tell'em you was in bed sleeping, and you don't know shit. Plain and simple."

"C, you ain't over in our unit," Weasel countered. "We need representation in our unit, just in case something jumps off during the evening when the yard is closed. They can't come and talk to you when the yard is closed."

"They can talk to Umkhonto," I told him. "I got what—over a hundred soldiers in Sunrise."

"Yeah, but they ain't leadership," Weasel countered.

Murmurs shot through the crowd, causing him to backtrack.

"I meant, they're not *civilian* leadership," he clarified. "We need civilian leadership to represent us."

I examined the crowd and found a face that would do. "Twin. He's been on the yard a long time. He's going to represent Sunrise."

Twin was from Lubbock, which was in the Texas Panhandle. Lubbock and Amarillo had about forty soldiers on the yard. And Twin had been on the yard for a while. He was quiet, he didn't get into any shit, had a good head on his shoulders, and the brother had been bidding for a while.

Several of the brothers patted Twin on his back. Weasel was fuming.

"I go to the hole, Ghirt takes over Sunset and the yard. Ghirt goes, then Twin has the yard. Umkhonto has its line of succession already spelled out. Just to let you know, Ghirt, Webber, Tamfu, Shorty, Scotty, Big Port, Shawn, Deuce, New Jersey, Gangsta, H-Town, Duck, Mice, Black, Jesse, Billy, and about a dozen other brothers in Umkhonto know what to do. Now, with that said, don't worry about nothing, we know what to do. Just keep quiet if they call you to the lieutenant's office.

"Oh, but in the meantime, when you see the lieutenants or the wardens or the captain, you need to go up to them and start bidding to get those brothers out the hole. That is our main concern right now, getting those brothers out of the hole."

I noticed a bunch of Mexicans walking by and getting scared. The sight of nearly four hundred brothers meeting on the side of the chapel was a frightening sight to them.

"Okay, that's it," I told them. "Let's break this shit up before we get these muthafuckas all nervous and shit."

The gathering broke up, with the majority of the brothers heading down to the cafeteria on the lower yard. I walked through the Control Gate, and two Fred Flintstone-looking guards were waiting for me.

"Alexander," Officer Starks shouted. "SIS wants to see you in his office ASAP!"

"Shit!" I said, turning toward Young Gangsta. "I go to the hole, pack my shit, hide what needs to be hidden, and keep shit organized while I'm gone. Tamfu!"

"Yeah, boss?" Tamfu asked.

"I gotta go and see the SIS lieutenant," I shouted. "You got the keys."

He nodded.

I sipped from my water jug, and then handed it over to Gangsta.

"I gotcha, C," he said, reassuring me.

I nodded, turned, and headed up the yard to the warden's temple, where the SIS had his office.

"In!" SIS shouted when I knocked on the door to his office.

I opened the door and stepped inside. He had his snake-skin cowboy boots propped up on his desk and a massive Confederate flag hanging on the wall behind him. A smaller Confederate flag sat on one side of his desk, with a matching Texas state flag on the other side. The U.S. flag was nowhere to be seen.

"Alexander, shit rolls downhill, you know that?" he asked, chewing his tobacco like a grazing cow. "Region gets shitted on by Washington, and then they shit on the warden. The warden then shits on the assistant warden, who then calls me into his office early in the morning and shits on me. Now me, I'm a good old boy. I was raised shoveling shit. But when I have to deal with a ton of it before I've had my morning coffee, well, that's when I get pissed. You ever seen a pissed-off SIS lieutenant before?"

"Let's see," I said, staring into space. "I seen pissed-off gangbangers, been shot twice and shot at about fifty different times by them. I've seen pissed-off cops, had one put a gun to my head and threaten to blow my brains out. Had another put a Glock under my chin and threaten to blow my brains out that way. I've seen pissed-off ATF agents, pissed-off drug task force agents, pissed-off DEA agents, pissed-off FBI agents, pissed-off U.S. attorneys, and even a few pissed-off judges. A pissed-off SIS … no, don't think I have."

"Well, you don't want to see one either!" he said, now angry because I had placed his threat within a menial context. "You know what diesel therapy is?"

I nodded. Diesel therapy is one of the Feds' favorite threats. They put you on a transfer bus and transfer you from prison to prison, all over the country, almost on a daily basis. You never get visits, your mail never catches up to you, your property never catches up to you, nothing. You basically spend your entire prison sentence on buses, in shackles.

"Good!" SIS nodded. "How would like to spend your fed time somewhere around Duluth, Minnesota, in the winter, and the Mojave Desert during the summer?"

"I'm from a tropical people, Lieutenant. We hate the cold," I told him. "What's the problem now?"

He leaned forward. "The problem is this fucking Umkhonto shit is all over the goddamned country now! And the BOP investigators are trying to say that it began here, in *my* prison! Can you imagine the asshole that makes me look like? Something like that, starting here in this prison, under *my* watch?"

"I don't understand what this has to do with me?"

"You know goddamned well what it has to do with you! You're in on this shit! You're probably in on it from the very beginning! But let me tell you this, son! The attorney general herself is coming down on you sons a bitches like stink on shit! Anyone caught being a member of this Umkhonto is going to be registered as a terrorist! Now how would you like *that* on your records? That means no camps, no low-custody, no halfway house, no drug program—nothing! You will be tagged as a terrorist for the rest of your natural-born lives if you're caught being a member!"

"Wow," I said, lifting an eyebrow. "That sounds like some J. Edgar Hoover-type of shit. Remember when he had a hard-on for the Black Panthers?"

"And you remember what happened to the Black Panthers?" he replied with a smirk.

"Geronimo has a grocery store in Atlanta, Eldridge Cleaver just passed away not too long ago. Angela Davis is a teacher, and so is Sonya Sanchez. Assata is still in Cuba—"

"They got crushed like a fucking bug against a West Texas windshield!" he said forcefully.

I turned up my palms. "I'm still at a loss as to how this has anything to do with me. Like I told you before, I just stick to myself. If I'm not in the library working, I'm lying in my bunk reading."

He nodded. "You're in on this shit, Alexander. I can't prove it, but when I do, you're never getting out of the hole."

"The hole? I get to lie in my bed all day and play with my dick while my food is brought to me. No work call, no more sleeping with one eye open or worrying about Mexicans hitting me over the head with a lock-n-a-sock. Where in the fuck do I sign up? I need some goddamned sleep."

The SIS smiled.

"So, they're putting pressure on you to bust up this Umkhonto stuff, huh?" I asked. "Why they ain't putting pressure on the gang lieutenants to bust up that Piasa shit? How many people have they gone to war with in the last three months? But they stressing over the brothers, huh?"

"Look, I hear you. And off the record, if it were me, I'd do the same goddamned thing. These fucking Mexicans are out of control. Hell, everyone knows that they're going to go after the brothers next, and then the white boys, and then it'll be us, the staff. We know what's going on here, and so does region. But you can't tell those egghead mutherfuckers in Washington nothing. They sit behind their desk, reading their fucking manuals, and try to tell us, here in the prisons dealing with this shit, how to do things. But like I said before, shit runs downhill."

SIS leaned back in his chair. "Apparently, some of your homeboys on the East Coast have gotten kinda rowdy. They also killed a couple of Aryan Brothers in Indiana, some Dirty White Boys in Minnesota, and some Border Brothers in Colorado. Some more of these Umkhonto fellas stabbed a guard in Alabama, and set a Mexican national on fire in Arkansas."

I don't know what it was inside of me that made my stomach flutter with pride. I was never one to take killing lightly. I guess it was the fact that Umkhonto had spread around the country, and that the brothers were standing up for themselves and fighting. Right or wrong, we were fighting back. And a people who fought back was a people who hadn't given up hope for a better tomorrow.

"There's no violence like that here," I said. "All the bullshit on this yard comes from those fucking Border Brother and Piasas. The rest of us are just trying to survive in here. You should have turned this muthafucker into an immigration joint and got us the hell outta here a long time ago."

"Spread the word," SIS said coldly. "I find any Umkhonto on my yard, I'm coming down on them like a ton of bricks. You got that?"

I nodded. It had been a warning. Keep the shit on the down-low and don't make him look bad. We went to war the very next day.

# Chapter Sixteen

The Border Brothers and Piasas hit us that next evening. G-Man was in the hole, and so was Rock, and so was Goodes. And so were a lot of our other soldiers, and all of the California brothers, and their Vegas and Phoenix flunkies. Our numbers were down, our leadership in the hole, and the Mexicans weren't stupid. They caught us off guard and hit us with everything they had. I got caught up in the dorm listening to the mix show on the radio.

"Christian!" New Orleans ran into my room out of breath. "It's going down, baby!"

I jumped up. "What's going down?"

"The *esses* and the brothers!" he shouted.

Suddenly I could hear the commotion. I lay on my bunk and kicked the steel bracing loose from the bunk above mine. It made a nice three-foot metal pipe. New Orleans and I raced through the building, shoving *esses* out of the way, and out into the yard where our people were fighting for their lives. It was on.

I hit the center of the yard and swung like a madman. I struck one attacker, sending him to the ground. And then I turned and struck another, splitting open his head. I dodged a knife blade then swung my pole at the knife wielder's hand, knocking the blade to the ground. No sooner had I parried that attack when I had to dodge another. I swung, striking the knife wielder over his head, and immediately turned and struck another attacker. Somehow, in this mêlée, I was able to bend down and pick up the massive blade that I had knocked out of one of the attackers' hand. From that moment on, I became an animal.

My mind went into autopilot, as did my body. Each of my senses became heightened to the point where I reacted before my enemies acted. Everything and everyone moved in slow motion. With my pipe in one hand and a knife in the other, I struck and slashed.

Barely conscious, I struck an attacker across his head and then swung my blade, slashing his throat. Another appeared in my vision. I struck him and then plunged my blade into his chest. Another one and I stabbed him in his stomach while crashing my pipe against his partner's head.

Suddenly, I was stabbed in the back. I turned and plunged my knife into that attacker's chest. Without a pause, I swung and struck his throat. His blood shot across my face, mixing with my sweat and saliva. I swung, and stabbed, and stuck, and hacked, until finally, there were no more people around me to wound or kill. Only silence.

My mind slowly regained consciousness, and I peered around the yard, finally realizing that I was being watched. Most of the Mexicans had withdrawn to the other side of the compound and peered through the chain fence as the last of their comrades died. My brothers, too, had finished their individual battles and watched. I felt eerily naked, standing in the middle of a circle of dead and wounded Mexicans, breathing heavily, covered with blood and sweat, saliva dripping from my mouth. Had I been shouting, growling, snarling, or making some other weird inhuman noises? To this day, I don't know. But what I do know is that as I slowly regained my humanity, I felt embarrassed. I felt like some creature from a nineteen fifties horror flick that had been caught by the townspeople. They now knew my true nature.

I stood erect and began to walk towards my people. I knew that I'd been stabbed once, but then realized that I had been stabbed twice more as well. I smiled, but the looks on the brothers' faces told me that they weren't buying my innocent smile. Their wide eyes and petrified looks told me that my own people were now scared of me.

Our battle with the Mexicans had been beyond one-sided; it had been a complete rout. Their loss had been complete. So complete, that once word reached other yards, there would definitely be repercussions. A wave of race battles would sweep through the system. And even on this yard, the battle would not be over. They would have to avenge such a sound defeat, or at least make a better showing in order to save face. But the next time, we would be ready for them.

Our victory that night turned out to be a pyrrhic victory. The SIS had to deal with a body count that was out of this world. He blamed it on radical elements in the African American prison population. He didn't want to say Umkhonto, because he had sworn to his higher-ups that there were no Umkhonto soldiers on the yard. He blamed these radical elements for introducing weapons into what would have been a mere fisticuff over a basketball game earlier that day. He was lying his ass off. He knew it, the warden knew it, the regional office knew it, but his report covered everyone's ass, so it was accepted without question. The radical elements were Ghirt and some of my top soldiers. I couldn't be transferred because although I was unofficially the head of Umkhonto, officially, I was the only shot caller on the yard for the brothers. The Feds knew how shit worked. You had to have at least one shot caller on the yard for each group in order to work things out and keep the peace. With G-Man, Goodes, and Rock in the hole over the California incident, I was it. So I remained. But losing Ghirt was a muthafucka.

"Are you sure Webber and Shorty are going to be able to handle it?" Ghirt asked.

I shrugged. "Until I find a replacement."

Ghirt smiled. "I can't be replaced. I'm one of a kind, kid!"

I laughed. "You're right. You're irreplaceable, but Shorty do a good job."

"I left him the training schedule, and he knows the routines, the workouts, and everything to get the new boots through basic."

I nodded. "Jersey will take over teaching them martial arts."

"Man, I'll whip Jersey," Ghirt laughed.

I nodded. "But he can teach them good enough to get their man."

"Tell him I said that," Ghirt laughed. He sat his property down at the door next to the property transfer office. I placed the boxes that I was carrying for him down next to the door as well.

"What we gonna do?" I asked.

"What the fuck you mean, what we gonna do?" Ghirt asked. "We gonna survive, man."

We embraced.

"I'm not good at good-byes, man," I told him with my voice breaking.

"You not gonna start crying on me, are you?"

"I might."

"Don't do it," he said, shaking his head and laughing. "That wouldn't be a good look."

"First Omene, and now you. You ugly muthafuckers keep leaving me."

Ghirt lifted his hand into the air. "Free world?"

"Free world!" I said clasping it.

"In the meantime, you got my folks' address and my sister's address."

I nodded and smiled. "Oh yeah, I'll definitely be writing baby sister, and big sister, too. See how close they really are."

"Fuck you!"

I hugged my brother once again. "You take care of yourself."

"I'm a soldier."

I shook my head. "Uh-uh. Soldiers follow orders blindly. You not a soldier, you're a warrior. Warriors think and use their heads."

He nodded.

"Still no idea of where they sending you to?" I asked.

He shook his head. "Wherever it is, you can best be sure that once I get there, Umkhonto is going to be put into full effect."

"Hell, the way the lieutenant is talking, it's probably already going to be in full effect. Just get their asses in order and make sure that they understand what Umkhonto is really about. It's about protecting our people. We are warriors for our people. We're not a fucking gang."

"I'll write as soon as I get to where I'm going."

I turned and began to walk away.

"Hey, old man!" Ghirt called out.

I turned back toward him and made a muscle. "Old men, don't have twenty-two-inch guns like these."

"Take care of your fucking self," he said solemnly.

Ghirt's departure hit me hard. I fell into a deep depression before he had even left the yard. I didn't feel like eating, I didn't feel like working out, I didn't feel like getting out of fucking bed. He was my brother. He had been with me since the beginning of my bid, and I never thought I would see the day when we would say good-bye.

I know that it sounds crazy, you know, developing that type of bond in prison. But when you see someone every day, share your hopes and your dreams, when you put your life into that person's hands and allow them to put their life in your hands, when you have each other's back, day in and day out, and when you go to war with someone, it's hard to not develop a bond with that person. Ghirt's transfer sent me into a deep depression.

My days blended together. I knew that it was only a matter of time before the Border Brothers tried us again. But even that didn't get me out of bed.

"Alexander!"

I raised up and removed my headphones. It was the guard, handing me a note.

"The chaplain said for you to call home," he told me.

My heart began to race. I jumped out of bed, put on my boots, and hurried over to the phone room.

"Hello?"

"Hey, what's going on?" I asked.

"Oh, we were worried about you," my mother said. "We hadn't heard from you in a while. Is everything all right?"

"Yeah, just been chilling."

"Chilling?"

"Yeah, just sleeping and waking up, that's all."

"Are you eating?" she asked. "What's the matter? You don't sound too good."

"Naw, I'm cool. Everything's all right."

"Your brother's here. You wanna talk to him?"

"Yeah, put him on."

I could hear the phone jostling as it changed hands.

"What up, dude?"

"Ain't nothing, what's been shaking?"

"Shit, bullshit. These niggaz is out here tripping."

"Same shit in here," I laughed. "What y'all been up to?"

"Trying to get this bread," he said. "You need some?"

"I can always use some," I answered.

"All right. I'ma give it to Momma before I leave."

"Appreciate it. Hey, send me some pictures, nigga!"

"All right. Wait 'til I go to the club."

"Nigga, go to the Kappa Beach Party and send a nigga some flicks of them hoes! Goddamn, y'all carrying me bad on the flicks."

"All right. I'ma look out for you."

"Nigga, you always say that shit."

"I'm for real this time. I'ma go get a camera, and I'ma hit the club."

"Let me seen them whips and shit in the 'Tone. I heard you got a new whip."

"Yeah, I busted out with this new BMW."

"Oh, yeah?"

"Hell, yeah. That bitch is tight, too."

"Send me some flicks. What T and them doing?"

"Same shit. Going to the mall and falling off at the strip clubs and shit."

I laughed. "Damn, them fools ain't gonna never change."

"Say, you know ya boy Lil J got killed the other day?"

"What?"

"Fool, them niggaz in the Rigsby rolled up on the side of old boy and served him."

"Bullshit!"

"I ain't bullshitting."

"Who? Who did it?"

"Monsta and them."

"You bullshitting, dude."

"Naw. They say that fool was tripping at the club with them niggaz right before it happened. They followed him and caught him right down the street. Fool crashed into that ditch right in front of the Rigsby."

"Man. So what is them niggaz talking about doing?"

"Shit, Capone locked up. And you gotta understand, man, Lil J was tripping out here lately. He was jacking fools and straight robbing muahfuckas."

"Say, let me make some calls real quick. I'ma hit you back in a little while. How long you gonna be over there?"

"I'll be here for a minute."

"All right, I'll holler at you later."

"All right."

I hung up the telephone and immediately headed for my room. If I had been depressed before, I was damn near suicidal now. Getting bad news from home was always fucked-up. As a matter of fact, you almost get used to it. When you're gone for a long time, people die. But you kinda expect certain muthafuckas to die: old people, ya niggaz wilding out in the streets. It's just certain muthafuckas that got death on them. But my nig, Lil J, I never saw him dying.

The crazy thing about my boy was that he was a stone-cold killa.

And as crazy as this shit might sound, it's always those types of muthafuckas who make it. It's the half-dedicated and completely innocent muthafuckas who always bite the bullet. The news that my nig was gone hit home hard. I just wanted to climb inside of my bunk and be left the fuck alone.

Young Gangsta tried to get me out to the yard for a walk around the track. I told him to leave me the fuck alone. Tamfu tried to get me over to the library for my French lessons. I told him to get the fuck away from me. Webber tried to get me roused up by talking politics. I told him to fuck off. One by one, I got the message across to my boys that I just wanted to be depressed. My prison time was wearing on me. I wanted to be out, I wanted to be home. I wanted to avenge the death of my friend, I wanted to make sure that I was able to hold my grandmother once again. I wanted to see my mother's smile. Most of all, I wanted to play with my son, I wanted to kiss his mother, I wanted my family.

"Get up."

I peered up. "Man, Old School, I don't feel like it."

Old School set the chessboard down on my legs, forcing me to sit up.

"Get up, youngster," Old School said in his raspy voice.

I sat all the way up. Old School started placing pieces on the chessboard and after a few moments, I began doing the same. After we had placed all of the pieces, Old School moved first.

"So, what's the matter with you, young lion?" he asked.

I shrugged. "Same shit; just tired of being in prison."

"That's good," he said, wiggling the toothpick around in his mouth. "Maybe then, you won't bring your ass back."

"I ain't coming back. That's for damn sure."

"Same thing I said about five bids ago."

"You've been down five times, Old School?"

"Six. This is my third rodeo in the feds, and I did three bids in the state."

"Goddamn, nigga! You couldn't get a job?"

He laughed, and it made me laugh.

"How's that little Darth Vader head son of yours?"

I laughed. "Fuck you."

"You know you cursed that baby, giving him that big-ass basketball head of yours."

Again I laughed.

"He's still playing football?"

"Running back; scoring all the touchdowns."

"He must get his athleticism from his mother."

"He gets it from his old man, nigga!"

"San Antone, you can't walk from here to there without tripping. What the fuck you talking about?"

"I know one thing. I can play chess!" I told him. "Check, nigga!"

"You over here wasting moves and shit," he said, moving out of check.

"Uh-uh, check," I told him once again. "Remember, you asked for this ass whipping."

He moved his king, and I took his queen.

"Damn it! I fucked up."

He moved his king again, and I swiped one of his rooks.

"You got this one, San Antone," he said, setting all of the pieces back up, so that we could start again. "Don't open with that Ruy Lopez shit!" Old School said, frustrated.

"How you gonna tell me how to open?" I asked. "Here," I said, running the Queens Gambit.

"How's that wife of yours?"

"Who the hell knows?"

"What'cha mean by that?"

"Hell, who knows what that muthafucka is up to. Shit, I don't know. I ain't got no letters, no visits, no pictures, nothing. Hell, she out there doing her thang."

"How you figure that?"

"She ain't doing me."

"Is she taking care of your son?"

"Yeah."

"She keep him clean, and fed, and with a roof over his head, right?"

"Yeah. Hell, that's what she's supposed to do."

"Yeah, but a lot of women don't even do that. Hell, my daughter out there strung out on that shit. She got my grandbabies all in the street. State threatening to take'em away from her."

"Damn, that's fucked up."

"So, don't complain about what she ain't doing. Think about what she doing. She ain't had no babies on you, have she?"

"She ain't crazy," I laughed.

"She ain't crazy? What you mean by that?"

"Shit, that muthafucka ain't crazy. Just what I said."

"San Antone, that's her pussy. You can't be getting mad over what she do with her pussy. I'm sure when you was out, you was doing what you wanted to do with your dick, nigga."

"Man, put your fucking cape away and play some chess."

"I ain't being no Captain Save 'Em. I'm just saying, nigga, you laying up in the bed like somebody done shot your dog when you got a good woman out there. She's taking care of your son, San Antone. That's all that matters. All that other shit is just extra."

I nodded. "I ain't tripping over that."

"You wanna be home with her?"

I nodded.

"You gonna marry her when you get out?"

"That depends."

"Depends on what?"

"If she don't have no more kids and shit. I might see what we can do."

"If she don't have no more kids? What kids got to do with it?"

"Shit, once you have a kid by somebody else after we done been together, then that nigga is who you be with."

"San Antone, you crazy!"

"Man, I ain't no old-ass nigga, Old School. I'm still a youngsta, and I still think like a youngsta. I ain't trying to deal with no niggas, and all that baby momma, baby daddy bullshit."

"You ever fuck a bitch with kids?"

"Yeah."

"Would you have been with her?"

I thought about it for a few seconds. "Yeah."

"So what's the difference? You love her, right? So you telling me that you wouldn't love her kids?"

"Man, what difference does it make? All this hypothetical-ass shit!"

"It's not hypothetical. We were talking about having a good woman. You ever play chess with your woman, San Antone?"

"Play chess with her?" I shook my head. "I don't think that she can play chess."

"You supposed to teach your woman, San Antone. Sit her down and teach her about life, about her role, about playing her position."

Old School started putting the pieces back into their starting positions.

"What are you doing?" I asked.

"You can get outta that?" he asked, peering down at the board. "If you can get outta that, you's a bad muthafucka."

I examined the board, and sure as shit, he had me in checkmate in two moves. I nodded and smiled. "You got that one."

He leaned in, cupping his hand behind his ear. "Huh? What you say? I can't hear you."

I laughed. "All right, you got that one."

Old School put the pieces back into place and started again.

"See these pieces?" he asked, pointing to the castles. "These are your houses. Just like in the free world, you keep your crib way out. That way, muahfuckas can't find ya shit. See these horses? These are your runners. They can't go too far. And that's how it's supposed to be. You gotta keep these muahfuckas close, so you can watch'em. And these bishops here, these are your main men. That's why they close to the king. You keep your niggaz close. See these white pieces over here? Their job is to destroy this black king. And her job?" Old School lifted the queen and laughed.

"Her job is to protect the black king. The most powerful piece on the board is the black queen. She is the most dominant piece on the board. Her sole reason for existence is to protect her king. She controls everything; she runs the board. And the smarter she is, the more dangerous she is. You just have to educate her and lead her. Let her know what position she has to play; let her know what the game is."

Old School lifted the black queen from the chessboard and tossed it to me.

I examined it and thought about what he had said. I knew that I had a phone call to make; I knew that I had work to do.

# Chapter Seventeen

Things went from bad to worse as the Feds continued their witch hunt for Umkhonto leadership. This time, it was Tamfu being transferred. They were hitting me where it hurt, taking away my top leadership. But more importantly, they took away my closest friends. The loss of Omene, and then Ghirt, and now Tamfu, was deeply depressing. In the space of less than thirty days, I found myself walking another one of my brothers to R&D to be transferred.

"You have my wife's number, right?" Tamfu asked.

I nodded. "She's in Atlanta, right?"

He nodded. "And I gave you my sister's number, right?"

"The one in Seattle?"

Again he nodded. "I gave you the number to my sister in Doula also, right?"

"I thought that you said she lived in Younde?"

"No, I lived in Younde right before I moved to Paris. My sister lives in Doula."

"You headed to Doula when you get out?"

"For a minute, then I'll be headed to Seattle to stay with my sister."

"She's the doctor, right?"

"Both of them are doctors."

I nodded.

"My sister in Seattle really likes you," he said with a smile.

I shook my head. "I wouldn't want to mess that girl's life up. Besides, your dad was the head of the Cameroon Secret Police. He ain't having me killed."

Tamfu laughed.

"I'ma come and visit you in Doula," I told him.

"Alexander, if I see you in Africa, I'm having you arrested," he said with a laugh.

"Why I can't go and visit the land of my ancestors?"

He shook his head. "I know you. I see you in Africa, you'll probably have that madman Ghirt with you, and your crazy henchman Webber, and about a thousand soldiers from Umkhonto. We ain't having that shit."

I laughed heartily.

"You know I'm just kidding," he said, turning serious. "I would follow you anywhere. And coming from me, that's not something to take lightly."

"I don't. Thank you for everything."

"Don't mention it. Just make sure that you stay in touch with me. You don't want to miss the big jump off."

I laughed. His big jump off was a running joke amongst the leaders of Umkhonto. He said that he was going to buy an island and start his own country. A place where there were no laws. Drinking, gambling, and fucking all day and all night would be the order of the day—total debauchery. He would charge people to live on his island, give them passports and protection, a tax haven, and a duty-free trade zone. He dreamed of creating a Dubai mixed with Vegas and Monte Carlos, with the lawlessness of the Wild West, and the debauchery of ancient Rome. Hell, if he could pull it off, I imagine there would be a waiting list longer than a muthafucka to get in.

Tamfu was a megalomaniac who suffered from delusions of grandeur. He truly believed that one day he would rule over an empire. Sick, yes, but it's what made him *him*. He could organize, communicate, teach, speak several languages, had lived on four continents, and had advanced degrees in computer science and engineering. He fashioned himself an international playboy. You could almost picture him in a white tux with a white scarf around his scrawny little yellow neck, standing at a baccarat table in Monaco. His insanity is what made us love him. It's what made him my brother. I, too, suffered from the same failings, vanities, and insanities.

There was a little bit of Tamfu in every one of us. And if there wasn't, there should be. It was this dreamer in each of us that made us believe that the impossible was possible. He was the lone voice in the room that always asked why not, when everyone else asked why. It was the Tamfus of the world that made life livable. I wouldn't want to live in a world where people didn't dream the impossible, and then went out to make it happen. Tamfu was the "can do" spirit of Umkhonto.

"You get that island jumping off, I'll be your first citizen," I said. "Not first paying citizen, but your first citizen."

"I don't think you'll be able to come then," he smiled.

"You're going to leave your brother out in this cruel world, homeless?"

"I'm sure you'll find your place. Besides, we may be able to make payment arrangements so that you can live on the island."

I laughed. He was West African through and through, despite how worldly he wanted to seem. Money talked, bullshit walked. West Africans were about getting their paper.

"I'm going to miss you," I told him.

"Don't. Soon, we'll be out in the free world making billions of dollars."

I sat his property down next to the door of the receiving and discharge office. He did the same. And then he did something way out of the ordinary. He embraced me.

I had never seen Tamfu display any kind of emotion whatsoever. It was always about business, money, proficiency, power, world domination. I had never seen him get angry, or upset, or heard him raise his voice, or anything. And now, we were locked in a strong embrace.

"You are the brother, I never had," he said in his deep baritone voice.

I was at a loss for words. I knew he wasn't prone to displaying this type of emotion, so it touched me deeply. In fact, it really fucked-me up.

"You're a good dude," I said, swallowing hard. "You take care of yourself, you hear me? You better take care of yourself."

"You keep taking care of the people."

"Always."

Saying good-bye to Tamfu had been hard. But as hard as that was, I felt like I was different for it. I was learning how to let go. Letting go was a powerful therapeutic tool. Letting go of my mistakes, letting go of my anger, letting go of my past, letting go of bitterness, distrust, hatred; letting go of all the bad things that had been poisoning my life. I wanted to step across that white line that divided my future from my past. But before I could do so, I knew that there was one more thing that I would have to let go of—my fear.

Being afraid to change was the deepest fear that a man could have. We are creatures of habit, and we are comfortable with what we know. We fashion ourselves brave, but in truth, we are cowards. If it were not true, then throwing off our prejudices would be easy. Deep down, I wanted change. But I knew that my fear would prevent me from any wholesale change. It would have to be incremental. My first steps to that change was letting go of my anger and bitterness. I knew that if I carried it with me, it would slowly eat me from the inside, like a powerful, toxic acid. I headed for the phone room.

"Hello?"

"Hey, how you doing?"

"Hey," baby momma said more animated. "Long time, no hear from."

"I just been doing my time."

"Why you ain't called and checked on your son?"

"I have. I asked my mother about him."

"You can call over here and talk to him," she said softly. "No matter what happens between me and you, I want you to be a part of his life. I won't deprive you two of a relationship."

"Thank you. That's big of you."

"I'm not a little girl anymore."

"I know. I'm not a little boy anymore either."

"That's good. So what are you doing with yourself?"

"Surviving."

"Surviving ... Me, too. I went back to cosmetology school."

"Oh, yeah? That's good, congratulations!" I was genuinely happy. I had pressed her for years to go back to school and do something with her life. Anything. I wanted her to prepare herself for the future. I wanted her to be able to stand on her own two feet and be able to take care of herself. And now she was doing it.

"Thank you. You still thinking about going to barber college in there?"

"Not really. I would have to get an educational transfer up north to Minnesota. I don't think that they would do it now because I'm too short. If I was going to do it, I should have done it years ago."

"Oh. I thought we was going to open up a shop together, like we used to talk about. You can go to Williams Barber College when you get out."

"Yeah, that would be fly. But shit, I'll be so busy working when I get out, I don't know how I'ma find the time to go to barber college."

"I'll be making some money doing hair. You can move in with us while you're in barber college. Your son would love that."

"And you? How would you feel about that?"

"I offered, didn't I?"

I didn't know where this woman came from. She definitely wasn't the spoiled little girl that I left on the streets. I guess life had toughened her up. Having to care for a child alone had matured her.

"I'd like that. I'd like to come and stay with you and my son. I won't be getting in the way or nothing, would I? You know, three's company, four's a crowd."

"I ain't got no nigga, if that's what you asking."

"Yeah, what happened to him?"

"Ain't never had one."

"Oh really? And what did you call David?"

"A friend. But why are we talking about him? What about us? What about your son?"

I had allowed my emotions to take over the first decent conversation that I had with this woman in years. "You're right."

"So what other classes do they have in there?"

"Here? Where I'm at now? They got a bunch of vocational training classes. They got masonry, carpentry, air conditioning, heating and ventilation repair, they got plumbing and electricity. Shit like that."

"You can make a lot of money fixing electricity or fixing air conditioners. Hell, plumbers make a lot of money too," she said.

I leaned back inside of the phone booth and closed my eyes. I saw me in a uniform, stepping out of my work truck with a lunch pail. I saw her doing hair. I saw us, with a tiny house, a used car, and a raggedy-ass dog. I saw us—being a family.

For the first time in my life, I saw myself in the free world, not selling drugs. I didn't have visions of reaching baller status or having piles of dope and money. I saw a humble man lifting his son in the air and twirling him around. After eight years in prison, I would die for that life. It was what I wanted now; it was what I needed.

"Where is my son?" I asked.

"He's outside playing."

"We gonna do this?"

"Do what?"

"Do the damn thing. I work as a plumber, an electrician, or a barber, while you do hair. We get us a crib, and we do the family thing."

"Living in sin?" she asked. I could hear the smile in her voice.

"No. I'll make an honest woman out of you. You just gotta want to be an honest woman."

"I am an honest woman."

"Thank you."

"For what?"

"For taking care of my son. I never said thank you for that."

"It's your turn when you come home. He's going to need his daddy."

"I know."

"Come home and do your part. Come home and raise him into a man."

"I can do that now," I said softly. "I couldn't do it back then, because I didn't know shit. What could I have taught him back then? But now—the world better look out."

"All right. Don't just talk a good game."

"I'm not just a talker. You'll see."

"We'll see."

That night, we went to war again with the Border Brothers. Again, they got their asses whipped. This time, we drove their soldiers to the upper yard where the panicking guards on duty locked the gate, leaving them up there. That meant that we were free to roll through the housing unit and beat the shit out of the cheerleading, half-dedicated muthafuckas. We kicked open lockers and raided their shit, like they did everyone else. It was fun. I won three radios and a bunch of fiend books. All the brothers came up on a little something at least.

The result of all those Piasas in the hole was that Special Housing was bursting at the seams. They had to kick some people out onto the yard. They let out the California brothers, along with a bunch of Texas boys that had gotten caught up when that shit went down. G-Man and Rock got let back onto the yard as well. Goodes, however, got sent to camp. *Can you believe that shit?* My nig went to a fucking camp.

Camps are located next to the prisons. They are for the lowest-security prisoners. They don't have fences around them, and they only have one fucking guard for the whole thing. Campers are a bunch of snitching, self-policing muthafuckas. Goodes was a soldier. I don't see how he made it out there.

"C!"

I turned. It was G-Man. He caught up to me, and together, we continued on to the chapel. On the way, we got stopped by a group of Dirty White Boys.

"Hey, G-Man, I need to holler at you fellas for a minute," Daley said. He was the leader of the white boys.

"What's up, Daley?" I asked, nodding.

"What's up, C?" he replied. "Hey, your boy Slim needs to be checked."

"What are you talking about?" I asked.

G-Man lifted his hand. "I don't want to hear it. Talk to Weasel."

"What?" I asked.

"Man, I ain't dealing with that shit any more," G declared.

I turned to Daley. "I'll have somebody come and talk to you and see what's up. We'll take care of it." He nodded and then quickly disappeared, knowing that G and I needed to talk.

"What are you talking about, G?"

"Man, Weasel pumped them dudes up and got them to vote over in Sunset. He wants to handle things, so shit, I'ma let him."

"He can't call for no fucking vote!" I said. "Who the fuck is he?"

"Man, C," G held up his hands stopping me. "Forget it. I'm tired of dealing with that bullshit. He wants to drive the car, let'em. Shit, C, we about to go home soon. We short timers, so let somebody else deal with all the headaches and petty-ass bullshit."

"He don't get the keys. Fuck him! Where was he when we were thirty deep, outnumbered, surrounded, and under the gun? He can't roll in here and try to take over the shit that *we* built, the shit that *we* organized! Fuck him!"

"C, I'm tired, man. I'm tired of arguing with them dudes all the time. I'm tired of him questioning my every decision, second-guessing me, always stirring up controversy and shit."

"I know how to handle him," I said coldly.

G shook his head. "Don't worry about it, C. Let him drive. Let him see that it ain't easy."

"Everybody on the yard respects you."

"Not these new cats."

"They don't know. They don't know how bad things were before you and Goodes got here. They don't know our history."

"They still tripping about Old School. They love to bring that shit up."

"Look, we made mistakes. We made a lot of mistakes back when we were trying to put this thing together. We were kids, G. We stepped up and put a lot of responsibility on our young-ass shoulders, and we did what we had to do. We weren't perfect, but we never lost a single brother."

"They don't understand that, C."

"I do." I turned and faced him and extended my hand. "You did a helluva job, G. A lot of people are alive today because of the things that you did. You stepped up and you represented us. You kept down the bullshit, and you kept your people safe. A lot of people went home because of you. You can be proud of what you did here."

He clasped my hand. "You too, C."

I shook my head. "On behalf of all the brothers … thank you."

# Chapter Eighteen

"Are you going to put a ring on my finger?" my baby momma asked.

"Yeah, I ain't got no problem doing that," I told her. "If everything is everything between us."

"Everything like what?"

"You know, we still got some issues to work out."

"Issues like what?"

"Like letters, like visits, like a whole lot of things. You know, it may not mean a lot to you out there, but it means a lot to me in here. I need you to support me."

She went silent.

"You don't know what it's like—"

"—And you don't know what it's like out here!" she countered. "You ever try to raise a child on your own? Do you know what *that's* like? Paying bills, putting food on the table, clothes on a child's back? And on top of that, working and going to school? It's not easy out here either. It's not easy being out here alone."

"Alone?"

"Alone! I'm out here *alone*! And that's hard enough. Seeing all of my friends get married, buy houses, and throw it up in my face. They talk like I'm crazy for sitting out here waiting for you!"

"Hey, hey, calm down. If they're throwing that shit up in your face like that, then they ain't your friends anyway. And don't worry about them bitches. It'll be your time to shine one day soon. I promise. You'll be able to invite all them hoes over to your house one day and show your shit off."

"Come home to me."

"I am," I said softly.

"Don't be giving me no jailhouse promises."

"I can show you better than I can tell you. You'll see."

"You know your mother talked to the lawyer."

"I know. That fool talking about winning my 2241 after I've been locked up eight fucking years? Fuck him."

"At least that's something. You won't have to be on probation when you get out."

A Border Brother walked into the room, eyeballing me the whole time.

"What the fuck you looking at, bitch?"

He turned away and began to use the phone.

"Who are you talking to?" my baby momma asked.

"This fucking, greasy-ass wetback," I answered. "He want his fucking ass beat."

"Christian! Why are you talking like that?"

"Man, fuck them muthafuckas! They need to line their asses up on the border and kill all them muthafuckas!"

"Who are you? Where is this coming from?"

"I'm just saying, baby, they need a goddamn electric fence along that fucking border. Fry every muthafucker trying to run across. Throw some sharks in the Rio Grande and some landmines on the other side of that son of a bitch!"

"Oh, my god! I can't believe you're saying this. What's happened to you? What have they done to you in there?"

"They haven't done shit to me. You don't understand how these muthafuckers are. They hate us. They think we dirty and shit. Can you imagine *that*? A fucking *Mexican* calling *us* dirty?"

"Christian, how can you talk like that? How can you teach your son to be a good person if you're talking like that?"

"I'ma have to keep it real with him, baby. He doesn't have to do anything bad, but there are always going to be idiots and assholes in the world that hate him simply because of the color of his skin! These people despise us. They hate blacks! That's just the truth."

"How can you say that? Enrique is one of your best friends."

"I'm not talking about Hispanics from over here. I'm talking about those border-crossing muahfuckas! They hate us. Hell, they hate Hispanics from over here. Henry sold us all out. He's one of them. Or at least he's acting like it."

She exhaled. "You can't fight hatred with hatred. You have to be the better man; you have to be the better person."

"That's all well and good, baby. But that 'turn the other cheek' shit only works in the free world, where you can get away from a muthafucka. I'm trapped in here with these bastards, so the only thing that I can do is fight fire with fire."

"Fighting fire with fire means that everybody gets burned. You can't do that. You have a child now. You have to step up, and you have to build a better world for him. Promise me that you'll stop being like that."

"Like what?"

"A racist asshole. That doesn't even sound right, not coming from you. That's not the Chris I know. The Chris I know is friends with everybody. He was a good person with a big heart."

That Chris died a long time ago, I wanted to tell her. But it was good to know that some people still believed in the old me. In my mind, I was a bigger asshole back then. But we each see one another through our own passions and prejudices. She saw the person that she wanted to see, and there was nothing that I could do to change that.

"I'm going to survive, baby."

"That's good. But surviving with a corrupted soul is not really surviving. I want you to come out here and teach your son how to be a good man, not one filled with prejudice and hate. It's no longer about you, baby. You have a son now, and everything that you do now has to be about him. What kind of world do you want to leave for him?"

"I'll try to do better. I'll give things a chance."

"That's all I'm asking. I know that you can be the bigger person."

"I'll talk to you later, girl."

"Love you."

"Yeah, me too."

I did get a letter from my lawyer, and that asshole was talking about winning my case. He was sure that the courts were going to decide in my favor. I had been locked up over eight years. What the fuck difference did it make now? I had done over two years in the federal detention facility, going to court fighting my case. I had spent two years fighting my appeal, and then another two years fighting it in a 2255 Motion. I spent my last two years fighting that in a 2241 Motion.

And now, I'm *finally* going to win? It was some fucking bullshit, and I didn't want to hear it.

I headed for my bunk, my usual place of refuge, and lay down thinking about the free world and what it would mean to get out. I ain't gonna lie to you, it was a scary thought. In the joint I knew what was what. There were rules and laws, and everything was pretty much straightforward. They provided the clothing, the meals, and the shelter. All I had to do was wake up, go to vocational training classes, and that was it. Breakfast, lunch, and dinner were all provided. I had a TV room and a sports TV room, and movies in the visitation room every Friday night. It was easy to just sit back and do nothing; to withdraw from the free world altogether.

The thought of having to go out from the safety of the prison world to the hostility of the free world was a scary thought indeed. In here, I had dominated; I had managed to become the apex predator. Out there in the free world, I was nothing. I was an amoeba, plankton, shrill. I was nothing but food to be eaten by the real apex predators of this world. To be able to stand up and face them was scary. But I knew that I had to do it. I couldn't leave my son out there alone to face those monsters. They would surely eat him alive. I had to come up with something. I had to come up with a plan for survival in the free world.

I was taking electrical classes and plumbing classes during the day. I decided to hit the library really hard at night. I could work as an electrician in the free world, and that would earn me enough money to take care of my family. But hitting the library at night would give me what I needed to really survive and to insure my son's survival.

I had to learn as much as I could about the world, about history, about math, about science, about computers, about everything. I was determined to be able to give him the tools that he would need to survive. There were so many traps out there waiting for him. I wanted to step up and teach him how to avoid them.

"Alexander."

I sat up in bed and pulled off my Walkman headphones. It was Pedro, and he was holding up a chess set. I nodded, and he set the board down on my bed, then we set up the pieces.

*"Cómo está tu familia?"* he asked.

*"Bien. Y tu familia?"*

*"Bien, gracias."* He held up a black piece and a white piece.

*"Deseas blanco o negro?"*

*"Quiero negro."* I told him, I wanted the black pieces.

*"Cuánto tiempo tú a en—"*

I lifted my hand, stopping him in midsentence. "We're not going to practice my Spanish today. Today is English Day. You're trying to be slick."

Pedro smiled. "How much time you have left?" he asked in broken English.

"I'm down to less than a year, I guess. And you? How much time do you have left?"

*"Tres meses.* Three months. And then ..." he lifted his arms into the air and began to thrust. "Pussy from *mamacita!"*

We both laughed heartily.

Pedro lifted his hand to his lips and stuck out his tongue, wiggling it around. "Going to eat some pussy!"

I shook my head and laughed again.

"What?" He slapped me across my shoulder. "You don't eat the fish?"

*"Si chelque chose sents, come du poisson, c'est tres mal!"* I said in French.

"What?"

"If something smells like fish, then that's not good!" I said in English, laughing.

"A little fish, but taste like chicken," he said laughing. "No taste like fish. Taste like fish ..." he shook his finger, "momma need to take a bath."

His English had me rolling.

"So, one year, you come to Mexico and visit me?"

"You're not going to remember me."

"Bullshit! One year, you come. You bring you family, we go to my family house. We ride the horses, we smoke a little marijuana, to drink Tequila, a little peyote, we eat the barbecue. A big hog for you and your family."

*"No puerco! No chancho!* No pork, no pig."

He slapped his hand against his forehead. "*Yo recuerdo! Tú musulmán. Bien, no puerco.* Steak then. Big cow."

I nodded. "Big cow. And you and your family come and visit me in San Antonio."

He nodded fervently. "San Antonio. I like San Antonio. Sexy Mexicanas in San Antonio!"

I couldn't help but think about Pedro in San Antonio—his wife in the kitchen cooking with my wife, our kids in the backyard playing together, he and I knocking down some beers and watching the Spurs on TV. But Pedro was Mexican. I was *supposed* to hate him. He was *supposed* to hate me. We were *supposed* to be enemies. How had we become friends? How did the friendship get past all of the racial bullshit in prison and foster into something real? How could I claim to hate Mexicans but want to visit and break bread with Pedro and have my family become friends with his? I was still having trouble reconciling what I felt about them as a whole with what I felt about Pedro as an individual. Crazy, right?

Well, my thoughts on the issue came to an abrupt end when I heard the commotion down the hall. I leapt out of bed and raced out of my room and down the hall to the TV room. Brothers were gathered in the hall in full gear, ready to rumble. I pushed my way through the crowd to find Weasel at the front and a bunch of white boys standing opposite him. They too were strapped and chomping at the bit, ready to roll.

"What the fuck's going on here?"

"Ask ya boy, C!" Powder shouted. He was third in charge of the white boys on the yard. "They fucking trippin' over the TV room!"

"We had NASCAR on the schedule!" Daley shouted.

"We had NBA basketball on the schedule!" Weasel countered.

The white boys produced a schedule and handed it to me. I took it and glanced over it. Then I handed it back to the white boys and turned to Weasel. He, too, produced a schedule. The white boys' schedule had NASCAR on it—the brother's schedule had NBA basketball on it. I turned and walked into the guard's office and grabbed the schedule chart off the wall and examined it. It had NASCAR on it.

"Move," I told the scary-ass guard sitting behind the desk. I opened his drawer and pulled out the TV schedule that said whose turn it was to draft the schedule for that TV room this week. It was a white boy's turn. I waved for Weasel to come into the office.

Weasel walked into the guard's office, hiding his shank in his sleeve.

"Close the door," I told him.

Weasel closed the door and then faced me.

"Where did you get this schedule from?" I asked, holding up the schedule that he had given me.

"Slick gave it to me."

"Slick? Your Dallas homeboy, Slick?"

Weasel nodded.

Slick was one of those muthafuckas who you never believed. That nigga lied just for the sake of lying. I wouldn't believe his real name unless I saw his birth certificate, talked to his momma, and had verification from the Social Security office. He was a lying, troublemaking son of a bitch.

"Yeah," Weasel said, growing indignant.

"You gonna start a war over a schedule Slick gave you?"

"Yeah, he my homeboy, and I believe him."

I threw the schedule book into his chest and he caught it. "It's the white boys turn to make the schedule this week. They put that fucking NASCAR shit on, like they do every fucking time it's NASCAR season. And every year, we move the basketball games into the BET room. And after NASCAR season, the brothers take over the sports TV room once again. We've been doing this shit for the last eight years!"

I walked out of the guard's office, brushing past him. "Yo, Daley. What's up?"

"What's up, C?"

"Why didn't you come to me, or Rock, or go to G-Man?"

"I thought Weasel was calling shots for the brothers now."

"Go to Rock or G-Man. If you can't find them, come to me. You got that?"

He nodded. "I got you."

"The TV room is yours."

A whoop and cheer shot through the white boys. They were way outnumbered and would have been slaughtered. But even knowing that, they were ready to go to war. I had to respect that. They were in the right, and they were willing to go to war for what they believed in.

I turned to the brothers. "Y'all go back to doing what y'all was doing. Everything is cool. They got the TV room." I nodded at Shorty.

Weasel walked past me, heading for the door leading to the stairs. I stopped him. "Hey, what the fuck are you doing over here in the first place? You don't even live in this fucking building."

He rolled his eyes at me like a bitch and then continued down the stairs. I turned to Shorty. “Slick almost took us to war over a bullshit TV room schedule that he made up. Discipline that fool.”

Shorty nodded and headed off to round up some Umkhonto soldiers to handle up on Slick.

Ghirt approached.

“Hey, find out who the highest-ranking Umkhonto member in Sunset is. He’s in charge of Sunset from now on. If G-Man doesn’t want it no more, then Umkhonto is taking over. From now on this joint is no longer under civilian leadership, it’s now directly under Umkhonto control until I say different.”

Ghirt nodded and raced off.

# Chapter Nineteen

The bus pulled up and offloaded another group of prisoners. None of us could believe our fucking eyes. The entire bus was *filled* with blacks. Seventy blacks climbed off the bus that day and joined us on the yard, including about ten from my hometown.

Baby Charles, Momo, Buggy, Lil Rat, and quite a few others showed up. It was crazy. Almost like a fucking family reunion. We also got a few Louisiana boys, some Georgia boys, some Mississippi boys, some Alabama boys, a few Carolina boys, and a couple of Arkansas and Tennessee boys. The South was *really deep*, which was a good thing, because we thought alike, and we all rolled together.

"C!" Momo shouted.

I rushed to my homeboy and wrapped my arms around him. "Man, what the fuck are you doing in here?"

He shook his head and smiled. "Man, got caught up in a fucked-up ass conspiracy. Man, this shit is crazy! They ain't find a lick a dope. All they had a nigga doing is talking on the phone."

"Nigga, you can't be on the phone talking about dope and shit!" I told him.

"I wasn't! That's the crazy shit! This time, I actually wasn't! That nigga BoBo called me and asked me what I wanted for my Mustang, and I told him that I'ma try to get five for it. And them hoes got up in court and said that I meant that I was trying to get five keys! I telling my lawyer, 'Muahfucka, I'm trying to get five thousand dollars for my car!'"

"He didn't tell them that?"

"Man, that muahfucka sold me up the river! All he wanted was his goddamned money!"

"Damn, that's fucked-up, homie. You got an appeal going?"

"My T. Jones is working on it. She gonna try to get me a lawyer."

"How much time you get?"

"Shit, they was trying to give a nigga a twinkie! Man, I hurried up and pleaded out for five!"

"*Five*, and you ain't even do shit?"

"Man, five—and all I did was get on the phone with some hot-ass niggaz! Shit, I wish I would've known them niggaz was being wired-tapped! I'd a stayed my ass away from them muahfuckas!"

I laughed and wrapped my arms around his shoulder, walking him to the housing unit. "What room they got you in?"

"Man, I'm in 308."

"We gonna have to change that and get you moved in with me," I told him. "How your brother doing?"

"Which one?"

"That black-ass, bug-eyed muthafucka that look just like you!"

"Hell, which one?"

Again we laughed.

My happy reunion was ruined by a Prince problem. Our resident grand wizard had been spouting his mouth off in front of some white boys, and some brothers and Mexicans overheard him. And apparently it wasn't the first time. I knew that he was still a racist son of a bitch by talking to him every night. His ridiculous belief in a variety of crackpots and the pseudoscience on race had shown me that the leopard hadn't changed his spots. It was really too bad for him that Momo had arrived and I needed his top bunk for my homeboy.

When I was approached by the brothers with the evidence, I didn't need much convincing. I got a couple of Louisiana and Mississippi boys together and headed for Prince's bed. I figured I'd let the brothers whose families had put up with his racist shit for all of those years have the honor of touching the fool up.

"Prince!" I called out to him. He turned and stared at me nervously. "I want you to meet my homeboys. This is Big Shreveport, this is New Orleans, this is Calliope, this is Big Mississippi, and this is Jackson."

Prince extended his hand.

"They're not here to shake your hand or be your friend."

"Oh?" Prince said, lifting an eyebrow.

"They're here to prove some of your theories about the black man.

Some of those books you've been reading, talking about how the black man is physically dominant. They're going to prove how right you are, my friend."

Prince eyed my cohorts nervously.

"I warned you to keep that bullshit off the yard," I told him. "But you just couldn't do it. I told everybody that you were an old man and that there were no points to be scored off whipping you. But you know what? I was wrong. So now, I'm going to let my homeboys from Mississippi and Louisiana have a crack at you."

"What?" Prince asked nervously. He slid off his bunk.

"You did a lot," I told him. "You created an atmosphere where it was acceptable to lynch black folks, beat up on black folks, and have black folks live in fear. Justice delayed is still justice served, Prince."

I gathered my belongings so that I could head to the phone room and started off, but then I turned back to Prince. "This is for James Byrd, for Medgar Evers, for *Martin Luther* King, for Emit Till, and for the thousands of other black men who died at the hands of muthafuckas like you. And when they bend you over and fuck you in the ass, I want you to think of all the sistahs that your people have violated through the years. I'll see you in hell, Grand Wizard."

And with that, I turned and walked away. Down the hall, I could hear his screams.

Inside the phone room, I called my girl. I could never tell her about what I had just done. She would have told me how wrong I was. She would have talked to me about forgiveness. She would have talked to me about not sinking to their level. She would have talked to me about building a better world. That was not the phone call that I wanted to have with her. I got another one that I didn't want to have either.

"Have you accepted God in your life?" she asked.

"Yeah, baby. I pray every day, six times a day."

"Six times a day? Yeahhh, right!"

"I do. I pray a lot. I talk to God all the time. That's the only way I've been able to halfway keep my sanity all these years."

"So, you go to church in there?"

I thought about the choir coming in from the outside. "Not all the time. I go every once in a while. But mainly, I pray by my bed every day."

"That's good, but you have to go to church too. Where two or more are gathered in His name—"

"I'm not big on organized religion, baby. In fact, I'm not big on religion period."

"What?"

"Don't get me wrong, I believe in the Almighty Creator, but I don't believe in organized religion. I don't believe that I need to go through anyone else to get to God. My God is all-powerful, all-hearing, all-seeing, all-knowing, and to believe that I need to go through a hierarchy of people or institutions in order for Him to hear me … I just don't buy into that."

"You have to go to church and pray. You have to pray the blood of Jesus."

I laughed at her. She gasped like I was the devil.

"Baby, let me tell you about religion. Man has done some of the most fucked-up things in the world to other men in the name of religion."

"God will take care of them. You can't judge all religion by what a few crazy people did a long time ago."

They had her mind. My woman was a good, obedient Negro. It would be up to me to turn her into that black queen, the one that could dominate the chessboard.

"I'm not saying that, baby. What I'm saying is that men have placed man-made creations, like churches, mosques, and synagogues, over what God Himself created, which is man. We kill one another, God's creations, over man's creations. We kill one another over doctrines, over tenets, over rituals. We kill one another because we disagree over the methods that we use to communicate with God, and God gets lost in the process."

"That's why we need to practice the true Word. We need to live our faith. Those people are using religion for their own purposes. That's why it's important for real Christians to stand up for what's right."

"You're right, baby, people should live their faith. We are in one hundred percent agreement with one another."

"I want you to start going to church. We need to pray together. You go to church over there, and I'll go over here, and we'll pray as a family."

"Okay," I lied. I would have to talk to her about my beliefs once I got out. Faith was important. And I wanted her to be able to lean on her faith. "What's my little man up to?"

"He's in there sleeping."

"Sleeping? Why's he asleep this time a day?"

"He's tired. I took him swimming earlier today. He swam and played all morning, and then ate and went to sleep."

"How's he doing in school?"

"He's doing good. He got a crush on some little girl."

"Already? What, he's eight now, and he's already trying to like some little girl?"

"Boy, he thinks he's eighteen."

"Tell him to slow his roll. He don't need to try and grow up too fast."

"Well, you'll be home soon enough. You can get him and teach him."

"I can't wait."

"I miss you."

"I miss you too."

My phone call with my girl had me feeling good. I was going to have Momo moved into Prince's old bed above me. My time was winding down, and I would be going home soon. I was in vocational training class, my girl was in cosmetology school, and for the first time in a long time, I felt good about my future.

The fear and uncertainty of leaving the place that I called home for eight years was significantly less. I felt ready to begin my life anew. I felt optimistic about getting my life started again. But I reminded myself that I had to deal with the situation that I was in. I had to keep my head in the game. All it took was one second of slipping and I could find myself being wheeled out of prison with a sheet over my head. I had to stay in the game until the very end.

The Mexican gangs acted as if my life were a stage play and they had just been shown a cue card saying act the fuck-up. The Mexicans had gotten rid of the Califas, the Texicans, the Aztecas, and all the others. Now, they were turning on one another.

Absent an external enemy, they now found themselves divided along state lines. *Mexican* state lines, that is. There were the boys from Zacatecas, Sinaloa, Oaxaca, Nuevo León, Puebla, Jalisco, Michoacán, Guanajuato, Chihuahua, and Coahuila—and they all hated one another now. Tonight's battle was between Zacatecas, Jalisco, Michoacán, and

Guanajuato. Chihuahua and Nuevo León sat on the sidelines, with one crew daring the other to enter into the fray. It was ridiculous.

I thought about human nature. All of these guys were united when they wanted to strike at Mexican American prison gangs. But as soon as that enemy was taken away from them and they had no one left to fight, they turned on themselves. Out of Mexican unity, they found state divisions. Guanajuato hated Tamaulipas. Tamaulipas hated Nuevo Laredo. Michoacán hated Zacatecas. Sinaloa hated Jalisco. And so on.

Was it in our nature to always fight amongst ourselves? Was prison just a microcosm of our broader life, just amplified because of its territorial confines? Why do we divide ourselves? Why do we fight when there is no real reason to fight? Are we really hell-bent on destroying one another? And if so, why? Are we destined to kill one another off until only one human remains on the planet? Is our violence something that is innate? Are we genetically predisposed to causing our own destruction? Is it something that we can fight, is it something that we can change, is there hope for tomorrow, is there hope for my child?

I sat in my window and watched a people who had fought together, men who had fought like brothers, turn on one another. I saw friends stabbing one another in their necks, their chests, their arms and backs. I saw men who were once brothers slice, stab, slash, and hack. I saw real-life cousins go at it because they were from different states.

I watched amid the howls, and cries, and burning fires, as men killed. The euphoria that I felt earlier dissipated and floated away like the burning embers from the trash can fires that burned near my window. So, too, went my hope for a better world for my son.

Was *this* what we really were? Is this what it all boiled down to? After all of our progress, after all of our technological advances, after all of our lofty proclamations, religious, and social enlightenments, we were nothing more than glorified primates. I looked out upon the yard, and I thought of William Golding's novel, *The Lord of the Flies*. The characters in that book had an excuse. They were children. We had none.

"The police retreated to the upper yard," Young Gangsta said, rushing into the room.

"I know," I said pointing. "The Mexicans started whipping on the police, too."

"C," Young Gangsta said solemnly. I could tell by his voice that something was wrong. I turned towards him. Behind him stood three Umkhonto soldiers, and Daniel, a young, twenty-year-old African American guard. I already knew it was going to be some shit.

"What the fuck?" I asked.

"He got caught down here, and now he's cut off," Gangsta told me.

"If he tries to make a run for it, they'll kill him," Jersey added. "There's no way he can make it out of this housing unit, let alone to that fence, before they get him."

I stared at him. His eyes were as wide as tangerines, and he was trembling like a category-five earthquake. I could give him to the Mexicans as a gift. It would earn a lot of goodwill. Or I could kick him out of my room and tell him he's on his own. They would kill him for sure.

My third option was that I could protect him. But protecting a guard from other prisoners during a riot would fuck me up for the rest of my life. We had a code. No matter what beefs we had between us, when it came to the police, it was us against them. Prisoners closed ranks—no ifs, ands, or buts about it. So, where was the dilemma? The dilemma was he was *black*.

I would never be able to set foot on another prison yard again without Umkhonto protection if I protected this muthafucka. The thing about that was that I had no intention of setting foot on another prison yard again once this rodeo was over. The other thing was that I didn't know how the brothers would take it or where they would stand on the matter once the smoke had cleared. My Umkhonto would back me. Our whole reason for being was to protect the brothers—to protect black people.

We were the spear and shield of our nation. Did that protection extend to our jailers was the question. Umkhonto was also meant to be a movement, something that we would take with us into the free world. We wanted to take that unity, that *die-for-one-another* spirit into the free world with us. We wanted Umkhonto to be so much more.

We wanted brothers to exchange the handshake, know that each was Umkhonto, and then do whatever it took to help one another. Whether it meant hiring a fellow Umkhonto member, promoting him, granting him a loan, lying for him on the stand, grabbing your pistol and going to war with him, it was always envisioned to be a true brotherhood. And if Umkhonto was meant to be more than just a prison gang, then my answer was really a given. Still, there would be hell to pay. From this day onward, I would be less than righteous in the eyes of many. I would be the equivalent of a snitch. Or even worse—I would be a muthafucka who saved the life of a guard. I would have violated the most sacred of all prison codes.

"Take off your uniform," I told him. I turned to Gangsta. "Get him one of your uniforms. Have him put it on. Then go and round up some soldiers. Have everyone on alert. Bring ten soldiers in here, have the rest nearby. Put them in various rooms nearby and the rest in the BET room. Break out the chess game, sit on my bed, and play chess with him until his people regain control of the yard."

Gangsta nodded and went into action. I turned and stared out of the window once again. I had just fallen on my sword. Not for a fellow Umkhonto member but for a young, scared black kid, who was from a small town, and who thought he found a leg up in life by getting one of the cushy federal jobs at the local prison.

Why I did it—to this day I still search for the answers. Many different ones have popped into my head since that night. Because he was black? Of course. Because I wasn't ready to give up on the world? Yes. Because he could have been my little brother under different circumstances? Yes, that too. I think the biggest reason was the second reason. I wasn't ready to give up on the world.

That night, I saw us regress into savages. I saw humanity divide itself and then commence to destroying itself. I wanted to say stop. I wanted to shout out of that window at the top of my lungs and plead for them to stop. I wanted a better world for my son, for their sons, for all of our children.

I helped him because I wanted to prove that we weren't all animals—that there was still a little bit of humanity left inside of me. I needed to prove that we could save instead of just destroy. Many people would hate my decision, and many times since, I, too, have questioned it. But in the end, I did the right thing. Yes, I stood up for my brother, but more than that—I stood up for our humanity.

The Mexicans did come into my room that night. They went room to room, searching for him and searching for their enemies.

"That's the guard, right there!" Lupe shouted.

The Mexicans roared through the hall.

"That's my homeboy from San Antonio," I countered.

"That's the fucking guard, *esse*!"

"That's my homeboy from San Antonio!" I said more firmly.

Lupe stepped into my room, eyeballing a scared Daniel who continued to play chess. Daniel was wearing one of Young Gangsta's uniforms that didn't have a nametag.

"That's the guard, San Antone!" Lupe countered. "You gonna play us like that, homes? You gonna take the fucking guard's side over another inmate's?"

"One thing, Lupe. You're a fucking inmate; me, I'm a fucking convict. I ain't no inmate. Two, that's my San Antone homeboy and a member of the Umkhonto. You telling me that you got a problem with the Umkhonto? Does Tamaulipas have a problem with Umkhonto?"

My soldiers rose.

Lupe shook his head. "I ain't got no problems with the brothers. Especially now that I know y'all rolling with the police. Snitch mutherfuckers!"

"You really want to call me that?" I said standing. "You *really* want to call me that to my face? I'm not sitting down anymore. Go ahead—call me a snitch to my face, Lupe."

I could see the fear in him.

"I'm just saying, homes," he retorted, pointing at Daniel, "that *maya* … muthafucker is the police."

He was about to say *mayate*, but caught himself. He knew that he had fucked-up.

"You, and the rest of your little greasy-ass, wetback homeboys get the fuck outta my room," I told him.

"Umkhonto!" Gangsta shouted.

The hallway shook as the thunderous sound of dozens and dozens of big black work boots came stomping down it. Lupe retreated into the hall and quickly led his people in the opposite direction.

Daniel exhaled. He was shaking badly. "Thank you."

I faced him. "You are a black man. No matter what uniform you wear, no matter what power you have, no matter where you're at, you are a black man. That is our common denominator. Before any religion, before any country, before anything else, we are black men. Remember tonight, and always remember it."

He nodded.

Eventually the guards did regain control of the yard. Before they made it to our floor, I had Daniel change back into his guard uniform, and I had some of my soldiers escort him to the stairway where his fellow guards were. I never told the guards the story, but he did. What I did that night circulated amongst the officers, counselors, case managers, unit managers, and wardens. After that night, I couldn't get in trouble for shit. And the witch hunt for Umkhonto members ended.

I survived what I did. The brothers were cool with it 'cause Daniel was a cool guard. He didn't fuck with anybody. He just sat in his office and changed the fucking TV when he was told. He was the perfect BOP babysitter. He didn't shake down our lockers, he didn't give us breathalyzer tests, he didn't give us random piss tests—he just sat in the office and minded his own business. The perfect guard.

Umkhonto really rode with me. I had proven to them that I was willing to make the tough decisions, and I was willing to take the hit for those decisions. They got a deeper meaning of what Umkhonto was about. We weren't a prison gang—we were the spear of our nation. We were warriors for our people, inside and outside. We were starting a *movement.* Umkhonto was going to be the shield and spear of *all* black people.

And the Mexicans? They hated me more than ever. The funny thing was I gave them a reason to patch up their differences and unify again. They came together and hit us two weeks later.

# Chapter Twenty

I woke to the sound of tennis shoes racing through the hallway. The tennis shoes and whispers instantly aroused my suspicions. I peered across the room at Young Gangsta, who was also awake.

"Momo," I whispered.

"I hear it," he answered.

I sat up in bed, slipped on my work boots, and grabbed my shank. Momo slid out of bed with his weapon and quietly put on his boots. Young Gangsta did the same. We all noticed that Pedro was missing.

"Ol' boy done crept out to be with his people," New Orleans observed. He, too, climbed out of bed. He didn't have to slide into his footgear, because he slept with his boots on. It wasn't that he was a Viking; he was just a fireman. He stayed ready to keep from having to get ready.

We all gathered in the middle of our room and kept our voices down.

"We need to get word to the others," I told them. "They're about to hit us."

New Orleans nodded and walked through the bathroom to the suite next door, where he woke the brothers up before returning to us.

"The *esses* in the next room are all gone too," he said.

I nodded. "You see anything in the hall?"

He shook his head. "No, they must be gathering up by the TV rooms or something."

The brothers in the next suite came into our room. "Hey, y'all split up, go room to room, and wake up all the brothers. Tell them to get suited and booted and to get ready. They about to hit us."

They nodded and raced out of the room. I turned to New Orleans. "Go out the door and take the outside stairs. Wake up all the brothers on the third floor and the first floor. Tell them to get ready and gather up in as few rooms as possible. And then get back here as soon as possible."

N.O. nodded and headed out the door. More brothers from my hallway poured into my room. "They about to hit us," I whispered.

I reached into my locker and pulled out a jar of coffee, took a pinch of coffee grains and placed them in my gums, and then passed the jar around for the others to do the same. The caffeine would help wake us up.

My jar went around the room and came back to me just as the first Border Brothers were entering into my room. I dashed the coffee in the first attacker's face, grabbed him, and threw him out of the window. The second one that came at me got my shank in his neck. I could see the brothers pouring from the room across the hall and from the door leading to the outside stairwell. They tried to hit us, but we were ready.

I stabbed another attacker in his stomach, and then another in his neck. I hit another Border Brother in his chest, and then struck another in his side. Next, I took a stab wound to my side, but fortunately, it wasn't deep. We quickly beat back their assault on my room, and then mopped up the rest of them on my floor. Finished, we headed to the stairs to help the brothers on the other floors.

We cleaned up our housing unit in efficient fashion. I was just hoping and praying that the brothers in the other housing unit fared as well. The lights on throughout the other housing unit told us that they were battling as well. We had managed to run our attackers to the upper yard, and now we watched and waited and hoped that when the guards opened those steel doors in the other housing unit, it would be Mexicans fleeing out of the doors instead of brothers.

"Let's go, C!" Young Gangsta shouted.

"And do what? Bang on the doors for the guards to let us in? We can't get in!"

We stood at our door, waiting. The Mexicans that we had driven out of the unit stood on the other side of the fence, watching and waiting as well. They, too, wondered how their comrades had fared. We all watched as the compound officer and one of the nighttime lieutenants ran over to the other housing unit with their keys. They opened the metal door, and no one poured out.

"What the fuck is going on?" Pink House Shorty asked.

"C, let's go!" Young Gangsta shouted again.

"Yo, let's roll!" Cabrini Green said.

I shook my head.

"They left the door open!" Shorty said, urging me to give the go-ahead.

And then our answer came. Mexicans poured from the building, followed by brothers chasing after them. A cheer went up from our side of the yard.

The stupid-ass guard at the gate separating the upper yard from the lower yard opened up the gate to let the Mexicans flee to the upper yard. Instead of that happening, though, the Mexicans on the upper yard ran into the lower yard, charging the pursuing brothers from the other housing unit.

"Let's go!" I shouted, charging into the yard. We rushed after them. Apparently the Mexicans had never heard of the Battle of Cannae. There were brothers to their front, and we had charged them from the rear. Our natural reaction was to encircle them and stab everything in front of us—and we did just that. They fell like wheat meeting a thresher. What had been a defeat quickly turned into a bloodbath.

The guards weren't going to try to break anything up and risk getting stabbed in the process. Instead, they got smart. They broke out the video cameras. Being caught on camera stabbing another prisoner meant that you could be charged with murder, or attempted murder. And if that person died, then the probability of getting a life sentence was very realistic. And life in the feds wasn't twenty years, it was *life*.

"Back to the housing units!" I shouted.

The brothers broke and ran for the housing units, leaving a lot of dead or wounded Mexicans lying on the compound. We ran into the housing units, and the guards locked us inside. The majority of us raced for the showers to wash the blood off, while others gathered our stripped off clothing and headed for the laundry room. It would be hours before reinforcements arrived to regain control of the yard. By then, we would have showered, wash and dried our clothing, and be in our beds acting like we were fast asleep. We had managed to break for the dorms before the guards got the camera up and running, so it would be a random witch hunt when the administrators arrived and started their investigation into the fight.

The guards officially restored control of the yard around six o'clock that morning. I got called into the unit manager's office around seven. They were calling prisoners into the various case managers' and counselors' offices to interview them and see what happened. Unfortunately, snitching on a prison yard is commonplace. They probably knew the full story within ten minutes of beginning their interviews. I got interviewed by the unit manager himself. His name was Stuart.

Mr. Stuart was a brother, and he was cool as fuck. He was less than a year from retirement, and he no longer gave a fuck.

"Alexander, come in," he said, waving at the seat opposite his. "Sit your big, ugly ass down."

I laughed.

"So, tell me what happened?"

I shrugged. "I was sleep."

"You were asleep. And the Border Brothers just ran past your room and left you alone. Try that shit with somebody else. Look, we already know what happened. They caught your asses sleeping in the middle of the night, ran into your rooms, but you were ready for them. You fought them off, kicked their asses, and then it really got fucked-up. Look, we don't care about the fight. And as far as the BOP is concerned, it was self-defense. We just need to tie this thing together in a neat report for D.C."

"I wish you the best. I wish that there was something that I could do to help, but I don't know anything. I was fast asleep, cuddling up with my Fee-Fee."

He laughed. "You sick son of a bitch."

I laughed. A Fee-Fee was a towel that had been rolled up tight like a pussy.

"Okay, okay, so you don't want to be a snitch," he conceded. "Well, we got to talk about something. I'm supposed to be in here twisting your arm for information."

I leaned back, stretched out, and got comfortable. "How about those Spurs?"

"Yeah, you think they're going to do it again?"

"I hope so. I don't see anybody stopping'em."

"I like Phoenix."

"You would—hater. So, what are you doing do when you retire?"

"Shit, I'm going fishing, man."

"Fishing?"

"Yeah, I can't wait. I won't have to look at your big ugly ass anymore. I think I'm going to buy me a Harley."

"A Harley?"

"Yeah, why not? My wife just bought an Escalade, so I'm going to buy me a Harley Davidson."

"You're going to get your fat ass up on a Harley?"

He laughed. "Yeah. Daddy still has a little bit of get-up-and-go in him!"

"You know what? I'm gone on that note." I rose and extended my hand. "You take care of yourself and be careful out there on that damn motorcycle."

He clasped my hand. "No, you take care of yourself, son. I don't want to hear about you bringing your black ass back to prison. You're so much better than this, man. You can get out there and do anything. There are enough of us in the system. You go out there and do great things."

I nodded. "I will. Maybe we'll go fishing together."

"I'd like that."

"You bait my hook for me?"

He shoved me out the door. "Get your big ugly ass outta here!"

There were lasting results from the Mexicans sneak attack on us in the middle of the night. They had been the aggressors against the Califas, the Aztecas, the Texicans, and now the Brothers. The region was pissed, and so was D.C. And so change was ordered.

The Border Brothers and Los Piasas were to be broken. They were going to be split up and shipped all over the country. In exchange, prisons from all over the country were to send inmates to the prison where we were. Over the next couple of months, Mexicans were loaded up and shipped out and replaced with busloads of blacks and whites. They even sent us a new captain, a black one. And a black lieutenant. It was crazy.

"He looks like a pimp," Gangsta said laughing.

"He *is* a pimp," Jersey said. "Look, that's his burgundy Cadillac out there in the parking lot."

"Bullshit!" I said laughing.

We were posted up on the stairs outside one of the housing units, just kicking the bullshit. The yard was changing rapidly before our eyes. It had gone from being even, to us being outnumbered ten-to-one, to us being outnumbered five-to-one, to us being outnumbered two-to-one. And now, we were quickly becoming the majority. Brothers were pouring in from the South and the East Coast.

"Man, I'm serious, that's his 'Lac."

"It has a CC grille on it, with a peanut butter rag, and those chrome disc and vogues," Gangsta added.

"Man, where did they get this cat from?" Big Mississippi asked.

"He looks like he one of yours," I told Mississippi. "Them 'ole loud-ass, country-ass pimp suits he be wearing."

We all broke into laughter.

"Aww, nigga, if he was from San Antone, he'd be wearing a fucking Mariachi suit, wouldn't he? I bet you know about that!"

Again we all laughed.

"Man, this cat is wearing a lavender suit," I observed. "Yesterday it was yellow, the day before it was lime green, and before that bright red. He has gold rings on each finger, gold bracelets, a gold watch, and a bunch of small-ass gold chains. And a fucking juicy-ass Jheri Curl! I know this nigga has got to be from the Walk."

"Naw, that 'Bama-ass nigga is from Chi Town," Chi-town told us.

"Bullshit! You for real?" Gangsta asked.

Chi-town threw his hands up. "As embarrassing as it is to admit, yeah."

The captain's pimp suits were legendary around the yard. He had more colors than a big box of crayons. And for some suits, he even had matching fedoras.

"I'll bet you these redneck-ass guards can't stand his ass," Big Austin said.

"A black captain?" Shorty asked. "Having to say 'Yes sir' to a nigga? Aww, hell, naw! You know they hating that shit, yo!"

Our numbers continued to grow over the summer. So much so, that we now outnumbered the Mexicans by more than a hundred soldiers. I had soldiers coming from other prisons who were already members of Umkhonto. It was bananas.

The blacks arriving on the yard weren't used to the way things were done. They had a problem, *they* handled it. They whipped ass and were genuinely surprised when brothers showed up to talk to them about what happened. They were surprised about the politics behind everything, they were surprised when they were told that they couldn't simply whip ass and keep on going. They had to talk to their 'shot callers,' who would, in turn, talk to me, or Rock, or G, and then one of us would go and talk to the *esses'* shot caller, who would handle the *esses*. It was political, and time-consuming, and a culture shock for brothers coming from prisons where the brothers had always been the majority.

For the brothers who were already on the yard, the change in demographics manifested itself in different ways. They released years of frustration and aggravation on the Mexicans. Brothers who had been here when it was a ten-to-one ratio, who had to bite their tongue and swallow their pride for years, started whipping Mexicans like it was free. Times got real bad for the Border Brothers and the Piasas. The brothers on the yard started carrying them real bad. They were mauled over the smallest issue.

I let my people take out their frustrations on an enemy that had carried us bad for a long time, motherfuckas who continuously threatened to go to war over small shit. When they had the numbers, we walked on eggs. They walked the yard with their chests puffed out, while we just wanted to survive.

I admit that if it hadn't been for the way they carried us and for the overwhelming odds that we faced, we wouldn't have come together like we did. We really formed a brotherhood here. And I'm not just talking about Umkhonto. All of the brothers came together and got each other's backs. It was beautiful. It was unfortunate that it took a life-and-death situation to make it happen, but sometimes that's the way life is.

I do have to admit that in a small way, I wish that brothers hadn't carried the *esses* as bad as they did. I wish that we could have had the power, and then shit on them by treating them fair. I wish that we would have shown them that we were different, that we were better than they were. My father always talked about how we would treat others if we had the power. How would blacks have treated whites if the situation had been reversed?

I remember reading a book by a cat named Stephen Barnes called *Lion's Blood.* In the book, a parallel world existed where blacks colonized America and Europe, and where whites were the slaves. Even in that world, there was a slave and a master. Something inside of me would like to think that if the situation had really been reversed, there would have been no slave and no master. Naïve? Yes. But I couldn't help the fact that I wanted my people to be better. I liked to dream that we were a better, more honorable, more spiritual people. Despite all that had been done to us, despite the truth of history, I held inside of me the hope that had the situation been reversed, there would have been no international slave trade.

I went to my bunk that evening to get some rest. When I walked into the room, I found Pedro with his head buried in his pillow, crying. One of his partners from his home state in Mexico was sitting on his bunk talking to him.

"Pedro, my man, what's up?"

He didn't answer.

I turned to his partner and nodded my head, asking him what was up.

"He got disciplined," Jesse told me.

"Disciplined?" I plopped down on my bed. "What the fuck for?"

"He got into it with a brother, and the brother went to our shot caller. So, in order to avoid any problems, they had him disciplined."

I felt like shit. "Man, that's fucked up. Why didn't you come to me? If you were having problems with one of the brothers, why didn't you come to me?"

Pedro peered up from his pillow. His lip was busted, and his eyes were puffy and red. I was pissed.

"Fuck!" I shouted, pounding my locker. "Who did it?"

"Alexander, I didn't disrespect your homeboy," Pedro said in broken English. "He said that I call him a nigra. I don't say that word. I never call him that. He lie. He want me to steal him tomatoes from the kitchen, and I say yes, ten *estampas*. He say, no, that too much. He always want me to steal, but he no want to pay for food. He call me names and tell me fucking wetback, but I no say nothing. I just walk away."

I nodded. "I know. Who was it?"

"Slick."

"*Muthafucka!*" I rose and walked out of the room.

I found Pedro's shot caller in the gym playing basketball. I walked onto the court and grabbed the basketball, stopping the game. I pointed at him. "You! Come here!"

Baca walked to where I was standing. He was the shot caller for the Piedras Negras clique.

"Throw us the basketball, San Antone!" Waco shouted.

"Get your ass off the court, San Antone!" Big Austin shouted.

"Yeah, get your Darth Vader helmet head ass off the court!" Charlie Hustle shouted.

"Hey! Pedro, my celly," I said to Baca. "You know who I'm talking about?"

He nodded.

"You disciplined him?"

He nodded. "We already took care of it."

"You don't take care of him again. You don't ever take care of him, you hear me?"

Baca recoiled, confused.

"He's not to be touched ever again, you hear me?"

"The Mexican?"

I nodded. "Yeah, the Mexican. My fucking celly, Pedro. You don't touch him, you hear me?"

"He's mines."

I shook my head. "No, maybe you're not understanding me. He's not yours, he's mines. He's my friend. You put your hands on him, you've put your hands on me. Do you understand me, amigo? Don't you *ever* touch him again! If he fucks up, you come to me. Pedro has the protection of Umkhonto on him."

"The brothers are protecting a Mexican?" he asked.

"I'm protecting my brother, Pedro," I told him. "Are we clear?"

He shrugged and nodded. He didn't give a fuck, he just wanted to survive.

I tossed the ball to Charlie Hustle, turned, and walked out of the gym. I don't know what I was thinking. How could I, the biggest bigot on the yard, threaten to go to war to protect a Mexican? I didn't know what was happening to me. I was comfortable being a racist pig. In fact, it was a reputation that I enjoyed. It kept the white guards away from me, out of my locker, and out of my face.

For years, I went around the yard ignoring the Mexicans and the white boys, only giving thought to them when it came time for war. But somehow, during that time period, I found a friend in Pedro. Was it one of those situations where Pedro was the good Mexican and the rest were bad? It was a situation that black people dealt with for years. White folks would go to war for their black maids and nannies. They would give them food and toys and all kinds of shit and genuinely had a benevolent type of affection for them, while hating black people in general.

But I can't say that I had that type of relationship with Pedro. I knew him, I knew his family, and I knew that he was a soldier for his people. I knew that he had been moved into my room to kill me. With all of those things on the table, we both bonded while simply trying to do time and get back to our families. He had hopes and dreams for his children, and I had hopes and dreams for mine. We were men in a world that made us kill one another, a world that told us that we should be enemies. And in that world, we managed to somehow create a true friendship.

I went back to my room, grabbed a face towel, poured some ice water on it from my water jug, and then kneeled down by the bed of my friend.

"You look uglier," I said, handing him the cold towel.

He took it and placed it on his lip. "Mamacita is gonna give me some good pussy for this."

I shook my head and laughed. "You freaky muthafucka."

# Chapter Twenty-One

"Man, I wanna hit them fools," I told Gangsta.

"What?"

"Man, I'm tired of their shit! That nigga needs to be put in his fucking place! They running around here fucking up, doing stupid shit, and this nigga is constantly bumping his gums."

Gangsta shook his head and smiled. "Leave it alone, C."

"Naw, man, that's some bullshit. That nigga wanna play shot caller and shit. Who the fuck is he?"

"C, what does it matter?  Man, leave that bullshit alone. You going home soon. So what who the fuck is he?"

"My point exactly! That nigga ain't running shit, and he needs to know it."

"Don't do it, C."

"Why do you keep saying that?"

"Because, that shit a work itself out. If he's the one, then he'll be the one. If he's not, then somebody else will work they way to the top. Crème always rises to the top, baby."

"That nigga is not taking over shit. We built this shit! We started this shit when he was still on the street sticking his thumb up his ass! And now he wants to run up in here trying to call shots?"

"C, if these fools listen to him, then that's on them. We leaving soon."

"It's not on them. He can't run Umkhonto. And if he can't have the backing of Umkhonto, then what kind of representative can he be?"

"C, if the brothers choose him, then what's the problem?  If he leads them the wrong way, then they'll get rid of his ass."

"Look, let's not change the argument!" I shouted. "His ass needs to be put in his place. He's the one that got us into it with the white boys that night over the TV, he's the one that had Pedro disciplined because of his shit starting homeboys, he's the reason why G stepped down. That nigga needs to be touched."

"Okay, touch him!" Gangsta said throwing his hands up in frustration. "It's your private army, so you do what you want to with it. Umkhonto isn't about the people, it isn't about protecting brothers, its all about you and what you want to do with it! You got thousands of soldiers all across the country ready and willing to do whatever you say. You don't like somebody, dead 'em. That's what Umkhonto is here for after all. We're here to beat up or kill whoever gets on your nerves."

"This dude is the problem, not me! He's the one causing division, not me!"

"Are you sure?"

"What the fuck you mean am I sure? Hell, yeah, I'm sure!"

"What the fuck are you doing? Go the fuck home! Leave this bullshit where it belongs! In here! Get your fucking mind out of prison, C! This shit is not your world, it's not your life; let it go!"

"What the fuck are you talking about?"

"I heard you talking about going out to the free world and giving it a try. What the fuck is that? You ain't going out there to give shit a try. What? If it's too tough for you, you gonna run back to prison? This shit ain't where we belong, C! This shit ain't *normal*. Out *there* is normal! Get your fucking head and heart out of this bullshit! Go home!"

I had been locked up for over eight years. I spent all of my twenties in prison. I became a man behind the walls. One-third of my life had been spent trying to survive that world. It had become my life.

"If you hit him, then everything we've built has been destroyed by you," Gangsta said calmly. "Not by him, but by *you*! Umkhonto was created to protect the brothers, not to stifle differences of opinion. Right now, to a whole lot of brothers, you can walk on water. Don't ruin that. Don't take away their hero. Don't destroy an organization that so many people love by turning it into your private vengeance machine."

"Fuck you, soft-ass muthafucka!" I said, knowing that he was in the right. I wanted to pick a fight with him. "Go to the state with that dick-in-the-booty ass shit."

"What? What, C?" he said walking up on me. "That's how we

carrying it?"

He was my best friend, my brother, and he was leaving for state prison the next morning. He walked up on me, and I stole on him. He grabbed a lamp and hit me upside my head, twice. I ran into him, tackling him, and caused us to hit the ground hard. We wrestled for position, getting in blows where we could. I was two hundred and thirty-five pounds of muscle, and so I was able to lift him up and toss him into the wall. He charged me, and again, we exchanged blows. Soon, we again found ourselves falling—only this time I had him in a headlock.

"Gangsta! Gangsta!"

"What, nigga?"

I let him go, and we both stood and stared at one another. A smile slowly crept across both of our faces, and then we embraced.

"I'm gonna see you in the free world, man," he said. "This shit ain't over. I'ma go and handle this shit in the state, and then we gonna hook up and become young black millionaires."

"I'm gonna miss you," I told him. We had done six years together. Seeing one another every day, gambling together, getting paper together, talking about our hopes and our dreams. I had taken him under my wing, and he had become my little brother.

"I'ma see what you really made of, nigga."

"What are you talking about?" I asked.

"You gonna be out in the free world while I'm locked up. I'ma see what you really talking about. If you gonna keep it real or what."

"Bitch, I kept it real while I was in prison. Why in the fuck I wouldn't keep it real outside of the walls?"

"You gonna forget about me?"

"Never."

"Young black millionaires?" he asked.

I nodded. "Young black millionaires." And that's where it came from. He took that YBM shit to the state with him. I didn't have a problem with getting paper, as long as it didn't exploit other black people. And this is how YBM came out of, and became a part of, Umkhonto.

Young Gangsta hopped up on top of Momo's bunk, lifted up the ceiling tile, and pulled down several bags. He tossed the bags to me and then hopped down.

"Five thousand books right there, C," he said.

"Five thousand books of stamps?" I was shocked. "Damn, nigga! Why you never sent none of these muahfuckas out to get cashed?"

"Send them to who? My sista? I don't know where she is. My grandmother? I haven't heard from her since her phone got cut off six years ago. My brother? That nigga could be on Mars for all I know. You the only family I got, ugly muahfucka!"

I nodded and wrapped my arm around him. "I'll take care of them. I'll send 'em out and have somebody take'em to the post office. I'll send you the cash."

He shook his head. "Just put the cash in a bank for me. That way, I'll have some money when I get out. Just send me a G and I'll make do with that. I'll hustle if I need more. You know how we do it."

I smiled. "Five thousand books, at six dollars and fifty cents to eight dollars and twenty-five cents a book. Hey, that's your Laundromat, your detail shop, and your car wash. You got your start-up money, baby boy."

"That's *our* start-up money, nigga. Damn shame a nigga had to come to the penitentiary to get his paper."

"That's 'cause you niggaz out here in West Texas don't know nothing about the dope game. You niggaz is just in the way."

"Fuck you, C!"

We shared a laugh.

"You ready for state?" I asked, wiping away the blood that dripped down from my head. "*Damn*, that lamp kinda hurt."

"It was supposed to, muahfucka," he said, wiping the blood off his lip. "You love me, C?"

I nodded.

"You betta. I don't wanna have to kill you."

"You ain't cut like that, nigga."

He smiled.

"You took care of me, C. You pull me in, showed me the real, showed me how to get money, talked to me and kept me outta trouble. You wasn't just like my big brother. Sometimes you was like a father to me."

"I know, Gangsta. Just bring your ass home safely. Don't get to the state and get caught up. Just do your time, stay out of the bullshit, and come home alive."

He nodded. "You taught me well."

Saying good-bye to Gangsta was the hardest thing I ever had to do. Before prison, the thought of loving another black man who wasn't a relative, or from my hood, or gang, never occurred to me. It was something I didn't understand, and if someone would have mentioned it, I would have thought them homo. But there is a love between black men that is possible. It is powerful beyond belief. Black men willing to stand up for one another, to kill for one another, to die for one another, is one of the most powerful things on earth. And even more powerful are black men willing to *live* for one another.

By living for one another, I mean living their lives in such a way as to have a positive impact on the lives of other black men. It meant living not only for their own children, but for the children of other black men. To do this, it took love between black men. I loved Young Gangsta as a brother and a son. And that's why it felt as though God had reached inside of me and pulled out my heart when I learned that he was killed in a riot two weeks after he got to state prison. He was twenty-six.

When I finally got out of bed again after recovering from word of Gangsta's death, I called a meeting with the brothers. The Mexicans were plea-bargaining. They were getting whipped if they sneezed wrong. We met in the BET room.

"Yo, this bullshit has got to stop!" I told them. "Man, you can't just go around putting hands on people like they're your children."

"Man, that's the way they used to carry us, San Antone!" Big Austin shouted.

"No, they didn't!" I countered. "At no time did Mexicans run around here putting they hands on no brothers."

"Yeah, but goddamn," Duck shouted, "they carried us badder than a muthafucka, San Antone! Had a nigga around here stressing and shit. Couldn't sleep. They always gathering up, threatening to go to war and shit. Now that we got the numbers, they want to cry and shit."

"Yeah, but when they had the numbers, they still didn't go around tossing brothers up and shit. Man, we need to calm this shit down. All I'm saying is that if you have a problem with an *esse*, holler at me or holler at Rock and we'll get that shit resolved with the quickness. Ain't no sense in going to the hole, ain't no sense in putting your hands on nobody, just take care of that shit and do your time. You don't want to roll with that, fine. It's your good time, and halfway house, and commissary, and phone that's getting taken.

"Look, they changed up the yard and brought in more brothers. Don't fuck around and have them change it up again and have this muthafucka turn into a yard full of white boys—or even worse—go back to what it was."

I peered around the room. "No more of that bullshit. Stop putting your hands on people. Muahfuckas act like you got some sense. Are we all good on this?"

Slowly, nods started appearing around the room.

"Good. Now let's watch the fucking Spurs game."

Saying good-bye to Gangsta was followed by saying good-bye to Pedro. He was finished with his Illegal Entry sentence and was now being deported back to Mexico. I helped him carrying his meager belongings up to Receiving and Discharge, where he would be escorted out of the prison and turned over to Immigration and Naturalization Services officers. INS would then take him to the U.S. and Mexico border and release him back into Mexico.

"Alexander, you coming to Laredo to visit me, no?" Pedro asked. "As soon as you go home, you get your family and you come and visit me."

"Laredo?" I asked, lifting an eyebrow. "I thought they were sending you back to Mexico."

He shrugged. "One, maybe two days, and back across the border."

"Back across the border. It's that easy, huh?"

He nodded. "My family, they in Laredo already. My wife, she have una casa in Laredo. My daughters, they born in United States. And my *novia* too. She have a job in Laredo."

I nodded. "So you have to come back."

"*Si*," he nodded and smiled. "And me *novia,* she's in Laredo now."

"You moved your *girlfriend* to Laredo? Are you nuts?"

"Two pussies in Laredo. One night here, one night here, one night with *una otra novia.*"

"Three? You dirty dog. Where in the hell are you going to get the energy and the money for three women?"

"*Drogas*. Sell *mucho* kilos. Sniff eight ball and *visita me novias, visita* my wife, *mucho* energy." He pounded his chest.

We both laughed at the same time.

"You promise, you me *visita*."

I nodded. "You take care of yourself. Don't get caught up in any bullshit."

"No." He shook his head and pointed toward the compound. "You keep head down. No bullshit for you."

He opened his arms, and we embraced. "You take care of yourself, my friend."

He nodded his head. I turned and began to walk away.

"Alexander!"

I turned back toward him.

"I no could do it."

"What?"

"I not could hurt you."

"I couldn't hurt you either, Pedro."

He walked to me and again wrapped me up in a big bear hug. *"Tu es mi hermano."*

*"Para siempre,"* I told him. For life.

My string of good-byes and bad news finally gave way to some good news. I got a letter from Ghirt. He was doing well. The Feds had transferred him to Alabama, which meant that he was closer to his family, so it worked out for the best.

The even better news, at least from my perspective, was that Umkhonto was already there when he arrived, and they had numbers. Umkhonto was in every prison throughout the South, as well as the East Coast. And in every prison that he had communication with, or heard about, they were doing what they were supposed to be doing, which was protecting and unifying brothers. And the best news was that it wasn't just a federal thing. They were all throughout the various state prison systems as well. I had thousands of soldiers in and out of the system. The question was what was I going to do with them?

If there was one thing that I learned from Gangsta, it was the promise of tomorrow. Gangsta and his dreams of getting out and taking care of his grandmother and building a better life for his young sister and her babies spoke of a better tomorrow. Despite everything in his life that he had been through, he still believed that he could make his tomorrow better than his today. He had dreams of bringing a Laundromat to his community, of building a car wash and providing jobs to the needy in his neighborhood. He had coined the phrase, "young black millionaires." It was what he aspired to be.

Taking Young Gangsta's hope and optimism and translating that into a vision for Umkhonto was important to me. I had an army of soldiers, and somehow, I had to turn that army into a real movement. I owed that to Gangsta. I owed it to my people. I owed it to my son, my woman, and myself. God, how I wanted to be better. A better person, a better father, a better man.

For the first time since I arrived in that place, I genuinely felt alone. I stood out on my balcony, peered up at the sky, and wondered if Gangsta was looking down on me. I wondered what Ghirt was doing, what Omene was doing, what Tamfu was doing. I knew what horny-ass Pedro was doing. My life had changed. I had changed. I was an old man in a young man's body. I was ready to move on with my life.

"I couldn't have hurt you either, Pedro," I whispered into the wind. On that lonely balcony, I prayed that the breeze would carry my words out to wherever my friend was. I hoped that it would carry my message out across the world, that two people of different backgrounds, different countries, different races, could become brothers. I prayed that that wind would carry my message of hope around the world. I was desperate for a new tomorrow.

# Chapter Twenty-Two

I had done over eight and a half years in prison. I had grown up inside the system. I went in before I was twenty, and I spent almost my entire twenties there. It is the place where I became a man.

My father used to tell me that prison was like a womb. That we go inside, and that we are formed into new beings. And then after we have fully formed, after a seed of consciousness has awakened our minds, we are then birthed into the free world. My new birth date was fast approaching, and I was scared as hell.

I had taken up vocational training, and I had my EPA certifications in air conditioning, heating, and ventilation repair. I had my journeyman's license in plumbing, and I was a certified masonry apprentice. I was also well on my way to being a licensed electrician. I had over a year of carpentry and furniture building under my belt, and I could frame a house, close it in, build the cabinets and furniture to go inside, and put the roof on the sucker. In truth, I could do all the air conditioning, plumbing, electrical wiring, and masonry work that the house would require. In other words, I had all the skills to build a house. What worried me was whether or not I could build a *home*.

I had a son waiting for me. Before I came into prison, I had nothing to teach him. And now, I had so much to share with him. I knew all of the traps that were out there waiting for him, all of the pitfalls, all of the bullshit that he was facing. In my conversations with Prince, I even got to go inside of the mind of the enemy. I could raise him up to be a man, a good man, but only if I were ready to be that man myself.

The world was a scary place for me now. Before, I thought myself a predator, but now that my eyes were open, I knew that I was really nothing more than a scavenger scampering through the underbrush, trying to survive in a world where the deck was stacked against me.

Before, I was violent; a danger for the local police force to squash like a bug. But now that I had educated myself, now that I had the power to save my son, my brother's sons, my sister's sons, and my neighbor's sons, I had become a dangerous scavenger. Even though the deck was stacked against me, knowing that it was stacked against me, and in what ways it was stacked against me made me a dangerous critter.

A self-educated black man who could educate, lift up, and enlighten other black men was a danger to the status quo. A black man who had the vocational skills to build a house, the emotional stability to build a home, the social passion to build a village, the historical foundation to build a nation, and the mental abilities to lead that nation, was Public Enemy Number One for many. Plus, I had an army.

I knew that I would be getting out soon, and I knew the things that needed to be done. I was going to take my son and teach him how to be a man. I was going to take my woman, marry her, build a home and a family with her, and I was going to help her, and protect her, and be the man she needed me to be. I was going to return to my community and talk to the youngsters, teach them, tell them of the dangers that awaited them if they walked a path of destruction.

I wanted to save the youngsters in my neighborhood. I wanted to save my people. For so much of my life, I had participated in their destruction. Now, I wanted to walk through my entire neighborhood and go door to door and apologize for the destruction that I had caused, for the hurt, the pain, and the letdown. I wanted to personally apologize to every human being that I had ever sold a piece of crack to, to every person whom I had ever sold weed to or smoked with. I wanted to apologize to every youngster who ever looked at me and thought that I was cool and wanted to be like me.

I had done so much wrong in my life, and now I wanted to do right. Prison had changed me. I had gone through the crucible—and the violence, and heat, and friction, and pressure had forged a new man.

"That's fucked-up, San Antone!"

I turned in the direction of the voice. It was Enrique.

"Some coward-ass shit you muthafuckas are pulling," he continued.

"What the fuck are you talkin' about?" I asked.

He had a small contingent of Border Brothers with him. We were inside of the restroom, and I was standing in front of the sink.

"I'm just saying, when we had the numbers, you niggas wasn't acting all fucking brave and bold. Now that you got the numbers, y'all quick to fight a muthafucka. That's some coward-ass shit."

"First of all, let that be the last 'nigga' that comes outta your bean-eating mouth, muthafucka. Second, when you wetbacks had the numbers, you was some bold-ass bitches, always threatening to go to war with the brothers. If you don't like what's going on, then threaten to go to war. That's what you always did in the past."

"You some punk-ass muthafuckas," Enrique sneered. "We wasn't going around here putting our hands on your people. Maybe we should have. Maybe we should have gotten you niggers off the compound back when we had a chance."

"I said, I didn't want to hear no more 'niggas'" I stole on him, striking him across his jaw. His people grabbed him, and the brothers that were in the restroom grabbed me.

Henry clasped his red jaw. "Fucking nigger! I'm *glad* my brothers killed your fucking uncle!"

"*What*?" I could feel the heat welling up in my face. "*What* did you say?" I yanked my arms away from the brothers holding me.

"I said, that's why my older brothers killed your fucking uncle, bitch." He was nodding and had a smile on his face that I had never seen before. "Yeah, they did it. They caught him and his homeboy walking down the street, and they killed him."

I don't know which one bothered me more—the fact that his brothers did it, or the fact that he had known all of these years.

"I helped my daddy destroy the guns and bury them in my backyard!" Henry blurted out. "I wish I would have gone with them that night. I wish I would have had the chance to kill your black nigger ass too!"

I hit him. I hit him with twenty-eight years' worth of fury and pain. It was as though I was trying to hit the wall behind him by driving my fist through his face. He collapsed instantly. I kicked him in his stomach as hard as I could. My kick caused a whooshing sound to flow from his lungs. I was going to kill Henry.

He clasped my leg, and then chopped me behind my knee, causing me to drop to the ground. We both rose and charged at one another with a fury that would make a wildebeest fight look like a ballet recital in comparison.

Henry and I locked arms. I was two hundred and thirty pounds of muscle. He was one hundred and seventy pounds of muscle. I was six foot one, he was five foot ten. I placed him inside a headlock, while he wrapped his arms around my legs and lifted me off the ground. We both fell once again.

I knew that only one of us was going to leave the bathroom alive that day. He had to have known it too. He had said too much, revealed too much for both of us to be able to walk away. He was one of my best friends, and his family had killed the only father figure I had while growing up. It was because of them that my life was the way it was. It was because of them that I was in prison right now. It was because of them that I had killed men and become a monster.

I rolled over on top of Henry and threw a punch to his face. I followed that blow with another, and then another, and then another. He rolled me off him, and then tried to dive on top of me. I used his momentum to keep him going and sent him flying into the wall. Then I jumped to my feet, raced to where he was getting up, and began to viciously kick him.

"Muthafucka!" I shouted. I kicked as hard as I could. I kicked him in his stomach, in his face, in his arms, legs, back, chest, ass, everywhere that I could. And once I had kicked the fight out of him, I grabbed him by his hair, pulling him up to his knees, and then rammed his head into one of the metal bathroom sinks. A massive gash appeared across his forehead. I rammed his head into the sink again, splitting it open like a melon. Blood shot all over the restroom. Most of those inside scattered like roaches. Being witness to a homicide, even in prison, was not something most people wanted to experience.

Despite his open head wound, I dropped down behind him and wrapped my arm around his throat. His hands flew to my forearm as he fought for air. I tightened my grip. I wanted him dead. I wanted his family to feel what my family felt that night. I wanted his mother to cry like my mother cried. I wanted his mother to hold her womb and reminisce, like when my grandmother fell to the floor and held her empty stomach the night she lost her child.

As the last throes of life left Henry's body, I clenched harder and wept. I wept for the little boy inside of me who lost the uncle who was like a big brother and father. I wept for the little boy inside of me who grew up without a father figure to turn to. I wept for the boy who had no one to talk to him about gangs, about drugs, about sex. They took so much from me. They had taken so much from my family. I sat in Henry's blood, and I wept, for I had just killed my best friend.

Webber had me cleaned up and had Umkhonto doctor the evidence. The Mexican witnesses were quickly caught and killed, and the whole scene was set up to look like an intra-Mexican gang fight.

And this was where Webber and I were different. He was brutal. He was about to kill the two brothers who actually stayed and saw the murder until they proved that they were Umkhonto members from another prison and that they could be trusted. Webber was all brains and business, and no heart or emotion. He had my clothing burnt and disposed of, and he even created an alibi for me, just in case. He was thorough and proficient. I was a mess.

"C, are you all right?" G-Man asked in his deep, countrified accent.

I peered up at him and nodded. He kneeled down just in front of me.

"Are you sure?" he continued. "I heard what happened. I'm sorry, man."

"Nothing to be sorry about," I said sadly. "He knew all those years, G. I spent nights at his house; he spent nights over mines. We played together, did everything together. We took karate together when we were kids. We used to go swimming together at the local field house when we were youngsters. My uncle even took us sometimes. We went to Catholic school together when we were youngsters. We used to go to the mall together, we used to steal our parents' cars late at night and sneak off to the teen club. And then we came to this place. This fucking place!"

I kicked my locker, and G grabbed me and held me.

"I want to go home!"

"I know."

"I hate this fucking place!" I shouted. "What kind of place is this? What kind of place turns a human being into an animal? What kind of place makes you kill your best friend?"

He embraced me tightly. More than anyone, he understood. He had been locked up for more than ten years. He was twenty-eight and had been dealing with bullshit for one third of his life. We had both stepped up when our people needed us, and we had done it at a young age. We had been deciding matters of life and death for many people before we were old enough to legally buy a beer.

The pressure of calling shots, of dealing with prison politics, outside relationships, of going home, of so many other things, had gotten to me. I was carrying a mountain on my shoulders, and he had walked in those shoes for many years. And through many of those years, although we didn't always see eye to eye on many matters, we still had one another's back. And now that he had tossed his keys to Weasel and given up representing the brothers, we found ourselves becoming closer. We had even begun counting one another as friends.

"Let it go, C. Let it all go. Go home to your family."

"I was trying to do that, G. I wasn't trying to do that fool. I was trying to get my head out of the fence. But these muthafuckas keep pulling me back in."

"You know what you have to do, C."

I nodded.

"Let this shit go for real, before it takes you over." He smiled. "Go home, go to Social Security, tell'em that you been locked up ten years and that you're institutionalized, and get your crazy check."

I laughed.

He was right. It was time to let go. Another bus had arrived that day, and eighty more brothers climbed off. The crazy thing about this busload is that fifty of them were Umkhonto members. My people on this yard were safe. We had done our job, and they were safe.

It was the first time that I was able to digest that fact or embrace the paradigm that we were now safe. I was no longer needed. It was time.

Later that evening, I walked to the upper yard where Umkhonto was jogging around the track, exercising on the football field, working out with the weight pile, and practicing martial arts in the gym. I found Webber walking around, inspecting everything. He had his clipboard in his hand taking notes. The sight of Webber caused most brothers to feel uneasy. I joined him in his inspection tour.

"We founded this out of our love for our people."

"I know, I was there," he said dryly.

"That's right, you were there. You were there in the beginning. You know the history, you know the key players, you know the reasons, you know everything."

"Is this going to be one of those emotional moments?" he asked coldly.

I smiled. Webber was Webber.

"Machiavelli said that he would rather be feared than loved. He said that love was conditional, and that it was something that the people control. They were free to give or not to give it. Fear, on the other hand, was something that he controlled. People would obey out of fear because it was in their best interest to do so."

"I read the book."

"He was wrong," I said.

"Oh, really?" He stopped and smiled, lifting an eyebrow.

"It's better to inspire, rather than to cause fear. Men will move mountains for you if your leadership inspires them to do so. They'll go that extra mile, they'll keep going long after they've given everything. But with fear, they'll obey until they find the opportunity to extricate themselves from their station."

"You're saying this to say what?"

"To say that you were my right hand; you were my hammer. And a hammer should be feared, but not the leader. The leader should be loved."

"They all love you."

"And now you should get them to love you." I waved my hand for him to continue walking. We stepped inside a room in the recreation building. All of Umkhonto's senior leadership on the yard was waiting for us.

"What is this?" Webber asked.

"You don't control everything," I smiled. "The leader can organize some things without you knowing, right?"

He walked deeper into the room. The senior leadership began clapping.

"What going on?" he asked, turning back to me.

"They are applauding their new leader," I told him.

"New leader?"

"The new head of Umkhonto," I told him. "Congratulations." I extended my hand, and he clasped it.

"What the fuck are you talking about?"

"I'm going home one day."

"Yeah, but not today."

"You were there in the beginning. You helped build this organization. You helped save a lot of lives. You are the leader now."

"When you walk out of that door, then—"

"Webber—"

"No, this is bullshit!"

"Webber, it's time! Turn around and address your men." I turned to the gathered leaders. "You all know Webber. You all know why we are here. I won't keep you; I won't be long, as I hate long good-byes. He is a good man and a great leader. Love him as you have loved me. Serve him and be loyal to him the same way you have been loyal to me. It has been the pleasure of my life leading you, fighting beside you, and calling you my brothers. I love you all. And I would die with you without thinking twice about it.

"I'm going to be participating in this year's Kwanza program. I've been given the topic of faith to cover. I want all of Umkhonto to be there, along with the rest of the brothers. It'll probably be my last speech to the yard. I'll say my good-byes to everyone then. Right now, your new leader will address you."

I turned to leave, and Webber clasped my arm.

"I am the leader of *all* of Umkhonto?"

"You are leader of Umkhonto west of the Mississippi. And you are the deputy leader of *all* of Umkhonto. Only Ghirt outranks you. He knows that he's been promoted, and he knows that you have been promoted. Stay true to the brothers, Webber. They'll follow you to hell and back if they respect you. People don't respect someone they fear; they will respect someone they love."

He nodded, and probably for the first time in his life showed some emotion. He hugged me.

"Thank you," he said.

"No, thank you."

I left the rec yard and walked to the chapel, which was empty. I opened the door and stepped inside. And for the first time since I arrived on the yard, I viewed the room as more than just a room. Its quiet peace gave me solace. I felt light, unburdened, and renewed.

Lifting a Bible and a Koran from the shelf, I sat down to read. For the first time in my life, the two books were going to share the same space. For much of my life, there had been too much focus on what divides men. Now, I was going to go through both books and have fun reading the stories that they shared.

There is so much in life that unites us, and I was going to rejoice in that. Henry's death had damaged me deeply. Sharing a history free of racism with Henry and developing a real friendship with Pedro had proven that men could do it. We could overcome our prejudices if we just tried. Black and Mexican, Muslim and Christian, Jew and Gentile, White and Black, Gay and Straight, Man and Woman, Republican and Democratic, Liberal and Conservative, Fundamentalist or Progressive, Sunni or Shiite—whatever our beefs, all we had to do is fucking try.

I saw Pedro trying to hang a picture of his daughters on his locker, and I offered him a free-ass tube of government-issued toothpaste. That single random act of kindness overcame a yard full of hatred. Others told us who we should be, but on our own, we decided who we were. We defied a yard, a history of prison politics that told us that we were supposed to hate one another. We reached across a divide of time and space, shook hands, and decided as men that we had more in common than we had that divided us. We reached across a divide that many said was unbridgeable and created for ourselves a brotherhood that men said couldn't exist. We clasped hands and said "fuck you" to a world bent on hatred and division.

I passed that evening in silent prayer, reading passages from both books of worship.

The following day I was summoned to my case manager's office.

"I got good news for you, Mr. Alexander," the case manager said. He slid some papers across his desk to me.

Peering down at them, I saw that it was a court order. "What the fuck is this?"

"You're going home. The court has overturned your case and has ordered the BOP to transport you back home at our earliest convenience for a retrial. The problem is, your halfway house papers came back. You'll be going to a halfway house in two weeks. You've basically completed your sentence.

"The government is not even sure if they want to spend the money to prosecute you again. They're wondering what benefit they would have to spend the money taking you to trial again when you've already finished your sentence. If you won, you would go home. If you lost, you would go home. So what difference would it make, right?"

"I did almost nine years in prison. I watched my son grow up through pictures and telephone calls. My woman has struggled for nine years to pay bills and raise a child by herself. I've lost friends and family members, people who I will never get the opportunity to say good-bye to. And now the judge wants to grant my 2241? Are you muthafuckas crazy?"

"Calm down," he said, extending his hands.

"Calm down? *Calm down?*" I rose. "I've spent one-third of my life in prison *fighting for my life*, and you muthafuckas want to decide that I *might* be innocent *now*? I go home in two weeks, and you want to open the gates for me *now*?"

"I know it's fucked-up," he nodded.

"Fucked up? *Fucked up?* Do you *know* what I've been through? Do you *know* what you've done to me? You've taken away ten years of my life! *Fuck you!*"

I raked the papers off his desk.

"Now you calm down!" he said, leaping to his feet.

"No, fuck you! Fuck the judge, fuck the prosecutor, fuck the Bureau of Prisons, and fuck this crooked-ass system of y'alls! Go home! Go home! Fuck you! I'm walking out of that door with the honor of having stood up and did my time as a soldier! And you muthafuckas ain't gonna take that from me! You muthafuckas ain't *sending* me home! I'm *going* home, 'cause I did my time! I took your best shot, and I survived this fucking plantation system! Yo, fuck you!"

I turned and stormed out.

# Chapter Twenty-Three

Kwanza came, and so did my turn to speak on faith. I was walking out the door the next day, and so I decided to use my speech on faith to speak to my brothers about life. I sat down the night before with my Bible and my Koran, and some books by Hazrat Khan, and wrote my farewell to the brothers on faith. My speech would primarily be based on Sufi teachings from the great writer, teacher, and Sufi spiritual leader, Hazrat Khan. I drew heavily from his work.

I had participated in Kwanza every year since I had been on the yard, always covering a different aspect of it. I would have liked to have covered love, or unity, or purpose, or one of the other subjects where I could have really delivered a powerful speech. But the luck of the draw had given me faith this year. Or perhaps it wasn't the luck of the draw. Perhaps I was going to deliver a message from The Man Upstairs. All we can do is prepare ourselves to be used by Him. I prayerfully wrote my words.

I was introduced by Brother Dexter, the head of the Nation of Islam on the yard. I hugged him and stepped behind the podium. The room was packed—so much so that brothers had to stand against the walls.

"I came here tonight to talk to you brothers about faith. Faith, as it pertains to Kwanza, means faith in our institutions, faith in our schools, our teachers, our leaders, our communities, and also, faith in God."

I had their undivided attention. The room fell so quiet you could hear a mouse fart.

"So many times we skirt around the issue of God, of religion, because we are afraid to offend," I continued. "We don't want to slight another person's beliefs, so we walk on eggs, we tiptoe around the issue. But those of you who know me know better than to expect me to tiptoe around anything, especially when it comes to telling the truth about us, about religion, about God. I'm going to shout the truth from this pulpit, out on the yard, in the unit, from the highest mountaintops, brothers, and I'm always going to give it to you raw and straight."

I paused and peered around the room. They were hanging on every word that I said.

"There can be no gathering of black men where God is absent. It's impossible, simply because of our nature; simply because of who we are. We are the people of the sun, man. We are the first, the select, the chosen. Every time the sun rises in the morning, God is renewing His covenant with you, with us. It's impossible for us to skirt around the issue of God, especially in any kind of discussion about faith, man. We can't do it!"

I had my Southern Baptist preacher voice in full swing now.

"Now, I'm going to talk a little bit about faith and about how important faith is. You can see the importance of faith in all of the other principles of Kwanza. Take *Umoja*, for example—'Unity.' You can't have unity unless you have faith in your brother. It's just that simple. Your brothers are going to have to believe in you, and you are going to have to believe in them before any form of unity can become manifest.

"Another example is *Kujchagulia*—'Self-Determination.' You can't have self-determination and strike out upon a path of independence unless you have faith in the *direction* in which you are headed. You have to have *faith* in order to do this, man!"

Nods shot through the audience.

"How about *Ujaama*—'Cooperative Economics'? You cannot pool your money and your resources together unless you have faith in one another. Your brother has to know that you are not going to mess over him, and you have to believe that your brother is not going to mess over you. You have to have faith in one another.

"Another one is *Ujima*—'Collective Work and Responsibility.' You have to have faith that all of the others are going to do their part; you have to believe that all your brothers are going to contribute equally, and that everyone is going to pull their load. That's what collective work and responsibility is all about—coming together as a community, as a people, to build. You cannot do that without faith."

Again, nods.

"*Nia*—'Purpose.' You have to have faith in our collective destiny, in our sense of mission, in our sense of purpose. And *Kuumba*—

'Creativity.' You have to have faith in your abilities in order to create something.

"So you see, faith plays an important part in a lot of things, man. Faith is what sustains us when the road seems dark, when our future, our direction, seems uncertain. Faith, man, is a rope that is attached to heaven, which is the only true source of safety. This rope, this *faith*, is your trust in the greatness and power of God, and the faith that God can move all things in time, in our favor. Do you hear me?"

They clapped and cheered and whistled as I gave them some of Brother Hazrat Khan's teachings.

"Now what I want to talk to you about is faith as it pertains to this celebration. We all know about faith in God, but what about faith as it pertains to one another? What about faith in our families, faith in our brothers, faith in our institutions? You cannot build a nation without faith in your people, without faith in one another.

"Let me tell you a story about a guy I met here a few years ago. His name was Jimmy. A couple of you may remember Jimmy. He had us call him JJ, for Jimmy the Jew. Jimmy was my celly for quite some time. We would often talk about life, about politics, about our people, our families, and things of that nature.

"Well, one day he and I were talking about him getting out of prison. I asked him, 'Jimmy, what are you going to do when you get out?' He responded that he was going to start his own business. He said, 'You know, there are a couple of Jewish banks that I can go to, and they'll give me a loan simply because I'm Jewish.' I thought about that. I thought long and hard about that statement. This man can go to his people, and he knows that they will loan him some money so that he can start his own business. He had *faith* in his people, and his people will loan him their money because they have *faith* in him!"

My delivery had been perfect. Again, they clapped and cheered.

"And because as a people they have faith in one another, they have been able to gain control of the world's banking and financial institutions. As a people, they have been able to sustain themselves, and their nation, and prosper while being surrounded by a people who want to drive them into the sea. They can do it, because they believe in one another; because they have faith in one another and in their destiny.

"Now, I want to contrast this with a story about us. This is a story about a man who was living in a small town, you know, back in the day. Back then, they had to buy blocks of ice to use inside of their iceboxes. That's how they used to keep their food cool and preserve it. Well, anyway, this one man would sell ice to the black people in the neighborhood so they wouldn't have to find a way to get all the way across town and pick some up. It was a very convenient service for those in the neighborhood, because a lot of people didn't have their own cars.

"Over the years, this man noticed that there was one man in particular who never bought any ice from him. He noticed that the man would drive all the way across town just to buy his ice. So one day, he decided to ask him about it. He said, 'Ray, I've been selling ice in the neighborhood for all these years, and I was curious why you've never bought any ice from me. I noticed that you'd rather drive all the way across town to get it, even though I bring it right here to the neighborhood.' Ray looked at him and rolled his eyes and said, 'Sam, you know the white man's ice is colder.'"

The brothers broke into riotous laughter.

"Imagine that?" I continued. "The white man's ice is colder. That's the type of mentality that many of us have when it comes to patronizing our own businesses, when it comes to having faith in our own people's products, when it comes to having faith in our own brothers. This is the mentality that we are going to have to throw off, man! You are going to have to believe in your brother, have faith in him, and not destroy his faith in you!"

More applause.

"You want to know how important faith in your brother is? You want to know what faith in one another really means? It means *brotherhood*, man! You know what brotherhood is? It's something that is divine! There is nothing greater.

"So many times we get caught up in our differences, in our doctrines, that we forget about God, man. We forget about the meaning of God. Jews want to kill Muslims, Muslims want to kill Jews. Christians have killed Muslims, Muslims have killed Christians, and Jews and Christians have slaughtered one another. Why? Because Christians say that you must pray this way, and Jews say that you must pray that way, and Muslims say that you must pray another way.

"When I was in Catholic school, I would have to walk into the cathedral, sprinkle myself with holy water, make the sign of the cross, kneel down, get up, go and get in line and make confession, have the priest grant me absolution, say my acts of contrition, and then go and pray to God through Christ. I had to go through thirty minutes of rituals for a five-minute prayer!"

Laughter went around the room.

"I later became a Muslim. I would wash myself, clean behind my ears, clean my hands, my forearms, my elbows, wash my feet, spread my rug on the floor, and make *salat*. I had to go through twenty minutes of preparation for a ten-minute prayer!

"We get so caught up in the methods that we use to get to God that we forget about God! We slaughter thousands of God's creatures because they don't pray the way we want them to pray! So now, have the rituals become more important than God? They must have, because every time you slaughter one of God's creatures, you are slaughtering God!"

More rapturous applause ensued. I decided to give them more of Hazrat Khan.

"Let me tell you something. Prayer, night vigils, fasts, all these things are wonderful, but *brotherhood*, man, is the *essence* of God!"

I had my Dr. King voice in full effect now.

"Every prophet that has ever come here has come for one purpose. All of their teachings, their works, their stories and actions, boil down to one thing. They came here to prepare you. 'Jesus didn't come to prepare me,' you might say; 'Jesus came for my salvation.'"

I paused and peered around the room for effect.

"Yes, but it was salvation through preparation. His sacrifice was to prepare your soul for the Kingdom of God. It's all about preparation. 'Preparing me to do what?' you might ask." I smiled at them, and they laughed. "Well ..., I'm gonna to tell you.

"The prophets were all sent here to prepare you for one thing. To prepare you to be an instrument of God! '*To be an instrument of God?*' Yes! To be an instrument of God, so that God can use you, work through you, fulfill His purpose for you. 'What is His purpose for me?' you might ask. 'What does God want?' God wants for His will to be done on earth, as it is in heaven. 'What is God's will?' God's will is that you obey His laws. 'His laws? What laws? God ain't got no laws, Brother Alexander; you tripping now!'"

They laughed with me as I used a comedic voice to ask questions to myself. I had my teaching hat on now.

"Yes, He does. They are called commandments. They are the laws that God gave to Brother Moses on Mt. Sinai., which, by the way, is in Africa. Before God gave Brother Moses those commandments, He ordered him to remove his sandals, because the ground he was standing on was holy. Now, if the land he was standing on was holy, and that land was in Africa, then that means Africa is the holy land."

The applause, whistles, and cheers were thunderous.

"Naw, let me stop," I said with a smile. "I'm not gonna go there! Bad brain! Bad brain!"

They laughed heartily.

"I can't give you that, man. But, God gave His laws to Brother Moses so that you may be in obedience to His will. Now let's think about this for a minute. When America passes a law, we all run to the newspaper, to the *Criminal Law Reporter*, and we *ooooh*, and *aaaaah* over it. In the streets, we were careful and terrified whenever we knew we were breaking the law. We trembled at the prospects of what America would do to us if it ever caught us breaking its laws. But we paid no attention, gave no thought about the wrath of God for breaking His laws! How much more powerful is God than America? You fear America, but you give little thought to the laws of God!"

They applauded thunderously.

"Now what does all this have to do with faith, Brother Alexander? you might be wondering. Well ..., I'm gonna tell you."

Again they laughed.

"Now, God gives us His laws, His commandments to follow so that we may be in obedience to Him, so that His will can be done on earth as it is in heaven. Well, you want to know what God's greatest law is? It's *faith*, man! Faith in and love of your neighbor! *Brotherhood*, man! Faith in your brother!"

I switched to my comedic voice once again. "'Now come on, Brother Alexander, where you get that from?' Well ..., I'm gonna tell you."

Again, they laughed.

"In the beginning, there was the Word. And the Word was with God. And God made the Word manifest itself into flesh. Jesus is the Word of God turned flesh! Now, being that Jesus is the Word of God manifested in the flesh, then that means all of Jesus' words and actions were the Word of God, follow me?"

"Preach, brother!" someone shouted.

"In the temple, Jesus was asked, what is the greatest commandment of them all? We're at Mark 12:28, if anyone wants to follow along."

The brothers laughed and applauded at the fact that I could recite passages and teach the Bible or Koran without having one in front of me.

"Here me, O Israel, the Lord our God is one," I continued, quoting Jesus. "The greatest commandment is love God with all of your heart, your mind, your strength, your soul, and love your neighbor as you love yourself. This is the word of God, man. Love your neighbor as you love yourself is the greatest commandment.

"*Brotherhood*, man! Faith and love in your brother. We're here today to talk about faith, man, the seventh principle of Kwanza, God's greatest commandment. Faith in and love of your brother. Do you follow me?"

Thunderous applause erupted throughout the hall. I waited until it subsided to continue. Then I opened up a book by Hazrat Khan and read from it.

> *If a man is not inclined to make peace with his brother, to harmonize with his fellow man, to seek to please those around him, then he has not performed his religious duties! For what can a man give to God, who is perfect? His goodness? His goodness is very little. His prayers? How many times will he pray? The whole day, man spends on himself, so if he prays three, four, five times a day, it's still not much.*
>
> *If a man can do anything to please God, it is only to please His creatures. There cannot be a better prayer and a greater religion than being conscientious in regards to the feelings of other men. If, when doing wrong, man would realize that he was doing wrong to God, and in doing right, that he was doing right to God, then all would be right in the world.*

Again, they applauded. I flipped more pages of Hazrat Khan's book and read again.

*This reminds me of a story about a teacher, a great holy man, who went with his students to visit a small village in the desert. While in the village, the holy man decided to stop in and pay his respects to an old man he had known for quite some time. Well, the old man, who was poor and lame, heard they were coming and decided to do something special for them. The old man, who had very little, prepared for them with great difficulty, an abundant meal. Now, this just happened to be a period when the teacher and his students were in a cycle of fasting.*

*The old man welcomed them with great joy, and the teacher and students went inside, and the teacher sat down with the old man and began to eat. The students refused and began whispering, "Teacher has forgotten his vow of fasting. Teacher is forgetful." But they dared not question him at that time.*

*Well, after the meal, they went out from the old man's hut, and the students began to question him. "Did teacher forget his vow of fasting?"*

*The teacher said, "No, teacher did not forget. But I would rather break fast than break the heart of that old man, who with all his joy prepared that meal."*

The brothers applauded.

"I want you to understand something," I continued. "Kindness in the hearts of men is the essence of God. Do you follow me?"

Applause and nods went around the room.

"Now, I want you to understand what I'm telling you, brothers. I want you to understand that the end sum total of all religions, of all philosophy, of all meditation and mysticisms, of everything one will ever learn and develop, is to be a better servant to humanity. Everything from the beginning to the end of what the prophets taught was about you serving mankind better.

"You will find, brothers, that true satisfaction of the soul comes from honest, humble service to one another. God's greatest commandment—love your neighbor as you love yourself—is nothing more than faith in and love of your brother."

Again, they applauded.

"Now, brothers, there's another kind of faith that I want to discuss with you. We've talked about faith in God and faith in your brother, and now I want to talk to you about having faith in yourselves. Faith in your future, faith in your destiny, faith in your ability to change the conditions that you are in, to change the conditions of your people.

"Sometimes the clouds hang low, sometimes our conditions are in such a state that we can't see any way out of them. But that's what having faith is all about. It's about hope, it's about believing in yourself, believing in your God, believing that all things change.

"One of the funny things about human nature is when good fortune befalls us, we can't believe it. We're like, man, I can't believe this is true! This can't be real! And the first thing we begin to think is that our good fortune can't last. That the good conditions will change. But when bad fortune comes our way, we can't see our way out of it. We can't see tomorrow. We think that this condition is going to last forever. That's crazy.

"Just think of the nature of life, man. From morning 'til evening, everything changes. *Everything*. So why do we not think that our unfavorable conditions will change also? We have to have faith, man. Faith in ourselves, faith in our God, faith in our destiny!"

They applauded thunderously.

"Brother Hazrat Khan tells a story about a young man named Timerlenk, a man whom destiny had intended to be great. Well, one day, tired of the strife of his daily life and overwhelmed by his worldly duties, he went into the forest and lay down on the ground to wait for death to come and take him.

"At that time, a spiritual man was passing by, and he recognized in young Timerlenk, the man that destiny had intended him to become great. So the holy man struck Timerlenk with his stick, and Timerlenk woke up and asked the holy man why he had come to trouble him there.

"Timerlenk said, 'I have left the world and have come into the forest, so why do you trouble me?' The holy man asked, 'What gain is there in the forest? You have the whole world before you. It is there that you will find what you have to accomplish, if you only realize the power that is within you.'"

I paused for effect.

"Timerlenk told him, 'No, I am too disappointed, too pessimistic for any good to come to me. The world has wounded me. I am too sore. My heart is broken. I will no longer stay in this world.'

"The holy man then told him, *'What is the use of having come to this world, if you have not accomplished something? If you have not experienced something?* If you are not happy, it is because you do not know how to live!'

"Timerlenk then asked the holy man if he thought that he would ever accomplish anything. The holy man told him, 'That is why I have come to awaken you. Wake up and pursue your duty with courage. You will be successful, there is no doubt about it. You simply must have faith.'"

Nods and murmurs went around the room. I held up Hazrat Khan's book before continuing with the story.

"This impression awakened in Timerlenk a spirit with which he had come into the world. And with every step that he took forward, he saw that conditions changed, and all the influences and forces that he needed for success came to him as if life, which had closed its doors, now opened all to him. And eventually, he became the Great Timerlaine of history and conquered all of Central Asia."

I closed Hazrat Khan's book and peered up at them.

"I told you this story because I want you to understand that conditions change with faith, brothers. No matter how hard times get, no matter how difficult things may seem, faith moves mountains."

They clapped and cheered. "Preach, brother, preach!"

"In the Bible, and I'm in Romans 5 for all those who want to follow."

Again there was laughter. They knew that I had all the books memorized.

"It says, glory also in tribulation, for tribulation breeds perseverance, and perseverance patience. Patience brings hope, and hope is never disappointed because of faith in the glory of God!"

Thunderous applause interrupted my speech.

"You have to believe!" I shouted over the applause.

I changed to my comedic voice once again. "Well, Brother Alexander, I don't know. You know, I got this conviction, and well, you know ..."

Laughter shot throughout the room.

"Yeah, I do know. I know whom God chooses to work through. I know that your conviction and you being labeled as a criminal means nothing to God, man! God has a destiny for you. And because the American government is putting labels on you, do you believe that that's gonna stop God's plan for you? Do you really believe that? Nations rise and fall, but the power of God is eternal. So don't you buy into this, 'Oh, my life is over; oh, I have a conviction,' mentality. Because God works through people like you, man!

"I'm gonna tell you a story about a young robber, the scourge of the earth, man. He was robbing old ladies, children, the blind, the cripple, whoever."

I opened up my Hazrat Khan book once again.

> *One day as a joke, a robber stopped by the temple and asked the sage for a blessing and for help in his occupation. The sage asked him what he did for a living, and he told the sage that he was a robber. The sage looked at him and told him that he had his blessing. The robber couldn't believe it. He was very pleased. He went away and had greater success than ever before.*
>
> *Happy with his success, he returned to the sage and greeted him. The sage told him that he was not yet satisfied with his success. He told the robber that he wanted him to be more successful and that he should go out and find three or four more robbers, join together, and then continue on with their work.*
>
> *The young man joined with five other robbers, and they had great success. Again he went to the sage and asked for his blessing. The sage gave him his blessing, but told him that he still wasn't satisfied. He told him that four or five robbers weren't enough, that he should go out and form a gang of twenty.*
>
> *The young man went out and found twenty robbers and joined together with them. Eventually, there were hundreds of them, and then thousands. The sage told him, I am not satisfied with the little work that you do. Why not attack the Mongol strongholds and push them out, so that in this country we may rule ourselves?*
>
> *The robber did so, and a kingdom was established. It*

> *eventually grew and became a great kingdom. That kingdom today has over a billion people and is a nuclear power. It's called India.*

I peered out and gazed at the faces of the brothers packed into the gathering hall.

"The moral to the story is the sage could have told the robber that he was a disgrace and that he should go and find some honest work. But he didn't, because he saw what the robber was capable of. Robbery was simply his first lesson, his A, B, C's. He had only a few more steps to take before he became the defender of his people and the founder of a nation. The robber didn't even understand what the sage was doing. He never realized at the time that the sage was simply preparing him for a great work. Now ask yourselves this, brothers, what are *you* being prepared for?"

Applause went around the room.

"If God used a robber to form a nation, what makes you think He won't use a drug dealer or a money launderer? You have a destiny, man! God placed you on this earth to fulfill that destiny! But you have to have faith in yourselves, faith in God, and faith in that destiny! Everyone and everything was created for a reason.

"There is a story that Brother Khan recounts; some of you brothers may have heard it before. Prophet Muhammad, peace and blessings be upon him, was lecturing his followers, telling them that all things and beings were created for a certain reason. One of his followers said, 'O Prophet, I cannot understand why mosquitoes were created!' And the Prophet answered, 'They were created so that you may get up quickly at night and engage yourself in prayer.'"

Laughter thundered throughout the room.

"So you see, brothers, everyone and everything was created for a purpose. You just have to believe, brothers. You just have to have faith in yourselves, faith in your destiny, *faith* in your abilities. You have the faith of God in you. I can't stress enough the importance of believing in yourself, in believing in your ability to effect change in your community, man. I don't want you to fall into that mental trap of believing that you are helpless, that you are powerless. You have a power inside of you that is beyond belief. It is beyond the ability of human comprehension. If only you knew your power.

"In the Koran, it is said that Allah offered His trust to the heavens and the earth and the mountains, but they refused, being unable to bear it. And then Allah offered His trust to man, who accepted it. Trust, in this case, is responsibility. The value of a man is as great as his responsibility. For what *mountains* could not bear, mankind has carried through life. Your power, brothers, is incomprehensible. For upon your shoulders you carry what *mountains* could not bear!"

The applause was thunderous.

"You just have to have faith. God put His trust in you, and yet, you won't even put faith in yourselves. Who knows more, man or God? You can do anything that you put your minds to, brothers, if you just have faith."

"Preach, brother!" shouts came from the audience.

"Brothers, what we have facing us out there makes it too important for you to give up. This is a winner-take-all game. I remember something the Honorable Minister Louis Farrakhan said one time, and it has stayed with me ever since I heard it. In fact, it pierced my heart and made me question everything that I knew, everything that I believed. He said, 'A man is not a real man if he cannot protect the women who gave birth to his nation.'

"I thought about that statement for a long time. I thought about what it meant. It made me think about our condition, about my responsibilities, about my abilities. We have to come together, brothers. We have to come together and form for ourselves a nation. A strong nation. And by nation, I don't mean a country, because a country is not a nation. A country is a piece of land. A people can form a nation without forming a country. The stakes are high."

Applause thundered throughout the room. The brothers from The Nation stood up and clapped and cheered.

"When the Minister made that statement, I want you to know that he wasn't only talking about physically protecting our women, he was also talking about protecting her spiritually, emotionally, and psychologically. He was also talking about protecting their dignity.

"Our women are not too dignified when they have to go downtown and hold their hand out for welfare, to put clothes on the backs of *our* seed. They're not dignified putting up with the flippant insults of old girl behind the counter, where they are applying for housing to put a roof over the heads of *our* seed.

*"C'mon, man, the daughters of Africa standing in a food stamp line so that they can get what they need to feed our seed? You better not give up! You better not!"*

The entire room erupted with thunderous applause. Every single attendee was on his feet. Even the guards and the chaplains were clapping and whistling.

"Don't you dare leave here believing that you can't make a difference! Don't you *dare* let these people put it in your head that you can't effect change in your communities! Your communities *need* you! Your communities *believe* in you! You carry upon your shoulders the hopes and dreams of an entire people! You're damn right you do!"

Again, they leapt to their feet in wild applause.

"Do you remember how you used to look at the little shorties out there playing basketball in the 'hood, and say, 'Man, that kid can hoop'? You thought, *Wow, he's going somewhere*. You just knew that he was going to be a millionaire by the time he's sixteen. Or what about your little niece or your nephew who could count before they turned two, or who could use a computer at the age of five? We said, 'Man, that kid's going to be a doctor or a scientist.' They carried our hopes and our dreams, man.

"Well, it was the same with you. But you took a wrong turn. Somewhere, things didn't work out, and so Mr. and Mrs. So-and-So who thought you were so great and so talented started rolling their eyes at you when you rolled by with the music bumping and the chronic smoke pouring out the windows."

Laughter shot throughout the room.

"But you know what? Our communities—they know about prisons. They know that prison is like a molten fire that forges new instruments. The know that you've gone through the fire, and they know, like Brother Weasel pointed out the other day, that prisons produce Malcoms. And so once again, they are happy to see you. They smile and wave at you once again. They know that you are a new man, and so once again, you carry the hopes and dreams of your community on your shoulders.

"You hear brothers talking about how the females are going to be all over them once they get out. How they are going to be choosing you, because you are fresh out of the joint."

Again they laughed heartily.

"They are trying to get at you, brothers, because they are hoping that these fires forged a new man. They are flocking to you, brothers, because they are hoping that you've become the man that you were created to be. Your community has put its faith in you again. And now, you have an obligation not to betray that faith."

Applause.

"God has great things planned for you. He's going to work great deeds through you. My mother used to tell a story that I want to share with you tonight. It's about a village that worshipped a volcano. Every year the village priest would select a young virgin to sacrifice to the volcano god in order to appease it in the hope that the volcano wouldn't erupt and destroy their village.

"Well, this particular year, they chose a young virgin from a family who didn't believe in the volcano god. They believed in another religion, a strange new religion where their God dwelled in a place called heaven. The priest took the young girl, examined her, and declared her eligible for sacrifice. You see, all of the sacrificial virgins had to be perfect, without any scars or blemishes on their bodies.

"Well, when the time came for the annual sacrifice, the entire village gathered and bathed the young girl in a nearby river, dressed her in a beautiful white gown, did up her hair, and placed white flowers in it. They led the girl up to the mountaintop, where the priest performed his rituals, and then turned to the girl to toss her into the volcano.

"As the priest took hold of her, a scar appeared down her cheek, right before their eyes. The priest was mortified. He ordered the girl to be taken away and another to be found because it would be sacrilegious to offer the volcano god an imperfect sacrifice.

"Years later, the little girl grew up, got married, and had a daughter who grew up and got married. That daughter got married and had a daughter who grew up, got married, and had a son whom an angel told her to name *Jesus*. The little girl's *destiny* was to be the great-great-grandmother of Mary."

Nods and applause went around the room.

"You may not understand your destiny, and God's plan for you may never be revealed. But you are here to serve a purpose. That purpose is to make yourself into the perfect instrument of God, so that He may use you. Never give up! Never lose *faith* in God. Never lose *faith* in your brothers. Never lose *faith* in yourself!"

I bowed. "*As-salaam Alakium!*"
I received a raucous standing ovation until I left the room.

# Chapter Twenty-Four

After my last speech to the brothers on the yard, it was time for me to go. Over the past few weeks, I had mailed all my important papers home. I had sent all of my stamps home, my journals, letters, and greeting cards. I had nothing left that I wanted to take home with me. My radios, tennis shoes, warm-up suits, and commissary remained. I left a good-bye note to my San Antonio homeboys, dividing my property among them. I walked into the prison with nothing; I was going to walk out with nothing. Nothing but my mind, that is.

Normally when a brother leaves, we all put in a bunch of commissary and cook him a huge spread. I kept my leaving a secret, because I wanted to avoid the good-byes. I wasn't good at saying good-bye. I wrote letters to the people I wanted to say a personal good-bye to. And because I had no boxes to carry, I could walk up to the Receiving and Discharge Office without raising any suspicions. At least I thought that I could.

Baby Charles was waiting for me outside of R&D.

"Fucked-up, C."

"What?"

"You trying to sneak up outta here."

"How you figure—"

He held up the letter I left on his bed, silencing me.

I shrugged. "You caught me."

"Why you didn't let us spread for you. I mean, *damn*, as much as you done for us."

I shook my head. "I just wanted to go. I can't say good-bye to y'all, man."

He nodded. "I feel you. We'll all be out there together in a minute.

Let me just give these people they issue, and I'll be out there with you and Ty."

"You take care of yourself."

"I will," he smiled. "You taught me well. You know, if it wasn't for you talking to me and showing me how to carry it, I'd a been up in here acting a fool."

"You're a good dude, Baby Charles."

We embraced tightly.

"I'm gonna miss you," I said softly. "I'm gonna miss all of you."

"You get out there and take care of little C. Keep him playing football and wrecking shit."

I laughed. "I will."

I pulled open the door to R&D. "Hey, do me a favor."

"Anything."

"Make sure the brothers stay together."

"We got this. Go home to your family."

I stepped into R&D, where I changed out of my prison clothing and put on some fresh gear that my girl had sent for me to wear home. The paperwork and fingerprinting took another fifteen minutes, and then I was walked up to the entrance at the Control Gate.

Walking through that series of electronically controlled metal doors was an experience that was surreal. There had been so many times during the past nine years when I thought that I wouldn't make it through those gates. I actually paused when I came to them, apprehensive about the world that I was about to step into.

When I left, there had been no Internet, only some weird thing called Prodigy. Cell phones were still bulky things that people carried around on their shoulders in bags. And now, there were cell phones with keyboards on them, there were cell phones the size of credit cards, there were cell phones that could hold my entire music catalogue on them.

I was stepping into a world that I no longer knew, a world now dominated by September 11; a world where everything was about bling. I left when Pac was alive and telling the world that he wasn't mad at them. Biggie was still Big Poppa, and the Luniz had five on it. Now Pac and Biggie were dead. I no longer knew the world that I lived in. I would be like a newborn baby, discovering everything as I went along.

The town driver was a cat from the camp whose job it was to drive prisoners to the bus station in the nearby town. I climbed into the Bureau of Prisons van, staring at the prison the whole time. Inside, I felt sadness so profound as to be indescribable. I missed them already. I wanted to take all of them home with me.

I wanted them all out in the free world right then and there. Leaving them behind to deal with the bullshit made me feel as though I were abandoning my brothers. Leaving behind a place that I called home for all of my adult life, and one-third of my total life, was hard, as crazy as that may sound. I even found myself touching the glass of the van window, as it pulled off to take me into the town.

I boarded the Greyhound bus that would take me back to San Antonio and found that I had been assigned a seat next to an old Hispanic woman. There had been a time in my life when I would have asked to be moved. I thanked God that that time had passed.

"Hello," she smiled as she greeted me.

"Hi," I replied.

"Where are you heading?"

"San Antonio," I told her.

"San Antonio, a beautiful place. Are you from there?"

I nodded.

"I am from Corpus Christi."

"A beautiful place," I told her.

"It's changed a lot since the last time I was there."

I nodded. My mind was elsewhere. For the last nine years of my life, I had walked everywhere. I hadn't been on a highway, or in any type of vehicle for that matter. Ten miles per hour was fast to me, and now I was in a bus doing sixty-five. Everything outside of the window was moving so fast. My life was speeding into the unknown, whether I was ready or not. I wiped the sweat from my palms and tried to stop my nervous rocking.

"What's the matter?"

I shook my head, and for some unknown reason, broke down.

I didn't cry when I was sentenced to ten years in prison. I didn't cry when I left my family and was thrown into a hard and cold prison. I never cried when my son would leave after a visit. With the exception of Enrique, I didn't cry when friends died in my arms. I really couldn't explain why I cried then.

Perhaps it was because I was going home to my family, perhaps it was because I had survived one of the worst experiences that a human being could go through. Perhaps it was out of exhaustion. I had given all my strength, all my heart, all my soul, in my struggle for survival. I went to prison, and somewhere along the way, I became a monster. And somewhere along that path, I found redemption.

I became a man in a world that breaks men. I found my soul in a place that corrupts souls. I found my strength in a place that eats the young. I gave up hatred, and prejudice, and bigotry in a place mired in those miasmic conditions. I found hope in a place devoid of hope. I found faith in a black hole that sucks away at the marrow of the human spirit. Perhaps I cried because that's what newborns do. In the fiery womb of prison, I had been reborn.

"You came from the prison?" the old woman asked softly.

I nodded and bawled like a baby.

She lifted my head and placed it upon her shoulder, wrapping her arms around me tightly. "It's okay, *mijo*. I understand."

And she did. Her tears began to fall and mix with my own. This Mexican woman, the woman who gave birth to the race of my so-called enemies, comforted me the entire way home. We laughed, we cried, we shared stories and experiences, and together on that long bus ride home, we celebrated our humanity.

# Epilogue

I climbed off of the bus and walked into the bus station. My woman and my son were standing in the middle of the station waiting for me. My son ran to me.

"Daddy!"

I scooped him up into my arms and lifted him high into the air, spinning him around. The next second, I brought him down to my lips, and I kissed him all over his head and face. I had made it back to him.

My woman came to me, and I kissed her with a passion that told of my promise for our future. It was a kiss that said "forever."

"I can't believe you're home," she said with tears pouring down her face.

"I told you before, baby, they could lock me up, but they couldn't eat me. They had to let me go sooner or later."

"I missed you."

"Miss me no more," I said, kissing her once again.

"Daddy, are you going to come to my football game on Saturday?"

"I wouldn't miss it for the world, son."

"I'm going to play football for the Longhorns, or for USC, or for Oklahoma, or Miami!" he said excitedly.

"I know you are," I told him. "You can do anything you put your mind to."

"You ready to pay for college?" my woman asked.

"I'm going to have to be." I smiled and caressed the old picture of Anna Marie inside of my top pocket. I was going to pay college for two kids.

I lifted my son onto my shoulders, grabbed my woman's hand, and headed out of the bus station. Together with my family, I walked down the street toward our car. I knew little about what the future held for me, but I knew that as I rebuilt the shattered pieces of my life, I would do things right this time. I didn't have to have any fancy cars or expensive jewelry. Everything that I needed, everything that my heart desired, I carried on my shoulders and held in my hand.

As I walked down that street toward an uncertain future, one thing was certain: we were going to get through this world together as a family. And I was going to be the man that my woman and child needed me to be. I was going to be the man that my community needed me to be. I was going to make the world a better place by being the black man that the world needed me to be.

God is great, I want to bear witness. God gives second chances.

Sneak Preview Of:

# *When Lions Dance*

Coming 2010

# Chapter One

The thunderous clap of the seven rifles roared across the gentle, green rolling hills of Arlington, Virginia. The rapport from the assault rifles hung solidly in the air, until being pushed away by a second thunderous clap, and finally, a third. The violent discharge of the twenty-one cartridges caused those gathered around the flag-draped coffin to bolt from the quiet subconscious of their solemn grief, back to the harsh realities of this chaotic, destructive world. The violent crashing of the rifles had the opposite effect on me. They made me drift into another time, another place, another world. I thought of a place in a very distant land. A dry place. A cold place. A rugged place. A place of violence, of destruction, of helplessness, and of fear. It is the place where my life was taken from me. It is the place where my child died.

The Army chaplain dutifully informed me that my child died without pain. The President told me that my child died a hero. The newspaper accounts stated that my child died cold, tired, frightened, and hungry. The one thing they all agreed on, however, was the fact that my child was dead.

I did not jump when the rifles of the honor guard cracked loudly across the lush rolling terrain of the cemetery, but I did jump when the bugler began playing "Taps". I had always dreaded that melancholy dirge. I had always hated the slow, hollow, solemn emptiness of it. I hated its finality. I hated it even more so now, because it was my child inside of that highly-polished chrome metal box that the bugler was playing it for.

I shuddered and closed my eyes when the honor kids lifted the flag off of my child's coffin and proceeded in their crisp, precise military movements to fold it. I knew what each fold meant, or rather what each fold meant to them. Bravery, sacrifice, dedication, and all of the other wonderful euphemisms, adjectives, and accolades that nations bestow upon their fallen. But, to me, each fold of that flag meant a step closer to a hard and cold finality that I would have severed my right arm to avoid. To the realization that I was about to lower my youngest child into a cold, hard, dark, and lonely ground, and then cover him over with dirt.

They called the valley of his death the Sha-e-Kot Valley. What it translated into, I had no idea. But, to me, it would always mean a stomach-churning, gut-wrenching pain. They say my child died fighting for freedom, for democracy, for a code of honor between he and his fellow soldiers. They say my child died fighting tyranny, injustice, and terror. They say he gave his life to protect us, our nation, our children, and our way of life. It all sounded wonderful, like my child was Superman or some other superhero. Still, it did not make it any easier for me to accept his death.

I do not know how to explain losing a child to you, and unless you have ever lost a child, you probably would not, or could not, understand it anyway. The morning the Army chaplain knocked upon my door and delivered that telegram informing me of my child's death is the day I, too, died. I felt as though God had reached inside of me, twisted all of my insides into a tight knot, and then yanked them out through my stomach. I was left with nothing but a numbing emptiness. I could no longer hear; I could no longer see; I could no longer breathe. All I could do was let out a silent, gasping scream, and cry burning tears of fire until my ducts became as dry and parched as that wretched, accursed land of my child's death. Today, I am still numb.

I was handed the pyramid-shaped flag by a four-star general, and I half listened as he mumbled something about a grateful nation. A grateful nation…

My mind once again withdrew into its own world, as I carefully pondered the significance of those words. A grateful nation…

My mind's reflection came to an abrupt end when I felt someone patting my hand reassuringly. I shifted my gaze to the left and received a smile from my friend and honored guest, our former commander-in-chief. Today, Bill was here as a private citizen to support me during this tragic time in my life. He was not here representing the grateful nation, as that job had been left to the vice president, who was seated just to the right of the former first couple. In fact, the majority of the government's luminaries were clumped to the left of me since the Secret Service had deemed it easier to protect them all that way. Today, Arlington was filled with senators, congressional representatives, mayors, a few governors, and many, many civil rights luminaries. They were all here out of respect for me and because of who I was, or rather who they thought I was. They really had no idea.

My name is Yimani Shaheed. I was born Mary Beth Wainwright, in a not exactly middle-class neighborhood in Birmingham, Alabama. Officially, our neighborhood was named North Smithfield. However, it was more commonly known by its unofficial name, Dynamite Hill.

Growing up in North Smithfield was like growing up in Beirut during the early eighties. The main difference between Smithfield and Beirut was that the people in Beirut knew why they hated, and more importantly, why they were hated. I grew up asking why the Klan hated me. I was a child, and I had done nothing. Still, the dynamite came.

"Yimani, the service is over," Martha Ray whispered.

I examined my surroundings, and sure enough, the people had risen and begun to form The Line. It was a long line. A line that snaked along a path through the cemetery and seemed to go on forever. It was the condolence line, where everyone would take their turn to stop, shake my hand, and tell me how sorry they were that my child was dead. Where the government officials would all stop, posture, and tell me what a hero my child was and how grateful this nation was. It was the line that would end and disperse, sending everyone but me back to their normal workaday lives. It was the death line, the procession of finality, the close of a ceremony that would take my child away forever. If I could have run away from that line of death, I would have. Trust me.

The former first couple went first. He hugged me tightly, and then she kissed me softly on my cheek. There were tears in each of their eyes, and unlike many of the other luminaries here, I could tell they were sincere. I thanked them for coming, and I thanked him for his support over the last few days. I knew he was busy, and I knew he had made a significant number of sacrifices to be here with me today. The vice president was next.

Once again, I was told how grateful this nation was. I smiled and thanked him politely, but inside, I wanted to scream. I wanted to shout at him with all of the fury that my frail and weary body could muster. I wanted to choke the living shit out of him. Not because of his politics, to which I was diametrically opposed, but because I knew he had sent my child away to die, whilst he hid inside of his undisclosed location. I wanted to lash out at him because I knew that from his underground fortress, he had sent the children of other mothers to die. And yes, I did hate his politics.

You do not piss off the entire world, stir up a cauldron of resentment, and then look back in befuddlement when it boils over into uncontrollable rage and hatred. The policies and actions of this administration resulted in the proverbial chickens coming home to roost. But damn it, why on me? Why on my family? Why my child? And yes, I was being selfish. But, as it was my child who I will never hear laugh again, who I will never see smile again, who I will never see walk down the aisle and create his own family, I have that right. We'll call it a mourning mother's prerogative.

The death line eventually petered out, and I was able to stand. I lifted myself with my birch wood cane, carefully stabilizing my knobby old knees and tired yet sleeping legs. My daughter Kaamilah took my hand into hers and led me towards the pathway that would take me to my waiting black Cadillac limousine, which in turn would take me to the airport to board the jet that would take me back home to Tuskegee, Alabama. It was a flight that I could not wait to take. I wanted to be out of this place. This land of conservative death politics. This land of lying politicians and dead children.

"Dr. Shaheed!" a voice called out from behind. "Dr. Shaheed!"

I stopped and turned in the direction from which my name had been called. Approaching was General Rodney Douglas Clarke, Commander-in-Chief of the United States Special Operations Command. I had known General Clarke since the early seventies, back when he was a dashing, young, red-headed, freckle-faced lieutenant. He extended his hand to me, and I clasped it gently.

"Dr. Shaheed, I just wanted to speak to you again in private, and extend to you my sincerest condolences," General Clarke said softly. "You have the sympathy of a grateful nation."

I laughed in his face.

"A grateful nation?" I asked. "A grateful nation? A nation so grateful that had my son been driving on the New Jersey Turnpike today, he would have had a ninety percent greater chance of being pulled over, harassed, denigrated, and even beaten because of the color of his skin. A nation so grateful that it refused to accept him as anything other than an athlete, a rapper, a drug dealer, a gang member, a nigger? A nation that is so grateful that it refused to give my college-educated son a job, resulting in his joining the Army and being sent off to some cold, hard, dusty, and desolate hell hole, only so he could be returned back to the grateful nation inside of a lead box? If this nation were truly grateful, General, my child would still be alive."

The General's eyes narrowed and he straightened his dignified shoulders. "I know you have a reason to be bitter, Dr. Shaheed. You've lost a lot in our nation's wars."

My own eyes narrowed, and I shifted my shoulders and turned my weathered palms toward the sky. "Which wars, General? The Cold War? That so-called war of containment? Or were you referring to Vietnam, the war you people sold to us based on some cockamamie Domino Theory? Or do you mean the war against Communism, where we invaded the tiny island nation of Grenada and justified it by asserting the so-called Monroe Doctrine, which somehow proclaimed us god over an entire hemisphere? No, General, you must be referring to the war on drugs. The war in which we invaded the sovereign nation of Panama, arrested its internationally recognized leader, brought him back to the grateful nation, and tried him inside of a drug court like a common criminal."

The General stiffened considerably, and his face turned the color of a summer rose. I was pushing all of the right buttons, so I decided to push some more.

"Or are you referring to the other drug war? The war against African American males, who make up only a tiny fraction of this nation's population, but constitute over eighty percent of its prison population. No, you must be referring to the oil war. Excuse me, I meant the Gulf War. The war that took place because the rich Texas oil companies wanted to continue to play the Middle East oil states off against one another. Profits first, General. We must not forget that. I imagine that one day we will come up with a proper name for the Gulf War, lest future generations see it for what it really was. In fact, I have a few suggestions you could take back to your superiors. How about, the war to save capitalism? It sounds a lot more dramatic, a lot more heroic, don't you think?"

"Okay, cut the crap, Yimani!" General Clarke barked. "Spare me the theatrics. I am not one of your students, so you can dispense with the liberal professor role, okay? Your son did not join the Army because he couldn't find a job and you know that! He volunteered to serve his country because that's the kind of kid you raised him to be. He volunteered, Yimani! He volunteered to go to jump school; he volunteered to go to scuba school; he volunteered to go to jungle training; he volunteered to go through special operations training; and he volunteered to be a special operations team member! He volunteered! And all of that volunteering doesn't sound to me like someone just looking for a paycheck. It sounds to me like a brave kid, Yimani. Like a patriot. Like a hero."

"Is that what a hero is to you?" I snapped. "Someone who gallops off into the sun to die?"

"Nobody wants to die, but sometimes, heroes do."

I nodded. "Yes, Rodney, sometimes they do. But I don't recall hearing a twenty-one gun salute at Martin's funeral. I don't remember hearing "Taps" being played at Malcom's. The heroes I know all died trying to make America live up to its promise of freedom and equality for all. The heroes I know died so that America would not be a lie. And you want to know the sad thing about it? They couldn't even sit at the same lunch counter as you or use the same restroom as you. They couldn't drink from the same water fountain as you, and in most cases, they couldn't even walk through the same goddamned door that you used. But they died, Rodney! They died so the idea that is America could live. Where is Myrlie Evers' flag?"

Tears fell from my eyes, and General Clarke pulled me close and held me. It was the second time in thirty years that Rodney Clarke held me inside of his arms as I mourned the loss of a soldier. The first time had been for my husband; this time was for my child.

"Don't hate your country, Yimani," he whispered.

"Hate it?" I lifted my head from his chest and peered into his steel blue eyes. "I risked my life to make it better."

General Clarke lowered his head and nodded. "Don't hate the Army, Yimani. Don't hate me."

"I don't, Rodney, but I'm too old to buy into all of this duty, honor, courage, and sacrifice crap. Heroes do not lift rifles and kill other human beings. I've never met a hero in a military uniform."

"Then allow me to introduce you to a few thousand of them," he whispered.

General Rodney Clarke placed his hands upon my shoulders and gently turned me around. He waved his hand out across the rolling hills of Arlington National Cemetery, as if showing me an estate-sized lot for a new home. It was then I realized how expensive the particular piece of real estate truly was. For the first time since the news of my child's death, my numbness slipped away from me, and for that singular moment I could feel again.

My eyes rolled across the gentle, green rolling hills and shallow lush valleys of Arlington, taking in the thousands upon thousands of white granite crosses and Stars of David.

"Your brother, the hero who died in Vietnam," General Clarke said softly, "he was buried in his uniform, was he not?"

It was a low blow. Yes, my brother Claude had been buried in his uniform, and yes, Claude had been a hero. His Congressional Medal of Honor had officially made him so. Claude was a hero to Marines everywhere, and for all times. Jodys had been sung about him; statues had been created in his honor; stories had been written about his actions. But even before all of those things, Claude had been my hero.

Rodney Clarke was a brilliant general, or so all of his superiors had attested. I'd never had the privilege to look into General Clarke's files or records, so I personally could not attest to his brilliance as an officer nor as a military tactician. However, what I could testify to was that the man had the timing of a precise Swiss chronometer. At my moment of vulnerability, he handed over my son's Silver Star, which had been awarded posthumously, and he also handed me the one thing I had been dreading the most…my son's last letter.

I had long ago heard of those dreaded 'In the event of my death' letters, and in my mind, I had always prayed I would never get one. Today, I received one.

"Read it now," he said in a voice that, despite its low tone, was filled with an impressive amount of command authority.

I took the wrinkled letter from the General's hand, and tried to control my shaking hands as I opened it. My eyes burned with fire as the tears welled up inside of them. Soon, they poured down my face in rapid succession, leaving liquid tracks of pain down my cheeks once I saw the first two words inside of my child's last letter. They were 'Hey

Ma'.

I stood there inside of Arlington National Cemetery overlooking broad fields of crosses, as I read my child's last letter. The letter made me laugh; it made me cry; it made me proud; and in the end, it made me die all over again.

Taj loved doing what he did for a living, and no matter how hard I tried to convince myself otherwise, it was the simple truth of the matter. He was part of an elite team. A band of brothers, he often called them. He was a first lieutenant on a special forces A-Team, a unit more commonly known as The Green Berets. Taj was an intelligence specialist, and his goal was to eventually work for the Central Intelligence Agency. It was something that he and I sparred about many times. I'd often wondered how my child could turn out to be the complete opposite of me. But, in the end, I realized it was not that we were complete opposites. To the contrary, we were just alike.

I served my nation by challenging its conscience, and by making it examine itself, its ideas, its beliefs, and its values. My child served this nation by believing in its ideals, its principles, its values, and its fundamental desire to more often than not, do the right thing on the world stage. We both believed in America. I, in what it could be, and he, in what it was. I spent my life serving it, fighting it, like a frustrated mother trying to get her child to be the best that it could be. My child wanted to spend his life keeping it safe and helping it to make this world a better, safer place.

Taj's letter made me look across that field of crosses in Arlington and not see soldiers, but see the lost sons and daughters of thousands of mother who were just like me. Reading my child's letter amidst a field of crosses made me understand the true preciousness of such a place. It was not about military pomp and pageantry. This place was about America's mourning of her lost children. About America's mourning of her lost innocence. About America's mourning of all that lost potential. Propriety be damned, I crumpled the corner of my child's last letter into my fist and turned to the one person who I knew would understand. I turned and fell into General Clarke's arms, where I wept like a child.

# Chapter Two

I left Virginia that afternoon and returned to my own tiny corner of the world. I lived in a place called Bending Oaks, on a street appropriately called Majestic Oaks. My home was a seven thousand, nine hundred, and thirty-nine square-foot Victorian style farmhouse. It was a white clapboard affair, with soaring turrets, three broad wrap-around porches with second-floor verandas, five copper-crowned bay windows, and a gorgeous standing seam metal roof that had weathered to a beautiful rich patina.

My home was nestled on an expansive five acre lot, within one of the most prestigious communities in Alabama. It was one of those communities where the overweight, middle-aged security guard, with the uniform two sizes too small, sat inside of a tiny booth eating junk food all day and waved you inside. This false sense of security cost me nine hundred thousand of my hard-earned dollars. And that price was only because of who I was and the position I held within the community. The builder originally wanted 1.3 million dollars for the place, but upon learning that I was the eminent Dr. Yimani Shaheed, famed civil right activist, former Black Panther, noted historian, and newly appointed president of Tuskegee University, he let me have the property with only a ten percent mark up.

Bending Oaks was certainly a far cry from where my life began. It was an even further cry from where I found myself living during certain times in my life. I remember times when food was a luxury and a warm, safe place to lay my head was a distant fantasy. But those days, thank God, were far behind me. Then again, those days, I had all of my children with me. They were hungry days, but they were living days. My baby was alive.

"Yimani, are you all right?"

I turned and ran my hand across my swollen, wet cheek. "Yes, Shaheed," I told my husband. "I'm alright."

He hobbled to the couch where I was seated and placed his frail arm around my neck. "I'm sorry, Yimani," he said in a weak, phlegm-filled voice, in between his deep, wet coughs. "I wish I would have had the strength to have gone with you."

"Oh, Shaheed, I'm alright," I lied. "I needed you to stay here and take of things, and to get your rest."

Shaheed removed his bone-thin arm from around my neck and smashed his trembling right fist into his balmy left palm. "What good is a man if he can't be there when his woman needs him the most!"

"Shaheed, you have always been there for me. You have always been my strength." I rose and extended my hand to him. "Come, let me help you to bed."

He waved his skeletal arm through the air, brushing off my assistance. So thin had he become that his small pajama suit hung loosely around his gaunt frame, as if he were some sort of teenage rap star lost inside of his fashionably baggy clothing.

"I'll be able to manage. I just heard you sniffling, that's all. What are you doing?"

I lifted Taj's last letter and the triangle coffin flag presented to me by the grateful nation. "I was just putting some things away, that's all."

I laid the crumpled letter down on the small Queen Anne style coffee table that sat before us, and I lifted my child's Silver Star. "The President awarded our child a Silver Star for heroism, above and beyond the call of duty."

Shaheed squinted his weary, sunken, saggy eyes. "Did you expect anything less of him?"

"Yes! I expected him to stay down, to not play hero! I expected him to come home!"

Although it had been said through teary eyes, it had also been said through clenched teeth. I knew I had slammed the door too hard. But being who he was, he simply ignored my bitterness, leaned forward, and lifted the crumpled letter from the cherry wood table.

"Is this what I think it is?" he asked in his deep, wheezing, phlegmatic tone.

I nodded. "Taj's last letter."

Shaheed's skeletal shaking hands unfolded the severely crumpled, well-traveled pieces of paper. And like a dagger piercing my heart, struck sharply with the words from my child, he began to read aloud.

*Hey Ma,*

*If you receive this letter, then I know that things are all bad! Forgive me for cursing, but some way, somewhere, somehow, things must have gotten pretty screwed up. You know what this reminds me of? It reminds me of the time when we were living in California, and you bought me that blue Super Shark skateboard. You used to tell me that if I went out and got myself killed, you were gonna whip me when I got home. Hey, Ma, don't whip me, okay? Trust me, it was an accident!*

*Ma, I don't want to sound brave, or gung ho, or anything like that. But I don't want you to worry about me. I'm all right, trust me. Hey, a long time ago, you taught me to believe in God, and Heaven, and angels. So, right now, at this very moment, (if everything goes according to plan) I'm an angel, and I'm smiling down on you.*

*Ma, I know how you are, and I know how you think. It's not the government's fault. It's not the Army's fault. It's not anyone's fault. Remember what you always used to tell me? You can die at home in bed, in the best of health, or you can survive on the most violent battlefield ever known to man. It's all according to God's plan. You remember that, don't you? Well, who are we to question?*

*Ma, I want you to do me a favor. I want to be buried in uniform, and I want to be buried with a military ceremony, in a military cemetery. I'm laughing right now because I know you're shouting at me because of my request. Ma, you'll never change. But that's good, because I wouldn't have you any other way.*

*Ma, I want you to know something. I really did love my job. I really loved helping people live a better life, and helping those who couldn't help themselves. I fought for those who couldn't fight for themselves, and I trained those who had the heart and courage to fight for the freedom but didn't know how. You want to hear something funny? Everybody thinks that what we do is sneak around and blow things up in the middle of the night. In my three years in the Army, I've built more things than I've blown up. Yesterday, I built a water-well in a village about three clicks from here. (Sorry, can't say where here is – Army censors). The look on those villagers' faces when they learned that they would have fresh, clean drinking water for the foreseeable future is something I'll never forget.*

*Ma, we did the right thing coming over here and helping these people out. The stories you told me about the things you went through don't even compare to what these people went through under their former government.*

*Ma, I don't really know what all I'm supposed to write in a letter like this. But, I do want you to make me a promise. I want you to promise me that you'll stay strong and keep on going. I want you to promise me that you'll live. You once taught me the difference between living and just being alive, and now I want you to remember it. I want you to go out and feel the sunshine for me. I want you to laugh for me. I want you to go out and sing, and smile, and dance for the both of us. Love for the both of us.*

*Ma, I don't want to sound all mushy and gushy, but I do want you to know this. If I had to do it all over again, I wouldn't have it any other way. If I get to Heaven, and I get to choose my next family, I'm gonna wait for you. You are the greatest Ma that ever existed. I love you always.*

*Your son,*
*Taj*

Again, I cried. I cried long after Shaheed had finished reading Taj's letter. I cried long after he had held me in his frail arms and I had assured him that I was all right so he could retire and get some sleep. I cried until my face hurt, until my eyes burned, until a numbing tone resonated throughout my ears and spread throughout my now aching head. I had to cry. I had to open the floodgates of my misery and mourn the part of me that was no longer a part of me, and yet would always be a part of me. But, even more than crying for my child and all of the things in regards to him that would not come to pass, I mourned for myself.

I spent my life protecting my children. I spent my life feeding my children, clothing them, sheltering them, nurturing them. Many times I went without food so that their bellies would be content. Many winters I walked through blistering cold so that they could have jackets and be warm. And God! God allowed me to bring my child this far, only to wrench him away! Why not then? Why not when I was hungry, when he was hungry, when he was a child, an infant, a seed? What kind of God allowed me to sacrifice, to grow attached, to love, to hope, to aspire, and then snuff out all of those things like a used, cheap, paper match? It was instantaneous, seemingly without much effort, consideration, or remorse. I cried because I felt cheated by God. I felt spent, used, *lied* to. What kind of God gives hope? What kind of God takes a child before its mother?

After my tears, I knelt down and told God that I hated Him. And then I asked Him how could He have done this to me. I had always been taught that if you just tried… If you tried to live right and to do the right things, then everything would *be* all right. That is why I felt as if I had been lied to.

I spent the first part of the night of Taj's funeral crying, pounding my fist against the coffee table, the sofa, and the floor, while cursing God. I spent the second part trying to find something to do to keep my mind from caving in on itself. Eventually, I decided to put Taj's belongings away.

I rose from my floral print sofa and walked across my living room to a large hall closet, where, with great effort, I began to remove boxes and boxes of materials in order to find the 'right box' in which to place the triangle flag awarded to me from the grateful nation. You see, I have a particular box in which my triangle flags are kept. Yes, I said flags with an 's'. I was presented a flag in exchange for the life of my brother; I was presented with another in exchange for the life of my husband; and last but certainly not least, I now had one to drape over the gaping hole in my heart, to cover over the void left by the now extinguished life of my child. As so, one by one, and again with great effort, I drug the large cardboard boxes over the plush-cut carpeting of my living room floor and sat them next to the sofa. This arrangement would allow me to sit down on the couch while conducting a search for my collection of coffin flags.

I seated myself on the sofa in front of the first dust-covered box, leaned forward slightly, and blew vigorously at the particles that had managed to collect themselves on the box in such a short period of time. I had only placed the boxes inside of the closet a few months ago, upon moving into my new abode. Nevertheless, dust had accumulated, as well as cobwebs, over those cardboard coffins that contained the keys to everything that I was and everything that I had become. They contained the memories of my life.

I gently raked my wrinkled, weary hands across the top of the first box, clearing away all of the cobwebs that my aged lungs no longer had the strength to clear away, and then I opened the box.

Inside, I had hoped to find a photo album, within which I could place one of my son's funeral programs. Of course, only after I had gone through it, saw pictures of my child as a child, and then cried my eyes out again. The thought had also crossed my mind that this first box would be the coffin flag box, within which I could place my son's flag and add to my collection. Imagine, most women my age would have built up a substantial collection of literature, art, or coupons even! While I, too, had those things, I somehow had, in the process of living, come to amass a collection of coffin flags, military decorations for bravery and courage and valor, and letters from presidents thanking me on behalf of the 'grateful nation'.

Inside of this box, my morbid collection of platitudes, posthumous awards, and coffin flags were not. Inside of this box, at the very top, lay things I had not seen in quite some time. Inside of this box lay the map of my life, the blueprints that deciphered who I was. Inside of this box lay my diaries.

I stared at the tattered volumes that lay before me. Part of me wanted to smile, reach out and grab the books, and flip through them. It was the part of me that thought of those books as a link to a pleasant past, far removed from this ugly present. They were a link to a time when my child was alive. A link to my brother, to my mother, my father, my childhood friends, and my innocence. But then, there was another part of me that was afraid of what those books held. There was a part of me that stared at those books as if they were a sleeping Frankenstein. There was a part of me that would not allow my arms to move, my lips to part, or my heart to beat, for fear of awakening the monster. That monster was the ugliness of my past.

I spent my life overcoming monsters. I spent my life challenging edicts, institutions, and dictates. All my life I've had to fight because I was born Black. I've had to fight because I was born a woman. I've had to fight simply because I was born. I now had a monster in my living room, and the most terrifying aspect of it all was that this monster lay not only in those tattered, colorful books before me, but he also had an outpost in my head. I knew that if I lifted the monster from its crypt, I would open a floodgate to a past filled with demons. And the most frightening of all the demons I would awaken would be the one that forced me to answer the question 'Who is Yimani Shaheed?'

Deep down, I had an idea who I was, and I even liked who I was. But the big question was, would I like who I was *before*? Would I still like who I had become if I re-examined the road that I took to get here? Could the façade that was Dr. Yimani Shaheed, university president, author, poet, activist, Presidential Medal of Freedom winner, still stand if it had to acknowledge that it had been built upon stones of desperation, poverty, prostitution, drug addiction, theft, and criminality? Could I still look the idolaters in the face, and would they be able to tell that the edifice that they had erected was really a temple built on ragged stone? Who was I? Who was I really, and by that question I meant to exclude the mountain of honorifics, titles, pre-fixes, and accolades that society had bestowed upon me. Not widow, not grieving mother, not professor, not university president, not doctor, not activist, not historian, not civil rights icon, not hero, not any of those things, but who was I? I was not a monster, although monsters had roamed the desolated war-ravaged battlescape that I called my life. I was not a racist, although I had hated men who hated me simply because of the color of my skin. I was not a feminist, although I had killed men.

I fretted over the answer to my question, although the answers lay before me like a constellation of stars waiting to be acknowledged, to be discovered, to be charted as much as those ancient navigators charted their way through the darkness of those stormy, ravishing, rocky seas.

With tepid resignation like those intrepid navigators of old, I embarked upon my task and lifted the astrochart so I could examine the path I took through the dark and stormy seas that I call my life. I touched the monster. I opened the first of my childhood diaries.